Praise for the Sophi

Sex, Murd
"Packs a bigger jo

"A terrific mystery. Kyra Davis comes up with the right mix of snappy and
tingling."
—*The Detroit Free Press*

Passion, Betrayal & Killer Highlights
"(A) high-octane hookup."
—*Cosmopolitan (A Red Hot Read)*

"Davis spins a tale full of unexpected turns and fun humor."
—*Romantic Times*

Obsession, Deceit And Really Dark Chocolate
"Wry sociopolitical commentary, the playful romantic negotiations between
Anatoly and Sophie and plenty of Starbucks coffee keep this steamy series chug-
ging along."
—*Publisher's Weekly*

"The tensions between Sophie and Anatoly is thick right from the beginning and
paired with the mystery it kept me turning pages to see if and when it would
explode."
—*Romance Junkies*

Lust, Loathing And A Little Lip Gloss
"A cast of quirky, wonderful characters, a well-crafted plot and a generous helping
of snarky humor make this one a winner. Sophie's sassy first-person narration is a
bonus—she's one of a kind.
—*Romantic Times*

"Humor, romance and an appealing, spirited protagonist"
—*Publisher's Weekly*

Vows, Vendettas & A Little Black Dress
"There's not a "normal" (read boring) character in the bunch, which is what makes
this series so much fun."
—*Booklist*

"If you enjoy an amusing and colorful story, this is the book for you. The read is
fast with gripping but funny suspense. I loved Sophie's devious little mind."
—*Freshfiction.com*

Vanity, Vengeance & A Weekend in Vegas
"...witty and funny...a fun read"
—*Alli's World*

"...I devoured this book...loved getting back into Sophie's world."
—*Mommy Snarks A Lot*

Praise for Davis' Other Books

Just One Night series

"…crackling with intensity. Davis...skillfully creates an uplifting story in which sex is presented both a freedom and as a metaphor for power, and where raw chemistry is the clear winner over bland complacency."
—Publishers Weekly (starred review)

So Much For My Happy Ending

"Davis' tragicomic tale is both entertaining and horrifying at once….harrowing…hopeful and even wildly funny at times."
—Romantic Times

Pure Sin Series

"I'm absolutely in love with this series…so much passion, so much intrigue"
—Jessys Book Club

A Sophie Katz Novel

CHAOS, DESIRE & A KICK-ASS CUPCAKE

NEW YORK TIMES BESTSELLING AUTHOR

KYRA DAVIS

TABLE OF CONTENTS

I dedicate this book to my readers. Your passion and loyalty to Sophie hasn't just kept her alive but caused her to thrive. You've also kept me smiling. Thank you!

# ACKNOWLEDGMENTS

I need to thank Ellie McLove for squeezing this book into her editing schedule at the last minute. Also thanks to Shannon Passmore for putting up with me as I constantly changed the dates in regards to when I would get her this book for formatting. I also need to give major props to my fantastic cover-design artist, Nicole of Cover Shot Creations. Sophie has never looked so good! And of course I need to thank my husband Rod and my son Isaac for patiently waiting for me to step out of the world of Sophie to join them in the world of reality. Lastly, I must thank my dogs who are never patient but always make me smile.

 # CHAPTER
ONE

*"I have a tendency to self-medicate. If I don't I suffer
from extended periods of debilitating sanity."
--Dying To Laugh*

"Well?" Anatoly asked as I stood in the middle of his new office, absorbing the room.

I turned, lifting my chin, seeing a shadowy reflection of myself in his dark brown eyes. He hadn't shaved that morning. There were strands of grey mixed in with the coarse black hair dotting his chin. It made him look more rugged than old. His arms were crossed against his black T-shirt and his legs crossed at the ankles as he leaned back against his new, but used desk. Even when relaxed he looked a little dangerous. He served in both the Russian and Israeli army before moving here. I learned not long ago that he had also done some work for the Russian mafia during the years of his reckless youth, although he assured me he wasn't truly part of the organization. More of a 1099 employee. He never killed for them which is not the same thing as saying he never killed.

You'd think that last part would be a problem for my

family but my sister, Leah, thought someone as temperamental and incautious as me should be grateful to be able to hold onto *any* man and my mother was so happy I was finally sharing my bed with a fellow Jew she was willing to overlook a few unreported felonies. People are always surprised to hear of her biases since my African American father wasn't Jewish, but then he did change his name from Christianson to Katz just to appeal to my mother's sense of cultural identity. As nuns change their names when they take a vow to live a life of poverty, chastity and obedience my father changed his name when he vowed to live a life defined by matrimony, family and general insanity. He died eighteen years ago yet the wound still stings whenever I allow my mind to touch it.

The muffled sound of a honking horn from the street below brought me back to the moment. Anatoly was waiting for my response and as patient as he was, he didn't actually *like* to wait.

"Do you really want to hear this?" My fingers moved from my bag to my black and white eternity scarf.

His jaw tightened ever so slightly. "Stop the games," he demanded, his Russian accent becoming a bit more pronounced.

I nodded and took a deep breath. "It's…cute."

The aggressiveness of the silence that followed was a little frightening.

"Cute," he eventually repeated, drawing out the word, making it sound like the venomous insult he perceived it to be.

I hesitated a moment before blurting out, "Oh my God, Anatoly, it's more than cute. It's fucking adorable. Your office is adorable."

"It's *not* adorable," he snapped. "It's conveniently located, it gets natural light, it has its own attached bathroom, it's a sophisticated space--"

"Weeeellll," I hedged as my eyes moved from the light yellow walls to the white painted trim of the paned windows. "It's sophisticated in a Simply Hello Kitty kind of way. But I do like it. The way they integrated the seashells and daisies into the crown molding…it's really…"

"Don't say it."

"It's *so* cute!"

He slammed his hand down on the desk and turned his glare to the window. "I'm getting a new office."

"You just signed a lease. Did it come with these furnishings?" I gestured to the only furniture in the room, the desk, a brown tufted leather office chair and two cushioned, wicker armchairs. "They absolutely fit the space. Totally charming."

"I'll paint the walls black."

"Then it'll just be adorably goth." I opened the door to what I assumed was a closet. It was a half bath with an old-fashioned pedestal sink that looked like it was plucked right out of a Victorian dollhouse. I got my smile in check before turning and walking over and perching myself on the edge of his desk, dangling my legs in his direction. "You know," I said in my most soothing tone, "you can be a pretty intimidating guy."

Anatoly made a noise that sounded like a half-hearted growl. He was nowhere near mollified.

"You *can* be," I insisted. "You have a mean glare when you're mad. You're like a hot James Bond villain." I shrugged off my purse from my shoulder. "It can be a problem."

"What are you talking about?"

"When you hire a P.I. you have to share a few secrets with him," I pointed out. "Open up the door to some of the more private areas of your life. It's hard to do that with an intimidating, tough guy. You need to take it down a notch. And you know how you do that?"

"I think I know where you're going with this."

"You need a super cute office," I continued with a nod. "When prospective clients come through that door they'll say, *okay, so he looks like he could kill me but those crown moldings of his are simply delightful!*"

He let his chin drop to his chest, his neck bent from the burden of my indictment.

"Who's the first client who gets to be enchanted by this place?" I asked.

"It's a new one," he grumbled. "He wants me to help him track down his stalker."

"You haven't had a stalker case in a while. Is the stalker a woman or a man?"

"He doesn't actually know." I tried not to giggle as I watched Anatoly's eyes wander up to the crown moldings and then dart away in shame. "He says someone put a miniature tracking device on his car. A very high-tech piece."

"Really?" Not many people would have the capability to do something like that. "Does he think the person who planted it is dangerous?"

"Very. But of course people's perceptions don't always match the reality, particularly if they feel threatened. In those cases they'll often exaggerate the danger in their own mind.

I'll get a better sense of the situation once I talk to him in person."

I let that sink in as I pushed myself to my feet and walked over to the window. The office was on the second floor of a classic three story San Francisco Edwardian. It had been converted to accommodate ground floor boutiques fitting of the recently gentrified little shopping area. The Thanksgiving weekend had just ended and the gift buying season was in full swing. From where I stood I could see the pedestrians wandering in and out of an organic, twelve-dollar-a-drink juice bar, an art gallery selling five thousand dollar sculptures made of recycled paint cans and a jewelry store that advertised conflict-free diamonds. Excess and apology all neatly wrapped up in one pretty little bow. Two years ago I had turned in a manuscript; *Dying to Laugh*, the final installment of my Alicia Bright murder mystery series, set on these very streets. My publisher packaged it, slapped a virtual bow on it and I sat back and watched as it ascended to the top of the New York Times bestsellers list. It was the sixth time an Alicia Bright mystery had reached the number one spot.

I had loved writing the series but it was time to move on. I needed to challenge myself, write new characters, prove to the world I could do more.

Except I hadn't done that. I hadn't written a word in seventeen months. There was something wrong with me.

From the corner of my eye I noted a figure standing a little too still, maybe looking up in my direction, but when I turned my head I saw that it was just a man in a black base-ball cap, looking down at his phone, not up. He quickly turned and walked away, head still bent toward his device.

Why were all these tech guys bothering to move to such a beautiful city if they were incapable of dragging their attention away from their screens?

"Does he have any idea who would *want* to stalk him?" I asked Anatoly, keeping us on a less depressing subject. "Or what they might hope to gain from it?"

"I think he does, but he didn't want to talk about it on the phone."

"Oh?" I ran my finger over the white painted wood that supported the squares of glass. "Because he thought someone might be listening in on the call?"

"That was the impression I got, yes. I don't anticipate that it'll be a dangerous assignment but it is…" he left the sentence incomplete as he drifted off into thought.

"Interesting," I said, electing to finish his statement as I turned back to face him. "That's a very interesting case."

"Yes," he said. Was that a note of guilt I heard in his voice? "It's been a while since I've had one of those."

It had been. Over the last few years, Anatoly has been offered an increasingly steady stream of cases dealing with insurance fraud, identity theft and wayward spouses. Well paying, low-risk cases. There was nothing to complain about. He was doing great.

We were doing great too, despite my writer's block (which I had purposely kept him in the dark about). From the moment we became a couple, Anatoly and I had either been on the precipice of a breakup or basking in the post-coital glow of reconciliation. His flaws have always scratched against mine in just the right way, igniting the most beautiful firework displays our city had ever seen. It all sort of came to a head in a chaotic, messy weekend in Vegas about two and a half years ago. We almost killed each other on that trip. But then some cartel chick named Margarita tried to kill me. Then a grudge bearing Russian dude named Alex Kinsky helped Anatoly save me from Margarita but also threatened to kill Anatoly and, well…it was just really complicated. After a rapid succession of near-death experiences, Anatoly and I decided that peacefully loving each other was better than strangling one another.

And now we had reached this place in our relationship that was just…different. We've fallen into a routine. A *good* routine. One that involves a lot of classic movie nights, reading the morning paper over cappuccino, the occasional ride along the beach on his Harley, glorious home-cooked meals (prepared exclusively by him) and great sex…although the latter wasn't happening as frequently as it used to and sometimes it seemed the intensity wasn't quite as, well, *intense*…but that was probably my imagination and it was still better than anything I'd had with *anyone* else by a *lot*. For the first time in over a decade, I had no deadlines hanging over my head, no conflicts, no drama, no chaos. This must be what all those fairy tales were talking about when they said *they lived happily ever after*.

But then, maybe not. I was hardly an expert on fairy tales. Only the dark ones interested me.

I smiled up at Anatoly and clasped my hands behind my back, the picture of innocence. "When's he coming?"

"In less than forty minutes and I believe you have a hair appointment in an hour. So if you're done insulting my office--" He gallantly gestured to the door.

"That's tomorrow." I self-consciously pulled at my hair. The fact that Anatoly remembered I had a salon appointment at all was an indication of how out of control my hair had gotten since my last one. "Today's my lunch with Dena."

"Great, say hello for me."

"Can I help?"

He hesitated, his jaw tightening ever so slightly. "Help with what?"

"Can I sit in on your meeting? You could say I'm your secretary. I could take notes."

His sigh was almost heavy enough to squash my hopes. Almost. "You're not my secretary, so no."

"Oh come on, I'll keep everything confidential. And maybe I'll have some good insights that can help you. I mean, I do have some experience with this kind of thing."

"Experience?" He shook his head and stuck his thumbs in the pockets of his jeans. "Stumbling upon a few crime scenes doesn't make you an investigator. It makes you un-lucky and accident prone."

I sat down in the chair behind his desk, swiveling it back and forth as I kept my eyes firmly on his. "I solved those crimes that I stumbled upon. I might just be a black Veronica Mars in the making."

"Yes, except you haven't solved a crime since that show was canceled. And wasn't Veronica Mars supposed to be eighteen?"

"It hasn't been that long and...okay, fine, I'm a little older than Veronica was," I said, coolly.

"Yes, by almost twenty ye--"

"Don't." I snapped. I rested my elbows on his desk and my chin in my hands. "Come on, let me be your secretary, just for the length of one meeting. Or even your assistant! It would be fun! Every Sherlock needs a Watson."

"You're not my Watson. And you have other plans this afternoon."

"I'll text Dena and tell her I'm going to be late. Come on, it'll be like old times."

"Sophie--"

"Please, Anatoly." But my tone had changed against my wishes. I had wanted to sound teasing but persuasive. I hadn't meant for that note of desperation to sneak in there.

Anatoly heard it. I could tell by the way he shifted his weight back on his heels and tilted his head half an inch to the side. He was going to ask me one of those horribly generic questions that people ask their lovers like: *What's going on with you?* Or *Is everything okay?*

I didn't know what was going on with me even though I felt the weight of it. I couldn't explain and I really, really didn't want to try.

And then, like a reprieve from God, there was a knock on the door. A giant grin spread slowly across my face. "Think our client's early?" Before Anatoly could respond, I was out of my seat, across the room and flinging open the door.

Before me, stood a fifty-something-year-old man only three inches taller than me. His blond, white streaked hair was unkempt and hung limply around his hollowed cheeked face. Everything he was wearing from his slightly-too-big Brooks Brothers chinos to his Tom Ford horned rimmed glasses implied a certain degree of wealth even as the missing shirt button and coffee stains that decorated the slightly frayed designer fabric projected something very different.

"I'm looking for Anatoly Darinsky?" he said, somewhat uncertainly.

"That would be the guy behind me. I'm Sophie Katz, his assistant." I caught a glimpse of Anatoly's expression over my shoulder and quickly amended. "Administrative assistant. Please come in!"

"I'm early." He stepped forward, hesitantly. Anatoly moved to shake his hand but the man rejected the gesture.

"My hands are sweaty," he said, his voice shaking slightly. "Is there somewhere I can wash them?"

"Right through here." Anatoly opened the door to the bathroom for him and the man excused himself briefly. We both listened while the water ran. I went over to Anatoly's desk and found a notepad and pen. Anatoly shot me a look and mouthed *You're unbelievable.* To which I responded by mouthing, *I know.* Although to be fair, this was the first time in, like, a year that I had done anything that was even remotely unbelievable.

But this wraith of a man in Anatoly's new, cutesy bathroom had me feeling oddly hopeful. Like I was perversely elevated by the promise of sharing in another's turmoil. I smiled broadly at Anatoly as he frowned, knowing I was pressing his buttons. Hoping that maybe, just maybe, this would be the first step to becoming truly unbelievable again.

# CHAPTER
TWO

When you hear hoof-beats it's usually horses. Occasionally it's zebras. But every once in a while it's some terrifying, previously unknown creature that will completely change the way you think about hoof-beats.
--Dying to Laugh

I sat next to our guest, Aaron London, as Anatoly examined him from behind his desk. Mr. London was polite but jittery and had already requested to see our drivers' licenses to prove our identities. But when we handed them over he seemed to have a tough time reading the words, holding them up this way and that in order to bring them into focus. My eyes kept wandering to his lips. They were so chapped they didn't even look fully human. A drop of blood rested behind a flap of dry skin near the corner of his mouth.

I offered him the Fiji water I had been hauling around with me in my purse along with an encouraging smile. He accepted both, taking a long drink before placing the bottle on the floor by his feet. I held my pen over the notepad in anticipation. "I'm sorry I'm so early," he said for about the fifth time.

"It's not a problem." Anatoly's thin smile didn't hide his irritation at being forced to repeat the reassurance.

"I believe it might throw them off if I don't show up where I'm expected when I'm expected."

"Who exactly are you trying to throw off?" Anatoly asked.

"The people tracking me," he replied after an uncomfortably long pause. "There are people trying to kill me."

I made a quick note: *homicidal tracking experts (bad guys).*

"Tell me about them," Anatoly requested, his voice was calm and even, "Why are they going to such extreme measures?"

London shook his head, a few strands of his hair moved with him, but it was too thin to really be whipped around. "I know things," he explained. "Things I'm not supposed to know." His eyes locked on me again and this time the anxiety there was so intense I found myself pulling back as if it might be contagious. Yes, I sought a degree of turmoil, but there was something off about this man. "What do you know about the pharmaceutical industry?" he asked.

I looked over at Anatoly who rewarded me with a barely perceptible shrug. "It's safe to assume neither one of us are experts," I admitted.

"I used to be in pharmaceuticals," London rubbed his hands against his wrinkled pants. "The way the business is run…it's not good, not good at all."

"I'm not sure I'm following," Anatoly said as I wrote *pharmaceutical industry: bad!*

"The amount of money spent on developing a drug, you have no idea. And when you spend all that money only to discover that your drug can have dangerous side effects, well the companies don't want to cop to that. They want to get their product to market even if it kills. And they *want* to kill me because I know that."

"What pharmaceutical company are we talking about, specifically?" I asked as I furiously scribbled away.

"Nolan-Volz is the worst of them, but there's a lot of collusion between these organizations. Anti-trust laws are being broken right and left. We just keep seeing the same story play out over and over again. Rispolex prescribed off label! Thalidomide! Doctors on the take! A medical ethics professor at NYU exposed how corrupt the testing system for drugs is but her reports were completely ignored! The whole medical establishment is in on it!"

"The *whole* medical establishment?" I asked, giving him the opportunity to pull back on the hyperbole. I would ask what the hell he was talking about in regards to the rest of it in a moment.

But rather than correct himself he nodded sagely and leaned forward, and urgently whispered. "The government is in on it too."

I looked down at my notepad and considered writing *government: Bad!* But these days that went without saying.

"They want me dead too! Our own government!" London continued.

Anatoly shifted his head toward the window as a siren briefly disrupted the more benign background noises of the streets. "I find that unlikely, Mr. London."

"Do you?" London retorted sarcastically. "Why is that? You think our government doesn't kill its own citizens? The death penalty! Covert operations! How many do you think they drove to suicide while testing LSD on unsuspecting Americans? What about eugenics? Where do you think the Nazis got *that* idea, huh?"

Following London's train of thought was getting harder by the second. My notes had become a jumbled mash up of conspiracy theory catch phrases. I was seeking turmoil, not incoherence. "Maybe we can put the drugs and Nazis aside for a moment and focus on what's going on with you in the here and now?"

He looked at me blankly and then fell back in his chair as if exhausted from his own ranting. "Of course. I'm sorry," he said, hoarsely. "I've been under such stress. It's not just that they're following me." With a slow purposeful movement, he ran his hand through his hair, then held up his flattened palm. It was covered with dozens of strands, apparently dislodged from his scalp with only the lightest touch. "I think they're poisoning me too," he whispered. "I'm not thinking straight. I'm weak and…" he looked down at the loose hairs, allowing the disturbing visual to complete his sentence. "I don't know how it's being done, how it's transmitted…I've taken to washing my hands immediately before touching another person. There could be toxins in my sweat. You know, Putin isn't the only government leader who poisons those who cross him. It can happen anywhere, to any of us."

"Maybe we can start with the evidence that you're being followed," Anatoly suggested. "Do you still have the tracking device they put on your car?"

I could tell by the way Anatoly said the word "they," that he was dubious of the pronoun's accuracy.

London looked up at Anatoly, surprised. "It's still on my

car."

Anatoly's stare chilled me and clearly shamed London who began fiddling with his glasses, pulling them down and then pushing them back up on the bridge of his nose. "Don't you think it's a good idea to take the device off?" Anatoly asked. "So *they* can't follow you anymore?"

"Of course it is," London conceded. "But I can't find it. I've taken it to a mechanic but they said they'd have to take apart the whole car to locate it. I took it to the police and they couldn't find it either and they weren't even sure if they had the legal authority to arrest anyone even if they *did* find it. Our legal system hasn't caught up with our technology! There are no laws against putting GPS tracking devices on *anything*. The politicians don't understand all the horrible ways technology can be applied! There's no regulation, no protections, no--"

"Evidence," Anatoly interrupted. "There is no evidence that there ever was a tracking device on your car. Maybe that's because there isn't one."

"No, no, it's there! I'll be driving around and no one will be on my tail. And then suddenly there's a Zipcar!"

"A Zipcar," Anatoly repeated.

"Yes! And it will follow me at a distance. Too much of a distance for me to make out the driver. Then if I do a U-turn or pull over, the Zipcar will drive off, in the opposite direction of course, so I can't see who's in it! And then maybe an hour later, maybe two, the Zipcar will be back! Sometimes it's the same one. Sometimes a different one. I know it wasn't following me all that time so how did it find me? It was *tracking* me!"

"There are a lot of Zipcars in the city." I was doing my

level best to point out the obvious without sounding patronizing. "Maybe that's the reason they keep popping up. Espe-
cially since you're not always seeing the same car."

"No, that's not how it works!" London said, imploringly.
"The driver must have a computer with them. A laptop
maybe. And they bring it from Zipcar to Zipcar--" but he
wasn't able to finish due to a coughing fit. It was a wet, ugly
cough and I found myself torn between wanting to pat him
on the back and desperately searching my bag for my bottle
of Purell.

"Have you gone to a doctor?" Anatoly asked. "To get
tested for poison or…anything else?"

"Didn't you hear me? The medical establishment can't
be trusted! Doctors are taking bribes from drug companies,
performing needless procedures on homeless people!" He
broke into another short coughing fit but then managed to
continue. "Did you know that right now, as we speak, people
are forming a New World Order? Oligarchs and their bought
and paid for politicians are going to try to take over everything!"

"Wait," I asked, "are you talking about Super Pacs?"

"No! Or yes, but no! It's going to get so much worse
than it is now! We can't trust anyone. No one has our inter-
ests at heart. Not the little guy, not blacks!" He jabbed his
finger at me with an almost desperate zeal. "They don't care
about what happens to the blacks!"

"Fucking Zipcar driving racists," I replied, managing to
keep a straight face.

"Mr. London, I think maybe we have to start again,"
Anatoly suggested. "Do you or do you not, have the names
of any *individuals* who might want to do you harm and do

you have *any* concrete evidence that someone is actively trying to?"

"They're poisoning me," he said, weakly. "Look at me. Use your eyes and see me dying. You're witnessing my murder."

Anatoly studied him for a moment and I could see the cocktail of pity and disappointment pouring out of him. "I'm afraid I can't take your case."

"But I've nowhere else to go," London whispered, blushing. The little bit of color actually made him seem less crazed and more, well, vulnerable. "You're the only P.I. of good repute who would agree to even see me."

"I'm sure others would take a meeting," Anatoly replied, perhaps a little too curtly.

I felt shame creep down my throat, settling in my gut. I had been attracted to the idea of a nefarious stalker that could be tracked down and held accountable. I had loved this stranger for the turbulence I assumed surrounded him. But the turbulence was within him. The demons stalking him could never be caught. This wasn't an adventure, it was a tragedy.

"It took me so long to work up the courage to come here,," London said, softly. "You've listened to me explain why I need help. Now all you have to do is see."

Anatoly *had* listened but with thinly veiled impatience. To be fair, that was the best this man could ever realistically hope for given the insanity of his story. And yet he had hoped for more.

Quietly I put the pad and pen on Anatoly's desk. There was no longer a need for note taking. Anatoly's silence in the face of this man's pleas was both firm and deafening.

"What will I do?" London whispered.

"I strongly recommend you speak with a doctor," Anatoly suggested and rose from his chair. "But that's up to you. Regardless, we should wrap things up here. I don't want to waste your time."

"No," London agreed. "After all, I may not have much left to waste."

There was an awkward silence as we all remained in our places, Anatoly and I both waiting for London to get up. But London seemed unaware that this was the logical next step. Sullenly meditative, he picked idly at loose hairs on his pant leg. Most looked like they were his, but I noted that others were short and black.

"Maybe I could walk you to your car?" I offered.

He stared at me blankly for what seemed like an eternity.

"It wouldn't be an inconvenience," I added. "I have to head out to make a lunch thing anyway."

Again nothing and then finally a nod. I mouthed *I'll call you* to Anatoly as London got to his feet. When he walked with me toward the door his movements seemed labored, like every step was a small challenge. Was he moving like that when he came into the office or was it just the mass of disillusionment that he was struggling under?

We left the office and took the stairs slowly. When he seemed to falter, I linked my arm through his, offering him support but masking it in companionship to spare whatever remained of his pride. The gesture stopped him in his tracks.

"Aren't you afraid?"

"Of what?" I asked.

"Of touching me. Even people who don't believe me, they don't want to touch me or be close to me. They see something's wrong with me and it scares them."

My mind automatically traveled back to my childhood when everyone was afraid to so much as shake hands with all the people in this city who were diagnosed with AIDS. We isolated them, made them feel like pariahs doomed to die alone. "I'm not afraid," I said, definitively.

I thought I saw the glimmer of a tear in his eye and I looked away, urging him forward. "Anatoly just moved into that office space today," I said in an attempt to lighten the mood.

"It's cute," London replied, absently.

"*Right?* I think there are apartments on the third floor. I'm sure they're lovely but I don't know if I'd want to live directly over a shopping district."

"You live in Ashbury Heights," he noted as I pushed open the heavy glass door that brought us to the street.

I turned and stared at him. "How?"

"Your driver's license."

The cool air touched my face and I found myself smiling at London as the shoppers streamed around us. "You're an observant man."

"Observant, yes," he started to lead me down the sidewalk, "but I'm beginning to question if I can still confidently call myself a man."

"Don't be ridiculous," I said, lightly. "You're just going through a rough patch, that's all."

"You mistake me," he said so softly I had to lean in to hear him. "What I mean is that there's so little left of the man I used to be it's as if I'm not fully here anymore. When I look in the mirror I don't see a person. I see a ghost, a corpse that doesn't have the sense to stop breathing."

Alllrighty then. That's not creepy at all.

He then went quiet for a few minutes as we continued to walk past a parallel-parked lineup of Prius and Teslas, Christmas wreaths hanging on each and every lamppost. I was about to ask him exactly where he parked his car when he piped up again. "Have you ever convinced yourself of something? Something that was unlikely?"

I exhaled in relief. I'm not sure it's such a horrible thing to occasionally be delusional but if your delusions are as dark as London's it's much better to come back to more mundane realities. "We all do that," I assured him. "Human nature."

"That's true," he agreed, thoughtfully. "After all, what is God but something we've convinced ourselves of with no evidence to support? What is the American dream but a fallacy to give the poor false hope? We're all convinced that we're going to be the exception to the rule."

Okay, so not exactly the direction I was hoping for. "What unlikely thing have you convinced yourself of specifically?"

He sighed as we walked by San Francisco's latest farm-to-table restaurant. "I convinced myself that you would help me."

Now it was me who abruptly stopped walking, pulling him to a stop with me before removing my arm from his. "I want to," I said, sincerely. "But I think the kind of help you need is different than the kind of help you think you need."

"You mean--" but before he could finish he started coughing. He lurched forward as the spasms violently wrenched away his physical control, causing the tip of his shoe to catch on a piece of uneven pavement. As he fell, his hands found the sidewalk in time to keep him from cracking open his skull. People around us stopped as I kneeled next to him, helpless as I watched his body shake and his face contort.

"Is he okay?" I heard a woman ask. Now on his hands and knees, London's coughs were getting worse. His glasses slipped from his face and dropped uselessly to the ground. He couldn't seem to stop. Whooping cough maybe?

"London? Should I call a doctor?" I asked. It was a stupid question. The man couldn't even talk. He looked up at me, his eyes fearful and milky, the convulsions racking through his delicate frame. "Call 911!" I cried out to the gathering crowd. But before I could fully get the words out he had fallen into unconsciousness, his glasses cracking beneath him. The coughs were now just gasps for breath and the time between each gasp kept getting a little longer. I looked up to see about five people on their cell phones, all calling for help. I reached into the pockets of London's jacket to see if there was anything useful there. An inhaler maybe? Could he have asthma? Maybe an EpiPen? But all I found was a crumpled up failed-payment notification from his car insurance provider and his phone in a camouflage patterned case. The phone was displaying one new text message from a number apparently not in his contacts.

Confusion hath now made his masterpiece

That was the whole text. No explanation, no laughing emoji to imply it was a joke. The damp wind must have been working its way through the cloth of my sweater because my skin suddenly felt cold.

I looked up at the street just as a Zipcar passed us by.

# CHAPTER
THREE

*"When I said I'd just go with the flow I didn't realize the
flow was created by the flushing of a toilet."*
--Dying To Laugh

It was complete madness. The paramedics arrived as I was
attempting to administer CPR. They were quick to load
London into the ambulance and while they found his car
keys and wallet in his pants pocket, presumably with his ID
and insurance info, they had somehow left me holding his
coat, phone and that stupid payment notice. I dictated a text
to Dena to tell her I had to cancel lunch and would explain
why later and then drove to the hospital as quickly as possible. Anatoly called but I had accidentally turned my Bluetooth off and couldn't deal with my phone at the same time
as I was racing through the narrow streets of the city. Besides, I wouldn't know what to say to him. I had no *clue*
what was going on. Maybe I'd get to the hospital and discover that London did have asthma and they had fixed everything in the ambulance. Or maybe he had cancer or some
other disease that he hadn't told us about.

Or maybe he had been poisoned by a person who was

following him around in a Zipcar.

As soon as I got to the hospital, before I even got out of my parked Audi, I tried calling the number the *Confusion* text had come from. I was greeted by an automated message telling me it wasn't a valid number. I dialed again, carefully entering each digit as it appeared on London's screen. But I got the same automated message. I tried calling from London's phone. It made no difference.

But you can't send a text from an invalid number, can you?

It was a question that kept running through my mind as I walked through the hospital entrance, clutching London's cell and jacket. The lobby was populated with people carrying Get-Well-Soon bouquets in their hands and brave smiles on their faces. The four women behind the sprawling reception desk seemed relaxed though, completely accustomed to being surrounded by the earth shattering events of human life.

"Hi," I said to the grey haired, sixty-something women sitting behind one of the desk's computers. "I'm here about Aaron London? He was just brought in through the emergency room."

The woman gave me a quick, sympathetic look as her fingers flew over her keyboard. "Relation?"

I blinked. I couldn't even truthfully call myself London's friend. "I'm his girlfriend."

As soon as the lie left my mouth I wanted to take it back. *Girlfriend* is not a relation. There was no value in *girlfriend*.

Besides, it made me look bad. If I had said wife it could have been assumed that we initially hooked up when he was still hot…or at least presentable. Now the doctors would think London was the best I could do.

Why am I this shallow?

"You can wait for him in the emergency room reception area," she said, gesturing to the left. "Go down that hallway and take a left at the very end of it. Sign in at the reception area there. If they move him to surgery they'll have someone let you know Miss...?"

"Katz, Sophie Katz." She gave me a visitor's pass to stick on my shirt and I followed her directions.

The emergency room waiting area was like all emergency room waiting areas: awful. Regardless of how well cleaned, they always stunk of sickness and distress. It was hard not to be envious of the ward's receptionists behind the glass, physically separated from the upheaval in their sterilized little bubble.

After signing in, I found two empty chairs a little ways away from anyone else, one for me and one for London's things.

Why didn't a guy as paranoid as London have his phone password protected? I would have thought he'd have one of those fingerprint things on it or maybe even new facial recognition technology. And aren't iPhones supposed to be harder to hack than Droids? What good was paranoia if it didn't at least make you security savvy?

I looked around the room as if I expected any of the people in there with me to have answers. The black man in the corner with the neatly clipped, short hair and downward turned mouth, frantically texting some presumably bad news, or the redhead chewing on her nails as she watched the doors that led to the exam rooms as if the strength of her will was enough to get a doctor to burst through with better news.

Nothing here was reassuring.

I picked up London's jacket again and started searching the pockets one more time as if something meaningful might have magically appeared in there since the last time I searched. But of course the pockets were now empty. Except...

I reached deeper into the inside pocket, something *was* there, halfway through a hole in the silk lining, making it easy to miss.

I pulled out two copper colored keys. House keys? Office keys? I shrugged and zipped them into the small pocket of my purse so I wouldn't lose them. Next I started skimming through the phone.

But there was nothing on it. Like, nothing-nothing. Not a single photo, the Facebook app had not been activated and if he had ever gotten a text from anyone else it had been erased. But maybe there would be something telling in his emails...

"Miss Katz?" I looked up to see the grey haired woman from the front desk. Her hands were clasped together in a worried fashion. Next to her was another woman in her early-forties, a blonde wind-blown bob hung around her long face as her cowl necked sweater drew attention to a small strand of pearls that lay slightly askew across her collarbone. Hanging back behind them stood a curvy teenage girl. Her thick mane of blonde hair fell all the way down her back, adding a hefty dose of femininity to her grey-striped hoodie and jeans ensemble.

The woman with the bob pointed a slender finger toward the chair next to mine. "I believe that's my husband's coat."

Husband? But this woman looked so...normal!

Well, maybe they hooked up while he was still hot. I stared at the coat and then the phone in my hand. "Maybe I should explain."

But the woman clearly had no interest in explanations. She crossed over and grabbed his jacket and then held out her hand toward me expectantly. "His phone?"

My own phone started ringing in my bag but I didn't reach for it. "I'm not his girlfriend," I croaked. "I was with him when he collapsed and--"

"I just want his phone." Her voice was restrained although I thought I detected a slight tremor. "I know that case, don't try to tell me it's not his. And I don't want or need an explanation."

I hesitated a moment and then carefully placed it in her palm. "He got a text--"

"Stop talking!" Her voice had lowered to a whispered yell. I shrank back, unnerved.

"Mrs. London?"

We all turned at the name. A doctor in a lab coat was standing by the doors.

"Anita," she said with a sigh. "Call me Anita." She glanced down at me one more time and then nodded at the teenage girl who approached the doctor with her. The three of them formed a small huddle, excluding everyone else in the room from the conversation. The woman from the front desk was now glaring at me and when I tried to meet her eyes she just gave a quick shake of her head, turned and left. Fantastic. If I ever had a medical emergency I'd have to tell the paramedics to take me to a different hospital.

I stood up and looked over at Anita as she put her arm gently around the teenager's shoulders, protectively pulling her close. She gave the doctor a curt nod and he turned to leave as she went to the window where the receptionists and administrators were. She quietly accepted a clipboard full of forms before crossing to the nearest chair to start filling them out. Tentatively, I approached, stopping several feet in front of them. They both ignored me, and I watched as she checked off the "Ms." box and wrote her name, Anita J. London.

"I was just the person who happened to be standing with him when he collapsed," I tried again. "I gave him CPR but…I'm not really trained in it. I don't know if it helped."

Mrs. London refused to look up. But the teenager did. She observed me through bloodshot eyes. "He has fluid around his heart and lungs," she explained. "A lot of it."

"You don't need to talk to her," Anita said, crisply.

"My father has to have emergency surgery." She looked over at the double doors where they kept the patients.

Anita finally looked up although she gave her entire focus to the girl. "Catherine Jaynes London, you do *not* share family business with strangers!"

"It isn't family business, Mom!" Catherine said, her voice rising. "It's life or death!"

"Don't be ridiculous, people don't die of pneumonia."

"We don't know that's what it is and they *do* if it's left untreated! You heard what the doctor said!" Catherine looked up at me again. "Why didn't you tell him to go to the doctor sooner? Why did you wait until he collapsed? Are you stupid?"

"I…" but my mind wasn't working fast enough to come up with an appropriate response.

"Life and death *is* a family matter," Anita growled, more

to me than to her daughter. "He's our family. You are not. You should leave."

"He got a weird text," I blurted out. Anita London was going to get this information whether she wanted it or not. "Confusion hath now made his masterpiece."

A rueful smile played on Anita's lips. "Now I see why he liked you, you're crazy too."

"I'm not his girlfriend," I said again. "I just *met* your husband today!"

"I don't care." Suddenly, she was on her feet again. "I don't care who you are. The father of my child is about to get emergency surgery. His pulse is…well, I can't remember the numbers, but it's *not* what it should be. Not even in the vicinity! So I don't care if you met my husband today or if you've been fucking him for years. What I care about is filling out this paperwork so they can stick a scalpel in him and save his life. Will you let me do that now?"

"Sure, yes, of course." I backed up and then slowly sat down in the row of chairs across from her. My phone started to go off again and I began to reach for it but Anita's voice stopped me.

"Leave!" she yelled and this time everyone in the waiting room, including those administrators behind their protective little window, were staring at us openly. Anita, Catherine and I were the train wreck and I was the one who had taken us off the rails.

I swallowed, hard, and adjusted the strap of my handbag on my shoulder. "I'm sorry you're going through all this," I said, quietly. I reached into my bag and pulled out a pen and a crumpled receipt I didn't need. On the back, I wrote my name and number. "When you're ready, I really think we should talk."

Anita started filling out the forms again, pointedly ignoring the paper still in my hand. Quietly I put it on the seat next to her daughter. "When you're ready," I said again.

And then I left. Because there was nothing else to do.

CHAPTER
FOUR

*"I want a man who will pour me champagne and distract
me from my problems and girlfriends who will buy me
shots while I wallow in them."
--Dying to Laugh*

Dena's text came in while I was sitting at a stoplight contemplating how all those poems and songs about the heart are completely off base. Whether it's the excited butterflies of love or the cramps of anxiety, it's clear that all our emotions live in or around our intestinal tract. It was going to take a bottle of Tums to deal with all the emotions currently swirling around down there. Nothing about my exchange with Anita or her husband before her was sitting well.

I picked up my phone and read the text noting for the first time the three missed calls from Anatoly. Dena's text read:

Is everything okay?

I texted back: *sort of yes, sort of no.*

As the light turned green Dena called. "Are you okay or not?" she asked, skipping the hellos and filling my car with her Kathleen-Turneresque voice.

"I'm fine," I reassured her. "Sorry I stood you up. But I mean, you will not *believe* what went down this afternoon!"

"You got yourself into a mess?" Dena asked, dryly. "I'm shocked."

"It's been some time since I've been in a mess."

She paused for half a second before conceding in a more conciliatory tone, "Fair enough. Lunch might have been hard anyway. A new shipment came in a day early and one of my salespeople called in sick. But Mary Ann's stopping by at six. We're going to try to catch one of the Happy Hours around here. Join us. You can test the limits of my belief."

The invitation sounded extraordinarily appealing. I had known Dena and her younger cousin, Mary Ann, since high school. Mary Ann never failed to make me smile and Dena…well, I could always count on Dena to give it to me straight without ever judging me. I needed that because at the moment I wasn't thinking straight and I was feeling a little judgmental of myself.

"Or do you have to smooth things over with Anatoly tonight?" she asked before I had even given her an answer to the last question.

"Smooth things over?" I repeated. "We're fine." I braked for a bicyclist who was trying to use the entire street as a bike lane. "We're totally and completely, disconcertingly fine."

"Oookay," Dena replied. "Sounds—"

But her next few words were cut off with the beep of another incoming call. Anatoly.

"That's him. I'll be at Guilty Pleasures at six." I switched over as I maneuvered up one of San Francisco's ninety-degree hills. "Anatoly? Oh my God, you'll never believe this but London might actually have a stalker!"

Silence.

"Anatoly?" I asked, a little more tentatively this time. "Is that you?"

"I called you three times," he finally replied, his voice even lower than normal.

"Oh, I saw that, sorry. But I mean, I'm talking about a really *evil* stalker," I clarified. "The kind that poisons someone and then sends him cryptically poetic texts. Of course it's possible…maybe even probable that it was coincidence, but still, it was all so weird! Am I making sense?"

"No," Anatoly said coolly.

"I was just walking London to his car and he collapsed into a coughing fit. Now the doctors are saying there's fluid around his heart and lungs. It's total insanity." As I reached the top of the hill I decided to turn on my headlights for extra visibility. The fog was so low and thick it was like driving through a cloud.

"Sounds like pneumonia," Anatoly noted.

"Oh don't be so mundane," I retorted. "I told you, he got a text. It said, 'Confusion hath made its masterpiece.'"

"Crazy people get crazy texts."

"Maybe," I allowed, "but here's the weird thing. I tried to call the number he got the text from and it was an invalid number. It's like someone disconnected their phone seconds before sending the text."

"Or they were using a fake SMS texting service," Anatoly said, impatiently.

"A…I'm sorry, a what?"

"There are apps that allow you to send texts from fake numbers. Sophie--"

"But why would anyone use a service like that unless they were up to something nefarious?"

"Because teenagers and trolls think it's funny," he snapped. "Sophie, I'm sorry London is sick, but that was obvious the minute he walked into my office. And you should have called me back."

"I told you, things got out of control."

"None of this was yours to control to begin with," he replied, more forcefully now. "You're my lover and my girlfriend but you are *not* my business partner."

I blanched, stopping a second too long at the stop sign. "You said you didn't mind my assisting you on this case."

"When exactly did I say that?"

"You implied it." I looked to my left to see one of Google's driverless cars.

"How?"

"By raising your eyebrows!" It was disturbingly tempting to try to run the car and its passenger off the road just to see what it would do.

"My eyebrows don't speak for me," Anatoly said, slowly. "And I don't insert myself into your work."

"Don't you?" I snapped. "I have missed an infinite number of deadlines because of you."

"You've missed two deadlines because of me," Anatoly growled.

"People have tried to *kill me* because of you!" I continued. "*That* has interfered with my work."

"I was *shot* because of *you.*"

"Please. It was a flesh wound." I waved at a pedestrian, signaling that it was okay to cross in front of me.

"*You didn't pick up your phone!*" he said again, raising his voice. Anatoly never raised his voice.

I tilted my head to the side. "Are you okay?"

"You walked out of my office arm in arm with a very troubled man and when I called you *three* times it went to voicemail. I called Dena but you didn't tell her where you were going. You didn't tell *me* where you were going. If you had been in my shoes what conclusion would you have jumped to?"

"You were worried about me?"

"Of *course* I was worried about you!"

"That's so sweet!"

"Sophie," he said, warningly.

"I'm sorry," I added, quickly. "I got distracted, but I should have picked up."

There was a long silence on the other end of the line. "You're apologizing," he said, carefully.

"I am," I confirmed. "I know I haven't done that in a while, but if you think about it, we haven't argued in a long time either."

"That's true."

"Now, can we get back to the stalker?"

"London doesn't have a stalker." The edge crept back into his voice. "He's obviously suffering from some untreated psychiatric condition and possibly from substance abuse."

I chewed gently on my lower lip. I could tell Anatoly that I saw a Zipcar but he'd only point out that wasn't exactly unusual in San Francisco. I could tell him about London's wife and daughter but he would tell me his personal relationships weren't any of my business and certainly didn't support any suspicions that London's health issues were brought on purposely by another. He'd be right about that too. Anatoly was being infuriatingly logical. "I may visit him in the hospital," I said instead.

"Don't. He might take your presence as validation of the merit of his convoluted story. The best case scenario would be for him to spend a few months in a psychiatric facility."

Anatoly was right. That might be the best outcome.

But it didn't *feel* right.

"I still think I might visit him," I pushed.

"It's a bad plan, Sophie," Anatoly sighed. "But if you have to, it should only be to give him back his wedding ring."

"Excuse me?"

"When he washed his hands it must have slipped off his finger. I just found it in the sink, halfway under the drain stopper. Since his wife is at the hospital maybe you can just give it to her and be done with it."

I told the hospital I was his girlfriend and when his wife goes to his bedside he won't be wearing his wedding ring. *Fuck!*

"Are you still at the office?" I asked, hopefully.

"Yes, but only for another hour. I have a potentially cheating husband I need to be tailing. I'm afraid I won't be done until at least nine so you'll have to get dinner without me."

"No worries, I'm meeting Dena and Mary Ann for drinks tonight anyway. But I'm coming over right now for the ring, okay?"

"Fine. If you over do it on the drinks give me a call and

I'll pick you up."

"Well, in that case, I'm doing shots," I joked.

"Don't get so drunk I'll feel guilty about taking advantage of you later."

I laughed and agreed to stay sober enough for consensual sex before ending the call and turning the car around. I had *no* idea how I was going to get that ring back to London, but I would figure out a way, a subtle way, so as not to make things worse for him. "I *am* going to help you, London," I whispered as I drove down the narrow streets. "This time, for real."

CHAPTER
FIVE

"You can reject Robert Frost's advice and choose the road most traveled, but it's still going to lead you to some unexpected and dangerously rugged detours. No one gets to stay on the paved road for the whole trip."
-Dying To Laugh

It says something about my friendship with Dena that I was unsurprised to find her absently doing bicep curls with giant dildos at the end of a work day, one black, one pinkish. She was standing in the middle of her store, Guilty Pleasures, studying a collection of colorful ball-gags hanging from hooks in the wall, her thick, Sicilian eyebrows scrunched together adding drama to her otherwise kittenish features.

"Ready for dinner?" I asked as I maneuvered around two giggling twenty-somethings hunched over the edible panties display.

Dena looked up, my voice pulling her out of her thoughts and then glanced at her wind-up watch, a subtle form of rebellion against the technification of the city. "Since when do you arrive anywhere early? That's Mary Ann's thing." She glanced back up at the wall. "I'm thinking about moving these further back and doing a vibrator display here instead." She held out the giant mechanical penises for my inspection. "I have these in eight different skin-tones now. Diversity."

I nodded and tapped the black one. "In February you should put the darker ones up front in honor of Black History Month."

Dena blinked down at the vibrators. "That's fucking brilliant."

"Do you have any black, Jewish dildos?" I asked. "To celebrate both sides of my racial and cultural identity?"

Dena held up the phallic device so it was eye level with me. "It's circumcised, isn't it? But if you're asking if I have any black dildos that will fuck you while playing Hava Nagila the answer is no."

"The limits of technology," I sighed as my eyes wandered over to a shelf holding a smiling, silicon creature with antennas. Its packaging read, *Flexi Felix for Anal Fun Days*! "I think Leah might be dating someone," I said, ideally. "She usually goes MIA when things are going really well for her and I haven't heard a peep from her in weeks."

Dena's gaze followed mine. "What is it about Flexi that made you think of your sister? Oh, is it because she's a tight-ass?"

"What? Okay, first off no and secondly *ew!* I was just thinking about how everything in my life has been so...I don't know...quiet lately. Getting a respite from Leah is probably part of that. Or at least it was quiet until today--"

The chime of the front entrance interrupted my stream of thought and alerted us to Mary Ann's arrival. She was half walking, half skipping in our direction, her chestnut curls bouncing enthusiastically around her shoulders giving her the look of a model from a shampoo commercial.

"Oh my God, I'm so glad you could come out tonight!" Mary Ann said, as she gave me an enthusiastic hug and then Dena a more tentative one as she carefully avoided contact with the dildos in her hands. "I have news!"

"Is it something I won't believe?" Dena asked, giving me a sidelong glance.

"Seriously guys!" Mary Ann's porcelain complexion flushed with excitement. "I'm going to have a baby!"

I froze in utter shock. Dena looked down at the black dildo as if it was somehow responsible.

"You're going to be a mom," I whispered. Then squealed, "You're going to be a mom!" It was enough to attract the attention of the giggling girls who looked up from the flavored lubes in their hands.

"I didn't even know this was something you were thinking about!" Dena said, the traces of suppressed emotion bringing her voice up an octave.

"Well, Monty and I have been talking about it for a while and we've decided it doesn't make sense to wait any longer. Now's the time!"

"We have to celebrate!" I stated firmly. "What should we do?"

"We can start by *not* going to happy hour," Dena gave Mary Ann a stern look. "No way in hell are you drinking during your pregnancy."

"Oh, I'm not pregnant," Mary Ann said, blithely. "I can have at least one cocktail. We have to toast this!"

Dena scrutinized her cousin and then looked over at me to see if I was as lost as she was.

I cleared my throat and shifted my weight from foot to foot. "Sooo…are you adopting?"

"No, what makes you think that?" Mary Ann looked at me, then Dena. "Oh, I see where the confusion is!" she added with a laugh. "I'm not pregnant right this second but I'm *going* to be pregnant. Probably by tomorrow."

The corners of Dena's mouth twitched "So your *news*," she said, gently putting the dildos down next to the anal beads, *"*is that you're going to fuck your husband tonight."

"That is so crude," Mary Ann said, irritably. "I'm going to make a baby with my husband tonight. It will be the first time I've ever had sex without any contraceptives."

"*Ever*?" Dena and I asked in unison.

"I've never had sex with anyone without a condom," Mary Ann further clarified. "I've never wanted to be pregnant before."

"My God," I whispered. "I've been friends with you for almost two decades and I never realized you were the most responsible woman on earth. Dena," I said, a little accusatorily, "you must have known. How could you not share that?"

"Because I *didn't* know!" she snapped and then gave Mary Ann a not so gentle smack on the arm. "You have *never* bought a condom from me! I have latex, polyisoprene, vegan-friendly condoms, condoms with cock rings, glow in the dark, extra thin, *everything!* It's like a fucking condom-copia in here and you never *once* hit me up!"

My phone started vibrating in my bag as Dena continued to rail against her cousin's refusal to involve her in her sex life. I didn't recognize the number but I was more than happy to use it as an excuse to step away. "Hello?"

"Is this Sophie Katz?" a girl asked. The young voice was

familiar but she spoke so quietly it was difficult to make out her words.

I moved several more feet away to better hear and to get myself out of the line of fire just in case Dena started hurling cock rings. "This is Sophie, who is this please?"

"It's Cat, Aaron London's daughter."

"Oh! I'm so glad you called! Look, it was a total misunderstanding back at the hospital. I'm not dating your dad. But I was with him when he…when it happened." I moved aside to make room for two more customers who were headed towards lingerie. "How *is* your dad?"

"Dead."

Dead?

My mouth dropped open and my fingers tightened around my cell. Behind me the new customers were chuckling. In front of me Dena was still gesticulating and yet all the sound in the room was now clouded in a kind of ringing silence. I took a step forward as if movement would help. As if there was some corner of this adult toy store that would be appropriate for receiving this kind of news. "But…the surgery? Didn't it work?" I asked, stupidly.

"I just thought you should know," she said, opting not to humor me by stating the obvious answer.

Again, I found myself struggling to find words. London's ring was in my purse, waiting for him to put it back on. I honestly hadn't expected he wouldn't be able to. I hadn't really believed that I could be talking to a man one minute and then have him just…die. Not from a gunshot or some sudden violent act but from something much quieter. A silent killer slithering through his veins.

Look at me. Use your eyes and see me dying. You're witnessing my murder.

"Is your mother with you?" I asked, urgently. "I need to talk to her. There are some things she should know."

"My mother is never going to talk to you." Catherine's voice was almost steady. "Not in a million years."

And then the line went dead. She was gone.

London was gone.

I watched mutely as Dena turned away from Mary Ann and started walking toward her office. Dena's limp was less severe than it used to be but still detectable. Odd, seeing Dena, the petite, athletic woman I've known since high school, limp with each step. It was a bullet to the back that had done it, years ago. A physical manifestation of a twisted metaphor. The things that scar us are never the things we see coming.

I hadn't seen this coming.

Mary Ann came bounding over, clearly unfazed by Dena's rant, but when she saw my face her expression immediately changed. "What's wrong?"

"Someone died today," I whispered.

Mary Ann's hands fluttered to her face. "Who? Who died?"

"No one you know. I didn't really know him either. But…but he asked me to help him. I didn't. And now…" my voice trailed off.

Mary Ann wordlessly pulled me into a hug. She was such a slender, small-boned woman you would think that a fierce hug might break her. And yet when her arms wrapped around me they felt reassuringly strong. I rested my chin on her shoulder and squeezed my eyes closed as I tried to just absorb the comfort she offered and block out the reason I needed it. It's like I had made it happen. I had wanted an adventure. A mystery. And now a man was dead.

Dena came back out and when she saw us in an embrace she let out an audible sigh. "Seriously, she spent her entire adult life having sex with cheap ass condoms. It's sad but it's not a tragedy." But then Dena too took a good look at my face. "Something happened." A statement more than a question. "Come on." She gently took my arm as Mary Ann released me. "Let's walk and talk."

CHAPTER SIX

*"The smart choice is almost always the cautious one.
I'm proud that I'm just stupid enough for bravery."
--Dying To Laugh*

"I'm the devil." I gripped my third Cape Cod in my hands. Dena, Mary Ann and I had found a small table in the corner of the dimly lit bar. The place was vibrating with the grating laughter of the Silicon Valley infiltrators, all decked out in the cheapest looking expensive clothes they could find. A virtual sea of white faces peering out of Nordstrom-bought hoodies. I had made a point of feeling superior to these so-called innovators for years. They were completely screwing up the vibe of my city. But as I watched them I couldn't help but think that their analytical brains would have found a much more effective way to handle the whole London thing than I had.

Mary Ann toyed with the leaves of sage sticking out of the artisan cocktail she had been working on for the last forty minutes. "You're not the devil, Sophie."

"Of course not," Dena agreed. "For one thing, Satan would have a better sense of what the fuck is going on. You were an innocent, clueless bystander. That's all."

"Wrong. I'm a guilty bystander. A *degenerate* bystander! He *asked* me to get involved and I rejected the idea out of hand." I slammed the rest of my drink.

"There was nothing to get involved in!" Dena insisted. "This London guy was sick and refused to get treatment from a doctor. You were in the wrong place at the wrong time. You're not guilty or a degenerate. What you are is drunk."

"Not yet," I retorted signaling to our passing cocktail waitress that I wanted another.

"Perhaps if you wait a few weeks and then call the daughter back," Mary Ann suggested, "maybe she'll talk to you. When she's, well, not less sad, but more calm."

"And after she's over the shock of finding out about your affair with her dad," Dena added with a humorless smile.

"And when they find he wasn't wearing his wedding ring they'll think it's more proof of that!" I moaned. "I have to straighten that out."

"You can ponder that one out tomorrow," Dena suggested, leaning back in her chair.

"Tomorrow!" I exclaimed. "Tomorrow? Who am I? Scarlett O'Hara? Annie? To hell with tomorrow!" Okay, so maybe I was a little tipsy. They were strong drinks. "I should have dealt with things *today*. I should have helped him somehow! I was so thrown by all the crazy conspiracy stuff…I just screwed up!"

"Jason always gravitates to the conspiracy theories out there," Dena noted, referencing her boyfriend and primary lover. Dena usually had a secondary or two on hand. It was an arrangement Jason seemed almost grateful for. After all, Dena might be a bit much for any one man to handle. "But you know Jason," Dena added. "He's a little eccentric."

I pressed my lips together and Mary Ann coughed softly as she stared pointedly into her cocktail. I had no problem with Jason. He was fun. But saying he was "a little eccentric," was like saying Muammar el-Qaddafi had been a little erratic.

"London had all these weird theories about how hospitals were performing needless medical procedures on the homeless," I began but was interrupted by the arrival of my drink, which required immediate drinking.

"Like Medicare pays out enough to be worth scamming," Dena said with a scoff.

"Mm," I put down my drink after downing a little over half of it. "London was also really concerned about a New World Order."

"Jason's always going on about that," Dena noted as the waitress walked off. "Oligarchs creating a secret society and taking over the world or some such bullshit."

"Wait," Mary Ann asked as she raised her martini glass for another sip, "What's an oligarch? Are they, like, a kind of ogre? Like in The Hobbit and Shrek?"

Dena took in a sharp breath and I could see her fist clenching by her side. She never had a lot of patience for what we euphemistically referred to as Mary Ann's unworldliness.

"Sort of," I said, giving Dena a subtle kick under the table before she let loose with something biting. "But these kind have money, so more in line with the ogres in Shrek II." A group of guys at the next table broke out in laughter. San

Francisco had become one of the rare cities where even the straight guys traveled in packs. Dena called them PGP, Proud Geek Packs. I shifted in my seat and brought my attention back to my own table. "London also thought the government is trying to kill us."

"Same with Jason," Dena noted.

I stared down at my drink. "I like Jason," I said slowly. "I mean he's crazy but I don't blow him off when he asks for my help."

"Yeah, well that's because he doesn't ask for your help," Dena said before taking a quick sip of her whiskey tonic.

"Okay, but I mean, I wouldn't," I explained. "And I don't treat him like he's a lunatic who needs professional help."

"Well," Mary Ann said, delicately, "I don't know if Jason getting a little professional help would be the worst idea…"

"I treat Jason with respect," I continued as Dena shot Mary Ann an icy glare. "I don't think I treated London with respect,"

"If I remember correctly, the first time you met Jason you thought he was a joke and treated him accordingly," Dena pointed out. "It wasn't until you got to know him that you came to respect the man under the conspiracy theories."

"Yeah, but I should have learned from that! We're in San Francisco! Half the people here think our government is homicidal!" My words started picking up speed until they were practically bumping into one another. "Every time there's a drone strike there's a protest on some street corner rallying against government sanctioned killing! We can disagree with them but that doesn't mean they're irrational.

Or even when they are it doesn't mean we should act like their concerns are stupid or silly. And that's what I did with this guy! *I dismissed him*! Why did I do that?" I fumbled around in my purse until I found the ring. I pulled it out and held it reverently in the palm of my hand. "I screwed up. I really, really, screwed up."

"No, you didn't," Dena said, definitively. "You were kind to an irrational man without encouraging his insanity. You did everything right…except for the girlfriend part."

I groaned again and made my hand a fist around the ring. "I can fix that much."

"How?" Mary Ann asked.

I opened my hand to reveal the ring. "If this fell off his finger, and that's got to be what happened, that probably means he had been losing weight. His clothes were too big and everything. And his weight loss, his family would have noticed that, right?"

"I would think so," Dena agreed.

I put the ring back in my purse and jumped to my feet, waving my arms in the air to get the waitress' attention.

"What are you doing?" Dena asked.

"I'm getting the check. We have to go to Aaron London's place."

Mary Ann and Dena looked at one another. "Um," Mary Ann said, running her fingers nervously back and forth along the edge of the table. "I don't think he's home."

"Of course he's not home," I replied. "But I've got to make it look like his ring fell off somewhere around his place! Or better yet, *in* his home!"

"I'm sorry, what?" Dena asked, flatly.

"I might have his house keys. I could just—"

"Yeah, *no!*" Dena said, cutting me off immediately. "You are not breaking into his house to return a ring!"

"Why not?" I demanded.

"For one thing, his wife and daughter are probably already there," Dena pointed out.

"But what if they're not? They could easily have gone to a family member's home while they process this. That's what my mom did when my dad died."

"Sophie." Dena said my name like it was a condemnation but I simply ignored her as I continued to make my case.

"It would be the opposite of a burglary! I would be like Santa Claus…if Santa gave you stuff that already belonged to you…and if he had a key instead of having to mess around with chimneys."

"Um," Mary Ann said again, "Dena may be right…about you being a little bit drunk."

"Of course I'm *drunk!* You think I want to deal with any of this while sober?" I retorted. "And look!" Again, I searched through my handbag until I found London's car insurance failed-payment notice, his name and address clearly printed in the corner. "See!" I slammed the paper down in front of my friends. "I have his address!"

The waitress came over with our check and I triumphantly put my credit card on top of it before she could even leave it on the table. "Drinks are on me," I declared. "Mary Ann, you'll have to drive us over there."

"*Listen to me,*" Dena rapped her knuckles against the table, "this isn't Christmas and nobody wants you busting into their living room no matter how jolly you are. We are not doing this!"

"But--"

"Do you even remember what happened the last time we tried to sneak around someone else's home?" Dena pressed. "That was at that guy Alex Kinsky's house in Vegas. The night ended when he held us at gunpoint and set the whole building on fire."

"That's really not fair," I countered. "The fire was a total accident."

"Sophie!"

"Fine!" I threw up my hands in mock surrender. "Then I'll…I'll just drop the ring by his doorstep."

"That's stupid!" Dena insisted.

"It's a free country! I can be stupid if I want to be!" Mary Ann and Dena looked up at me doubtfully. Frustrated, I put my hands on my hips. "I swear to God you two, I will go on a full sobriety boycott until you agree to help me handle this! Right now, the only important thing is the ring!"

"Oh make up your mind, are you Santa or Golem?" Dena muttered.

I stared her down, letting her know I was not going to let this go.

She sighed and shook her head. "Let me just ask you this, if we drop Precious by his front door, like, by the mat or something, will you let this go?"

"Yes," I said, without really thinking about it. "Sure."

Dena and Mary Ann exchanged looks. As the waitress came back with a receipt for me to sign, Dena gave a little shrug. "Okay. Looks like it's time for us hobbits to go on an adventure."

# CHAPTER
SEVEN

"The willingness to take great risks can lead to great accomplishments and an air of youthful vitality. Or it can lead to great failure and serious wrinkles."
–Dying To Laugh

London's place turned out to be a four-plex two blocks from the beach in the outer sunset district. As we pulled into a parallel spot across the street, we noted there were lights on in three out of the four apartments.

"It doesn't mean the dark one's his," Dena noted. She was sitting in the backseat. Mary Ann was sitting behind the wheel tapping her fingers to Kelly Clarkson which, according to the deal she struck with Dena, she was allowed to play after every two Kendrick Lamar songs. "His wife and daughter really could be home. Or maybe they're in the dark apartment but went to sleep."

"It's not that late," I said, uncertainly.

"It's not that early either," Dena reminded me. "Besides, they're in *mourning.* They have reason to just crawl under the covers and black out the world. Just drop the ring off by the front door and let's go."

"But…what if the wrong person finds it," I asked. "What if they take it?"

"Sophie, this is *your* plan," Dena reminded me. "If someone steals the wedding ring he'll have bad juju for the rest of his life. Let's do this and move on."

I nodded. Sobriety was making a very gradual and unwelcome comeback. Time was of the essence.

"Okay, you guys stay here for a minute. I'm going to look around to see if there's a good spot for it, if not…" my voice trailed off.

"If not?" Mary Ann repeated, urging me to finish my thought.

But I didn't have a finish for that thought. I shook my head, uncertain and then opened the car door. "Just five minutes you guys."

"Wait, you went from *a* minute to *five* minutes in less than three sentences," Dena protested. "Five minutes is not--"

I jumped out of the car and closed the door before she could continue. As I walked up to London's building I could hear the muffled sound of a dog barking from somewhere inside. The various buzzers listed the apartment numbers. Living so close to the beach in San Francisco meant living in a fog bank for approximately three hundred sixty days of every year. But then London didn't seem like a man who longed for the sun and perhaps his daughter enjoyed holding beach bonfires with friends like I did when I was her age. As for Anita…I didn't have much of a read on her at all.

I ran my fingers lightly over the buzzers. *Were* Anita and Cathy home? At a friend's? A loving family member's? I lowered my gaze to study the steps leading up to the building, then the walkway…surely there was some place to plant this stupid thing. But of course, there wasn't.

But if they weren't home, and the key really was to their apartment...

I gave my head an energetic shake to clear it. Dena was right, breaking into the apartment wasn't a good idea.

But what if I just broke into the apartment *building*? Like maybe the ring could have slipped off his finger while he was clinging to the banister, or fiddling with his mail after collecting it? I could go in and just drop it in a plausible location.

My little voice, which was apparently a lot more sober than I was, told me that was a ridiculous and reckless idea.

I glanced over my shoulder at Mary Ann's car, still parked serenely across the street. I gave them a little wave, letting them know I was fine. Not that they couldn't see that for themselves. The only thing they could be worried about was that I might be thinking about doing exactly what I was thinking about doing.

I reached into my bag, as subtlety as possible, and fished out the keys. I sort of strolled up to the front door, keeping my head bent toward the ground as if looking for a place to drop the ring. Keeping my body angled so Dena and Mary Ann couldn't see exactly what I was up to, I tried one of the keys. It fit into the lock but didn't turn.

By that point, there was no way Dena and Mary Ann hadn't caught on to what was up. Quickly my fingers closed around the other key, just as Dena was opening the car door and started crossing the street toward me. I fumbled with it as I tried, then succeeded to get it into the lock. It turned. This was *the* key! I was about to triumphantly push open the door when it swung open on its own, pulling away from me.

I squealed and jumped back into Dena who had caught up with me and she fell back into Mary Ann who let out an even louder squeal. We all stood there, regaining our balance as a man wearing sweats, a T-shirt, Vans and spiky black hair, gelled to an inch of its life, stared down at us from the now open doorway.

"Can I help you?" he asked, irritably.

I blinked, a little stunned.

"I'm really sorry," Dena began. "We have the wrong--"

"We're friends of Aaron London in unit 4," I interrupted, straightening my spine and pulling out a smile. "We're expected. His wife gave me the key." I held up the keys as evidence.

The man barely even looked at them. "Bullshit."

My smile disappeared. I hadn't expected to be called out that fast. Behind me, I heard Mary Ann squeak out an *uh-oh.*

"No, really," I said, trying to maintain at least the façade of confidence. "She gave it to me this afternoon. I don't think she's home yet...or, she may be sleeping..."

"Look, I don't know who you are, but you didn't get those keys from his wife," he retorted.

I took a sharp breath, tasting the salt in the air. "What makes you say that?"

"Unit 4 guy? Aaron London? He's in the apartment right next to mine and he doesn't have a wife."

For a few seconds, I just stared at him, unsure if I had heard him correctly. When I finally glanced back at my friends they looked every bit as stunned as I felt. My hand went to my purse where the ring was. It was a wedding ring. I mean, it *looked* like a wedding ring. Anita was London's wife. That's what made sense. "He…doesn't have a wife," I repeated, slowly.

"No, that dude lives alone…except for the dog. Is he married to the dog? Is that the bitch you're talking about? Because if it is, I wish you could get her to shut the hell up."

It was everything I could do not to pull the wedding ring out of my purse and shove it in Gel-Head's face. He *had* to be wrong. And Anita must have been listed as an emergency contact in London's wallet or something otherwise how would the hospital know to call her?

Mary Ann raised her hand as if she was a student in a classroom. "Um, sorry, I'm a little lost. Is the bitch that won't shut up, like, a *dog*-dog? Or are you just being really mean about a woman you don't find attractive?"

"What?" the guy shook his head. "I'm talking about a *dog*. I think it's a Lab or something…maybe part pit. I don't know, but it's got a pink collar so I'm guessing she's a girl, and do *not* tell me I'm gender stereotyping. People have been trying to lay that shit on me ever since I moved to San Francisco."

My eyes moved past him to the apartment building. I could see the lobby painted a utilitarian beige, metal mailboxes lined up neatly on the wall, the frayed carpet on the steps that led tenants up to their apartments. I tried to imagine the angry woman I met at the hospital latching on her pearls before descending those steps. But it was like trying to picture Audrey Hepburn in an Adam Sandler film.

"Um, how long have you lived here?" I asked. Maybe he had just moved in a few days ago. Maybe Anita and Catherine had been away visiting potential colleges or ailing grandparents.

"I moved in four months ago. And…look, I don't know what your relationship is with Unit 4 but there's something wrong with that dog. She's been barking since I got back from work. I have to be on the Google bus at six-thirty tomorrow morning and now I gotta go out and buy earplugs just so I can sleep!"

But it was like the quiet roar of the ocean was pulling his words away from me. I could barely hear anything other than my own screaming thoughts. *Had* the hospital called Anita? Or had she just shown up, because maybe, just maybe, she knew he was going to end up in the hospital.

Or maybe she had been following him. In a Zipcar.

But that was crazy…wasn't it? Of course it was. It had to be crazy.

Gel-Head was still talking. It took effort to drag my attention back to him.

"Barking, whining, then barking again," he was saying. "There is *no* sound insulation in this place. Maybe she's in distress or something, I dunno. I haven't heard her do this before." He sucked in his lower lip, revealing a wisp of a soul patch. "Look, if you think you can get it to shut up and you really have a key, just give me some plausible story about how you got it. Something so when the cops ask me why I didn't report a bunch of suspicious looking women entering my neighbor's apartment I'll have an out. Seriously, I don't care. I just need that thing to be quiet."

"You really shouldn't call living creatures *things*," Mary Ann scolded.

Gel-Head's mouth curled down into a cartoonishly frustrated glare. "I really hate this city."

"Aaron London was admitted into Mercy Hospital

today," I said, choosing my words with obvious deliberation. The wind picked up, brushing wet air against my face. "He gave us his keys so we could get some stuff for him and take care of the dog."

Gel-Head studied me as a new force of wind tried and failed to tousle his hair. "That's your plausible story?"

"Pretty much."

He considered it, then shrugged. "It'll do. Just keep in mind, if the dog doesn't shut up in the next fifteen minutes I really am calling the police."

"Fair," I agreed. Gel-Head stood back and held open the door for us. I went in right away but Dena and Mary Ann hung back.

"Guys," I said, impatiently, gesturing for them to follow.

"Sophie, we don't know what we're walking into," Dena pointed out.

"She's right," Mary Ann agreed. "I do want to help the dog but…what if it's a scary dog?"

"Yeah," Dena agreed then narrowed her eyes and faced Gel-Head. "Is the barking bitch Lassie or Cujo?"

"I don't know," he said, clearly exacerbated. "Neither? Maybe more like that dog in *Marley and Me*?"

"Oh, I loved that movie!" Mary Ann cooed. "I cried so much at the end."

"Are you guys going to do this or what?" Gel-Head snapped.

I gave my friends an imploring look. "Please?" I asked. "If not for me, then for Marley."

Mary Ann gave me a firm nod and marched past Dena into the building. "For Marley."

Dena exhaled loudly and followed. "This is so fucking

crazy."

In the minute that it took us to get to the apartment, the dog had gone from barking to whimpering and scratching at the door. Mary Ann placed her flat palm next to the peephole. "That poor thing! Do you think she's psychic?"

Both Dena and I looked at her as Gel-Head, who had been trailing behind us, let himself into the apartment on the other end of the hall and slammed his door closed.

"Maybe that's why she's so upset," Mary Ann explained, ignoring our enabler's dramatic exit. "She knows her human died. Animals are different than us. They understand things we don't."

"We're *all* animals, but I'm completely sure that dog understands things you don't," Dena grumbled.

"London was in bad shape when I saw him." I chewed on my lower lip, shifting my weight from foot to foot. "It wouldn't surprise me if he hadn't been home the night before."

"Oh, that poor thing!" Mary Ann said again. "Open the door, Sophie."

"Wait a minute, what's the plan here," Dena interjected. "Are we just going to take the dog out for a short walk, feed her and then leave her for someone who actually *knows* London to take care of her?"

"Maybe?" I said, uncertainly.

"Because you know we can't just take the dog, right?" Dena asked. "We don't have enough information about what's going on here to do that."

She was right, we had *no* idea what we were about to walk into. I still couldn't get my head around Anita and Catherine being frauds…in fact I didn't really believe it. It's not like Gel-Head looked like the kind of guy who was particularly observant. And yet, not to notice the existence of two people who theoretically lived down the hall from you…

"Hold on a second." I pulled out my phone and went through my recent call log. "His teenage daughter…or the person who might be his daughter, is the one who called me with the news." I found the number and pressed call. I put it on speaker so we could all hear.

It went to voicemail after one ring. "Hi, I can't get to the phone right now. You can leave a message which I probably won't listen to or you could just be normal and text."

"I don't know if she's his daughter or not, but she's definitely a teenager," Dena muttered. I shushed her right as the phone beeped.

I opened my mouth, then shut it and then promptly hung up. "I don't know what to say or how to say it," I admitted.

Dena let out a short laugh and took my phone from me. After a few seconds of tapping, she showed me the text message she had come up with:

I'm so sorry about your dad. Will you be taking care of his dog or do you need help with that?

"That'll work, yes?" Dena asked and then pressed send before I could weigh in.

The scratching at the door was getting frantic. What if the dog *did* bite?

"That animal needs help," Mary Ann said, sternly. "Open the door, Sophie."

Mary Ann could be a ditz at times but no one could say she wasn't brave and efficient in the face of a crisis.

The doorknob trembled slightly with the efforts of the animal inside. "Here goes nothing." Slowly, carefully, I slipped the key in the lock and inched open the door.

Immediately a black furry snout squeezed its way through the crack and forced the door all the way open.

The snout was attached to a large, pink-collared dog, built like an unusually barrel chested lab with Richard Nixon jowls, wagging her stub of a tail as she sniffed my shoes and pant legs. There was not even a whisper of hostility in her manner. I leaned down and scratched her behind her ears as she stared up at me with big, black, puppy dog eyes. She was strong and gorgeous…and smelly. In fact, the stink was pretty intense.

The dog moved on to Mary Ann, but the smell didn't let up. That's when I looked up and saw it. The majority of the stench was coming from the apartment. Although it looked a lot more like a toxic waste dump than anyone's living quarters. There were dirty paper plates on the floor, a dog bowl inexplicably placed in the middle of the room that, even in the dim light, looked crusty. I spotted a cup on a pedestal table by the door, still partially filled with old, neglected coffee. Empty water bottles had been cast carelessly about.

But mostly there were papers. Papers and papers and papers. Printed out articles crumpled up on the floor, newspaper articles pinned to the walls with certain passages circled or highlighted, torn out pages of magazines piled on chairs. A wastebasket overflowing with shreds of ripped up sentences. Pamphlets and business cards scattered across the coffee table. If someone set off a bomb in a Kinko's you'd have less paper and more order than you had here.

Dena stepped up next to me, peering into the space. "I think we have confirmation of Aaron London's crazy."

I felt Mary Ann come up behind me, the dog now nudging against the back of my legs. "It's like an episode of Hoarders," Mary Ann observed, "except…worse."

"We can't just leave this dog here," I whispered.

"It's not our dog!" Dena snapped.

I gestured to the junkyard London had made out of his apartment. "This is animal abuse." I paused to think about how best to handle things before adding, "we have to go in there."

Dena balked. "I think I'd rather spend a week in prison than a second in that hole."

I squared my shoulders. "We have to take the dog out. So we need a leash. I'm sure there's a leash in there."

"Oh for Christ's sake." Dena dug into her oversized-bag and pulled out a short, chain-link leash. "If we truly have to take her, we can use this."

Mary Ann did a quick double take. "You don't have a dog."

"I have a boyfriend," Dena replied.

"Wait..." Mary Ann began, but I cut her off.

"Please don't ask her to explain that," I requested.

Dena leaned down to put the leash on the dog. As soon as she did, the dog managed to give her a lick on the nose. "Chill," Dena said sternly to the mutt. "I don't even let Jason do that."

"He definitely doesn't live here with a woman," I said quietly.

"It does seem unlikely," Mary Ann agreed.

"Maybe they were separated," I suggested. "Maybe he moved in here while they were taking a break and he sort of," I glanced back at the apartment, "let the bachelor thing get out of control."

"*That's* highly likely," Dena straightened herself back up to standing, keeping the dog close to her side. "Can we go now?"

I swallowed hard and bit my lip. I was *so* curious. But the smell was not getting better with continued exposure. And there might be bugs in there. I wasn't sure if I could handle a lot of bugs. Still… "Let me just place the ring."

I took several steps away from the door, pulled out the ring, inhaled a deep breath and then, holding it, walked into the cesspool. I didn't have the courage to turn on the light to see things more clearly. Instead, I made do with the lighting coming in from the hallway and skirted around shadows and shapes as I made my way to the coffee table. On the couch was a pile of clothes, each item too dark to be distinguishable from the others in the dim light with the exception of a red, checkered winter scarf that seemed to be slithering off the pile as if attempting a slow moving escape.

I glanced down at the coffee table. Pamphlets touting holistic medicine and homeopathy were scattered about along with a few business cards. I picked one up and narrowed my eyes to make out the words. It was for a blogger for a site called Corporate Evil. That sounded like London's cup of tea. Another business card was for the *Founder Of Citizens Against (Legal) Drugs.*

The *legal* part, in parenthesis no less, made me want to smile. But I resisted just in case moving my mouth inadvertently led to my accidentally inhaling.

That breath I was holding was beginning to hurt. Still, I reached for one more business card.

Gundrun Volz

Nolan-Volz
Co-Founder, CEO

Seriously? I put my hand on my chest, partially out of shock and partially because I really was going to have to inhale soon. Was this truly the card of the Nolan-Volz CEO? Or was it a fake? It had to be a fake, right? I mean, no one would really name their kid Gundrun Volz.

"Sophie!" Dena yelled from where she stood in the hall. "We can't be hanging out here!"

She was right. Plus, I really did have to breathe. I put the Gundrun Volz card in my back pocket and carefully placed the ring in the center of the table where it could be easily seen before quickly walking out of the apartment. As I closed the door behind me, I finally released my breath with a gasp, desperate for air that wasn't weighted down by the stench of slovenly neglect.

I looked over at Mary Ann, still holding her nose. "I think Dena's right. Going would be good," she said in a nasal voice.

"You did everything you wanted to do," Dena pointed out. "You returned the ring and we're rescuing the dog. Plus I'm pretty sure we have just confirmed that he wasn't living with his wife. There's no reason to hang out."

"Oh, my God," Mary Ann squealed. Dena and I both looked over to see Mary Ann, crouched down by the dog, studying her tags. "You won't believe what her name is!"

"Marley?" I guessed.

"No!" She stood up with a big, bright smile. "Her name is Sophie!"

CHAPTER
EIGHT

"If you play tennis like a pro, it's not fun to play with amateurs. By the same logic, I refuse to sleep with virgins. "
--Dying To Laugh

By the time I got home, I was sober enough to drive but exhausted enough to pass out. Still, I had managed to retrieve my car, drive to a 24-hour CVS and load up on dog food, poop bags and the like. Ms. Dogz, as I was now calling her, was calm enough, but occasionally she would let out a whine and once, when I looked back at her while at a stoplight, I noticed she was shaking.

When Ms. Dogz and I finally stumbled up my front steps and sort of fell through the door of my Victorian, Anatoly had already been home for hours. He was waiting for me in the living room, reading some WWII book on our leather couch, one foot propped up on the dark wood coffee table. "I thought you were going to call and have me come get you," he said, not looking up quite yet as he marked his place in the book. Mr. Katz was snuggled up by his side but when my feline saw what I had brought with me, he was immediately on his feet, back arched.

Anatoly noticed and followed Mr. Katz's glare. "You got a dog?" he asked, incredulously.

"Not exactly," I hedged. "She needs a bath."

Ms. Dogz managed to pull away from me, but once her freedom was obtained, she didn't exactly go wild. Instead, she carefully sniffed the area rug covering the recently re-polished hardwood floors, then the chair closest to her. Finally, she approached Anatoly and Mr. Katz.

"You're beautiful," Anatoly told her, appreciatively. "But she's right about the bath."

Mr. Katz leaned forward and swapped his claws across Ms. Dogz's nose.

Ms. Dogz looked stunned and took several steps back as Anatoly swiftly picked up Mr. Katz, ignoring his flailing attempts to try to strike once more at his new adversary. "Looks like she needs a bath and a Band-Aid now. What's her name?"

"I'm calling her Ms. Dogz. We're just fostering her until I can figure out if she belongs to someone," I said, side-stepping the question. I went up and examined Ms. Dogz's nose. Only a minor scratch. Still, it was ironic that I had thought Mr. Katz would be the one who would need protection.

Anatoly nodded and walked back to our only downstairs bedroom, otherwise known as my office, and shut Mr. Katz in there.

"I don't want him to think he's being replaced," I said, urgently.

"He can stay in the office until he calms down. Where did you find her?"

"She was trapped," I hedged. "Want to help me bathe her?"

He gave me a quizzical look.

"I don't know if she has fleas," I said quickly, not wanting to give him a chance to ask too many questions, "but I bought some Dawn dish soap because apparently, Dawn kills fleas. Did you know that? Isn't that weird?"

"Why don't you want me to know where you found her?" Anatoly asked, flatly.

"I told you, she was trapped...inside." I shifted my weight back onto my heels. "I really think we should wash her."

"Inside where?"

I bit my lip and looked over at the dog.

"Inside where, Sophie?"

Immediately Ms. Dogz's ears perked up and she trotted over to Anatoly's side. It brought a small smile to his lips. He was such a sucker for dogs. He leaned down to look at her tags and then burst out laughing.

"I know what it says. We're still calling her *Ms. Dogz,*" I said, irritably.

"Have you called the number on the tag?" he asked.

"I have, but the person at that number...isn't available."

He shot me another look and then slowly straightened back to standing. "Why so cryptic? Where exactly was she trapped?"

I swallowed hard, and then mumbled, "Inside an apartment."

There was at least five seconds of silence. "You want to try that again?"

I held up my hands in a request for patience and understanding. "I didn't do anything significantly illegal."

Anatoly's eyebrows shot up and then he muttered some Russian curse.

"Look, I can explain *everything* while we wash the dog." I pulled out the Dawn and held it out for him as if the dish soap would clarify everything. "We have to get rid of the theoretical fleas."

In the upstairs hall bathroom, Anatoly and I were both on our knees, wet. This was the first time we had been in this position together when sex wasn't involved. Although Anatoly did *look* like sex on a stick. He had removed his shoes, his socks, his shirt, so now it was just him in his jeans and a perfectly chiseled torso all wet from our efforts to clean this mutt. I was probably looking a little less enticing in bleach-stained yoga pants and a Race For A Cure 2012 T-shirt.

Mr. Katz had been freed from my office and was now sulking in our bedroom. Ms. Dogz was before us in a tub full of soapy bubbles looking extremely unhappy. Almost as unhappy as Anatoly. I had told him the whole story. As stories go, it wasn't his favorite.

"This isn't the big mystery you think it is," Anatoly insisted as he massaged some of the soap into the dog's fur. "Anita and Aaron London are probably separated. He might not have even been wearing the ring, just carrying it around while they figured things out."

"And he dropped it in the sink from his pocket?" I asked incredulously. Although by that point I was close to positive that the couple had been separated. At the hospital, Cat London had asked me why I hadn't taken her father to the hospital sooner. I had assumed she meant sooner in the day, but now that I thought about it, I wasn't sure she meant that at all. It was more than likely she meant I should have taken him earlier in the week, maybe even earlier in the month.

I scrubbed some more soap into Ms. Dogz's neck. She gave me a look similar to the one my sister gave me when I set the table using paper napkins. It was a *why-are-you-doing-this-to-me* look. "Maybe London died of natural causes and Anita's on the up and up," I said. "But it's also possible you're wrong, isn't it? Shouldn't we look into that?"

"No."

"No?" I balked. "You don't believe there's even the slightest chance you're wrong?"

"It's highly unlikely," he amended. "But now, thanks to you, I have to track this woman down anyway and figure out how to explain to her why we have her husband's dog. You could have saved us a lot of hassle and legal liability if you had simply called the SPCA."

"I didn't need to call anyone. I had a key." *And it had been* fun *being reckless again.*

"You understand we're going to have to return her, yes?" I might have been mistaken, but I thought I heard just a tinge of regret in Anatoly's voice. He had been wanting a dog for a while but I had been hesitant to impose something like that on Mr. Katz. It wasn't an unrealistic concern. I could tell by the look Mr. Katz gave Ms. Dogz as she came out of the office that a dogicide was being plotted.

"Maybe not. I mean, yes, if London had the dog before

their supposed split, Anita will want her back," I reasoned as I moved on to Ms. Dogz's back. There were soapsuds clinging to Anatoly's bicep and I was trying really, really hard not to stare. "On the other hand, if Ms. Dogz was Anita's replacement…" I let my voice trail off, allowing Anatoly to fill in the blanks.

Anatoly reached for the hand shower, his arm brushing up against mine as he did although he didn't even glance my way. Ms. Dogz treated Anatoly to a baleful stare. I wondered how much she understood. If she was waiting for London to come knocking on the door and rescue her from this water torture.

"Anyway, you can't say there isn't *any* reason to at least consider the possibility that London sorta, kinda knew what he was talking about," I pressed. "That maybe someone was out to get him. That he was being poisoned. He *is* dead, after all."

"It wasn't that long ago that you tried to convince me that Alex Kinsky sorta, kinda knew what he was talking about." He turned on the stream and started rinsing the suds off Ms. Dogz. "But he was conning you. He almost ended up killing both of us."

"First off, that has absolutely nothing to do with this," I snapped. "Alex is a man with mafia-ties who offered to help me through criminal means. London was an individual who asked *us* for help through legal means. Secondly, Alex didn't exactly con me. It's just that he only gave me part of the story. Maybe that's what London did."

"London didn't give us *any* story," Anatoly corrected as he rinsed off the last of the soap. I leaned over and drained the tub. My shirt was drenched and clinging to me in all sorts of inconvenient places. It might have been construed as an invitation if Anatoly bothered to take his eyes off the dog for one flippin' second. "Ranting and raving is very different from story telling."

I angrily swiped at a wet curl that was sticking to my cheek. "Why are you so resistant to even considering the possible veracity of the facts of this case?"

"What case?" Anatoly put the hand shower back with much more force than necessary. "For it to be a case, there has to be a client. London didn't hire me--"

"Because you wouldn't let him!" I jumped to my feet and grabbed a towel throwing it over a now confused-look-ing-but-fresh-smelling Ms. Dogz. She was probably wonder-ing what new kind of madhouse she had wandered into.

"I think we can both agree he won't be paying me," Anatoly continued as he vigorously dried her. "This isn't our business. No one wants us involved and there's no upside in forcing the issue. There most likely isn't an issue to force." He carefully helped Ms. Dogz out of the tub. She immediate-ly shook herself off, splattering us both and making a mock-ery out of our attempts at drying. "We have no solid reason to believe that anyone poisoned or even stalked London. This is over. At least it would be if you hadn't broken into his apartment and stolen his dog!"

"*Saved*. I *saved* his dog!" I turned on my heel and stomped out of the bathroom. Ms. Dogz was right behind me, then in front of me, then behind me again as she sprinted up and down the hall in a burst of energy, shaking herself every two or three seconds, making sure the whole second floor shared in her bathing experience. I threw open our bedroom door with the energy of unbridled frustration. Ms.

Dogz rushed into the room, startling Mr. Katz who had been curled up on the bed. He looked at the expression on my face, then at the wet dog and jumped to the floor, storming out of the room just as Anatoly stormed in.

"We have an obligation," I said in a voice that wasn't quite a yell, but loud enough to let the world know I wasn't messing around.

"To whom?" Anatoly asked, coolly.

"To London."

"He's dead."

"So what?" Ms. Dogz had stopped running around, undoubtedly captivated by the strength of my argument. "That doesn't change the fact that he asked us for help! It doesn't mean we didn't screw up when we blew him off! And it doesn't mean we get to turn our backs on his dog!"

"Again, all you had to do was call the SPCA! Or you could have called the police and told them there's a dog stuck in a dead man's apartment! That's what you do. What you *don't* do is break into a man's house! If you had been caught, you could have ended up in jail or worse!"

"But I wasn't caught!" I took a step closer, glaring up into his eyes. "An animal was in trouble and so I did what needed to be done. It's called being responsible."

"Are you suggesting that I'm being irresponsible?"

"I'm suggesting that you're being an asshole."

"Careful, Sophie."

Ms. Dogz perked up her ears. That animal's insistence on responding to my name drove my agitation up to the next level.

"Or what?" I challenged, my hands now clenched into fists.

Anatoly stared down into my eyes, letting the silence stretch. I had forgotten how forceful his silences could be. He could infuse them with tension and threat…

…and sex. Anatoly could do with a silence what Otis Redding could do with a moan. Goose bumps were prickling my arms as my breath quickened. I was fully aware of the rhythm with which his uncovered chest was moving and yet my eyes were locked on his, absolutely unable to look anywhere else.

"Anatoly," I whispered "I--"

But I didn't get a chance to continue. In an instant, I was up against the wall, my arms pinned above my head as his lips found my neck and his body pressed against mine. His mouth found that spot that made me positively squirm and I let out a little squeak as I was suddenly unable to speak. His lips moved up to my ear and his teeth scraped gently against the lobe. When he released my arms he lifted me up so that I was still pressed against the wall. My legs wrapped themselves around his waist as my arms encircled his neck. *I can't remember the last time I wanted him this badly.*

He crushed his mouth against mine, parting my lips with his tongue as I let my fingers run through his short, coarse hair. I bit down on his lower lip, my nails digging into his flesh. There was an energy to this that had been missing lately. A whirl of excitement was spiraling up from my stomach through my ribcage, making my heart beat too fast and my breathing too shallow.

I loved it.

He moved me from the wall and half carried, half threw me on the bed. He was on top of me in an instant and my fingers immediately traveled to the button of his jeans, reaching into his pants, feeling the proof of his desire as my other hand greedily ran down his shoulders, his back, his beautiful biceps.

"Sophie," he said in a growl as he began to lower his face toward mine.

Except our lips never touched because the dog shoved her face between ours, causing me to accidentally press my mouth against black fur.

"Whaat da ferk!" I sputtered as I spit out wet fur. Anatoly busted out laughing, harder than he had in ages. I looked at him, looked at the dog, who looked back with innocent enthusiasm and in an instant I was giggling too, then laughing, then pretty much breathless with hysterics. Anatoly and I were both laughing like hyenas as Ms. Dogz pranced back and forth, periodically leaning in to lick one of our faces as she rejoiced in the commotion she'd caused.

"You might have to take a nickname," Anatoly said as he sat up, wiping both dog slobber and tears from his face.

I scooted myself up, pressing my back against the headboard as I attempted to catch my breath. "I already gave her an alias," I reminded him. "Ms. Dogz."

"I'm not talking to the dog, I'm talking to you."

"*I* should take a nickname?" I balked, although I could feel the giggles threatening an encore. "I'm not giving up my name for a dog, not even if we get to keep her."

"Well, the dog clearly isn't giving up her name for anyone," Anatoly chuckled. "I could call you baby."

"*Baby?* What is this, a 1970s porno? Millennials use the word, bae."

"We're too old to be Millennials."

"Oh my God, there you go again, being all realistic and

honest about our age." I moved forward and straddled him, using my left hand to push him flat on the bed and my right hand to cover his mouth. "If you stop talking, I think we can make this work."

I could feel his smile against my palm and then, without another word, he reached up, unhooking my bra, slowly pulling it off me so the straps tickled my skin, tossing it to the floor where, with a little luck, it wouldn't become a chew toy.

He cupped my breasts, his thumbs moving slowly over my nipples until they reached for him. His eyes moved steadily up and down my body before finally, they once again locked with mine.

Without saying a word, he told me I was beautiful.

Anatoly really could do wonderful things with silence.

# CHAPTER
NINE

"There's a reason I'm afraid of the dark. When I can't see the tangled mess that surrounds me, I start thinking about the tangled mess that is me."
--Dying To Laugh

I woke up to the quiet whine of Ms. Dogz. Anatoly's arm draped over my stomach, his breathing deep and steady, his body completely relaxed into sleep. I felt the weight of Mr. Katz curled up above the covers. There was just enough light for me to see Ms. Dogz outline on the makeshift bed of spare blankets we had set-up for her. Her head was on her paws, her eyes too black to make out. But her whining...steady, mournful, rhythmic, it was heartbreaking.

Such a whirlwind of emotions. The ecstasy of the evening that topped off a day filled with confusion, daring, thrills, loss and guilt.

All fun aside I still felt so much guilt.

"There's nothing I could have done," I whispered aloud, to the dark, to London's dog. *Even if we had agreed to help him, we still wouldn't have been able to save his life. It's not our fault.*

But the last few moments of his life…those *could* have been filled with hope. Anatoly and I filled them with disappointment. Now, with nothing around to distract me, I couldn't escape that truth.

Anatoly mumbled something incoherent and turned to face the wall, dragging his warmth away.

Carefully I pulled my feet out from underneath my cat. With practiced stealth, I managed to creep out from beneath the blankets without waking either of my bedmates. I crouched down by Ms. Dogz and ran my hand over the top of her head and back. She smelled cleaner than I felt. "You're going to be okay," I assured her.

How many people had said that to me after I lost my own father at nineteen? And, assuming she really was his daughter, how many people must have said that to Cat London within the last ten hours? All those people were right of course. But in an odd way, they were totally wrong too. When you lose someone who is that central to your being you have to change the definition of what it means to be okay.

Ms. Dogz's whining was getting softer with my touch, less plaintive. The quiet gave new amplification to the thoughts forming in my exhausted mind:

Maybe Anatoly's right.

London was probably separated from his wife, which didn't mean there still wasn't love there. Not necessarily. Yes, he was clearly in the middle of a breakdown but if she was the mother of his child, Anita was his family.

If London's family wanted my help, I would owe it to them. But they quite clearly didn't. Would London want me to upset his family? Now, just as they had begun to grieve?

Yes, yes he would if it meant uncovering the truth.

But it was hard to figure out if that was the voice of reason or that of my own stubbornness. There was no question that I was incredibly tempted to pursue this. To investigate and see if I could solve a murder or at the very least prove that it *was* a murder. But why? What would be the point? No matter what I discovered, London would still be gone. His last moments on this earth would still be defined by disappointment. The latter's my fault but I couldn't change what was done. I couldn't help him.

But I could still make it worse. I could hurt his daughter.

So if I did pursue this, who would I be doing it for? Me? Today should have been purely awful. And it *was* awful… except…it was also so much fun. I had felt…*energized.* More so than I had in a while. Even the resulting conflict with Anatoly had ended up amplifying our lust. What was wrong with me that I could get an endorphin kick from something so dark and twisted?

I removed my hand from Ms. Dogz's back and sat quietly by her side. "It's possible I'm a monster," I murmured. Ms. Dogz tilted her head, looking up at me with eyes that were still perfectly camouflaged by the darkness. Then she shifted her weight and put her head on my lap.

I *loved* this dog.

I would have to think about what I needed to do to deserve her.

CHAPTER
TEN

*"Everyone is beautiful in their own way...but good hair
products help."*
--Dying For Laughs

My whole office was flooded with morning sun. Anatoly was gone and I was still in my nightshirt, my hair an ill shaped frizzy halo. I had an appointment with Marcus that afternoon so I had zero incentive to try to do anything with it. But then, I hadn't really done much with it for some time now.

I ran my bare foot over Ms. Dogz's back, letting her fur tickle my sole. To her left was Mr. Katz, giving her a hardcore kitty glare. Still, his proximity to our newest resident was progress.

My laptop sat before me and was open to Microsoft Word. Microsoft called their software Word because that was its raison d'être; to hold words. And my raison d'être was to *create* words. I should have been looking at a page filled with *my* words. Words that carved images into readers' minds, gave life to new adventures, words that created colorful characters, pain, hilarity and love. But the only thing on my screen was a bleak, empty page and a cursor blinking at me accusingly.

I ran my fingers over the keys, once, then twice.

Once upon a time…

I let out a wry laugh and hit the delete button. I looked down at my furry friends. "I have never wanted to be an accountant," I told them. "But there are many days when I've wanted to want to be an accountant."

Ms. Dogz tilted her head in a manner that was clearly doggie language for *explain.* Mr. Katz blinked his eyes, which was kitty language for, *you don't have to explain. I get it.*

"If you're an accountant you just do your job," I went on, for Ms. Dogz's sake. "You don't need to be inspired. You don't have to create a new world every year. You just do what you know how to do. Sometimes you have to put in an insane number of hours, sometimes you don't. But you *do* understand what you're doing. But being an author, you have to relearn your craft with each friggin' book." I looked back at the computer screen and the soft grey background to my unadulterated, white document. My imagination was failing me. I had become as dull and empty as the screen.

"I'm lost," I whispered.

Mr. Katz looked up at me and blinked his eyes once. Kitty language for, "No shit."

My phone rang and I looked down at the screen. Mama. Oh boy. My mother was a little nuts and it was rare that she called me for any purpose other than to complain that I wasn't calling *her.*

"Hello, Mama," I said upon picking up. "How are you?"

"Good mamaleh!" she said, using her favorite Yiddish term of endearment for me. "I'm just calling to hear your voice."

I waited for her to tack on the prerequisite passive-aggressive admonishment. Something along the lines of, *I've nearly forgotten what you sound like!*

But…nothing. She added nothing. Huh. "I guess I should be the one calling you," I said slowly, trying to spot the trap.

"You called me Sunday! What, now you should spend every minute of every day on the phone with your mother? You have a life, already! Speaking of which, how is your Anatoly?"

"He's good," I answered, still wary.

"Good!" she gushed. "Is he ready to make an honest woman out of you? Nice Jewish girls shouldn't be living in sin with gangsters, Sophie. You should marry the man and make it proper."

And there it is.

"I'm pretty sure gangsters only marry their girlfriends when they're worried they'll be compelled to testify against them. But Anatoly doesn't have to concern himself with that."

"Why because he's not a real gangster?" Mama asked with a smile in her voice.

"No, because I'm not a real snitch," I volleyed back.

My mother laughed, for once not taking my joking literally. "Such a troublemaker you are. Well, as long as you're happy mamaleh. I just spoke to your sister. You know her party planning business is going like gangbusters? She's like a real Martha Stewart, that one! So wonderful to have two happy daughters. And your little nephew, Jack? He's a genius. Let me tell you what he did at school the other day…"

I listened to her detail Jack's lists of accomplishments. This was by far the least contentious call I'd ever had with my mother. Although to be fair, she had been a lot less pushy in general lately. Her appetite for doling out hefty portions of Jewish guilt seemed to be diminishing with age. As a result, I had less and less call to be snarky or to bicker.

It was a good thing. It was something to be grateful for. But I didn't feel grateful, although I really wanted to. I just felt…numb.

Three hours later, Marcus was studying my hair, his mouth curved down as he reached out to touch one of my frizzier curls. We were in his salon and the music of Prince was intermingling with the sounds of confidences being exchanged between patrons and their stylists. The exposed brick walls made the place seem both elitist and rustic. Marcus was also a mix of those two sensibilities. His short dreads and muscular form denoted a man who didn't need to spend time primping in the morning, but his AX Armani T-shirt paired with his fitted white jeans said that he did anyway.

"You haven't been using your product," he growled.

I sighed, my mind elsewhere.

"It's like you've been taking styling lessons from Don

King."

"Oh come on, it's not that bad," I snapped, the insult bringing me back to the here and now. "I ran out of product a few days ago. I was going to pick some more up yesterday but things got hectic."

"Did we have a nuclear holocaust that I missed?" he asked. "Because short of that, there's no excuse for going days without product. We live in a civilized society, Sophie. This," he held out my curls so that they formed wings on either side of my head, "is not civilized."

"What is your problem today?"

"My problem?" He leaned back on his heels and stroked his chin, pretending to ponder the question. "Well, it starts with my assistant calling in sick this morning with an upset stomach…too much vodka will do that to a person. So I rescheduled the client whose appointment layered over the end of yours for another day, and then my next three clients, *three,* canceled on *me.*"

"Three?" I repeated, surprised. Marcus's services were always in high demand. Most people had to wait months for an appointment. It was hard to imagine three of them canceling at the last minute. "What's going on?"

"One of them has some sort of work emergency and her boss won't let her leave until it's handled. Another just found out that her son's about to be expelled from his elite private school so she's running over there with an endowment check and an accompanying plea for leniency. And the last just found out this morning that her husband has been screwing their dog trainer." He spit out the last sentence with particular vehemence. The stylist working nearest us cast a bemused look in our direction before pointing her hair dryer at her client's head. "I understand why you might have to cancel a hair appointment in order to save your job or your kid," Marcus said, raising his voice to be heard over the dryer, "but if you find out you're being cheated on the *first* thing you should do is fix your damn hair! What, you're going to confront your husband and his mistress on a *bad* hair day? Who *does* that?"

"It does seem like an ill conceived plan," I agreed.

"And then to top it all off, you come in here looking like you just went skipping through a thunderstorm with a lightning rod all because you can't be bothered to get your butt over to Target to buy some product!"

"Oh for…" I shook my head, already bored with my role as a temporary punching bag. "Look," I said, steadily, "I'm here, aren't I? Or is all this too much for you to handle?" I patted my hair protectively. "Because there's a new salon on Maiden Lane that supposedly specializes in miracles."

Marcus made eye contact with me through the mirror. "Oh touché." He stepped back and examined my hair even more carefully. I stared pointedly at the blown up Rolling Stones covers that decorated the walls. Much better than seeing Marcus' perfect nose wrinkle in distaste.

"All right," he finally grumbled. "I've vented, I'm calmer and I've formulated a plan of attack."

I gave him a small smile. "You still love me?"

"Always and forever," he said with a sigh. "Okay, let's Beyoncé you out."

He stepped forward and started combing through the disaster, his eyes narrowed with focus. "I'd like to do some color, but if we do you have to promise me you'll deep condition once a week. Your hair's going to start getting drier now that the grey's coming in and---"

"The grey's coming in?" I leaped to my feet and faced him. "Is that supposed to be some kind of sick joke?"

The patrons in the chairs nearest me all jumped, surprised by my outburst and then quickly started whispering to their respective stylists.

Marcus gave me a withering stare. "We all go grey sometime, honey. Anderson Cooper went silver fox before he hit thirty."

"But that's not me!" I insisted, banging my hand against the revolving chair. "I'm not going to go grey for another decade! I don't have a single strand of—ow!"

Marcus had reached over and yanked out one of my hairs from the back of my head and held it up for my inspection. "What color would you say that is?"

I bit down on my lower lip and glared at the hair. "Slate."

The corners of Marcus' mouth twitched. "It's a little light for slate. You might have to amend to silver."

"Fuck."

"Sit."

"Fine." I dropped back down in my chair, disgusted.

"It's really not a big deal," he assured me, my own outburst calming his mood.

"Whatever." I sounded like a petulant teenager. Did London's daughter sound like that? How was she doing? "Are there a lot of…hairs like that back there?"

He hesitated a little too long before replying. "Have you been stressed lately?"

"No! Not unless I grew this within the last twenty-four hours! With the major exception of yesterday, everything has been smooth as silk. I have no deadlines. Excluding last night, Anatoly and I haven't had an argument about *anything* in like, a year. Everyone I care about is doing well. Financially I'm totally fine. My family has been acting suspiciously sane. Mr. Katz is thriving. I have absolutely zero to be stressed about."

"Ah, that explains it."

I turned my head so I could figure out what the hell he was talking about but he firmly turned it back toward the mirror. "Artist at work. Stay still." He started working through a particularly stubborn tangle with the business end of a comb. "The good news is that with me on your team you never have to go…slate. You'll only get blonder with age."

I started to nod in appreciation then remembered myself and went into mannequin-challenge mode, only allowing my eyes to wander around the room. I noticed for the first time that, with the exception of the Eurasian receptionist, Marcus and I were the only people of color in the salon. Thanks to Silicon Valley and sky rocketing rents the whole city was becoming *blonder with age.* We used to be vanilla, chocolate chip ice cream with caramel swirls. Now the chips and swirls were becoming a little more sparse. If we kept it up, we might morph into plain ol' vanilla.

Until yesterday, your life had become a bit vanilla too.

I blanched and cast my eyes down. I didn't know where that little voice had come from but it was wrong. As wrong as the silver hairs on my head.

"All right," he sighed once the knots were gone and my hair was divided up into several different sections. "Stay here while I go mix some color. When I get back you can tell me about the last twenty-four hours that were…less than smooth?"

"They weren't even in the vicinity of smooth."

"Oh goody. I'm crossing my fingers for scandalous. Be right back, love."

He turned and disappeared into a back room where all the chemicals were kept. I lifted my eyes again to see my reflection in the mirror. I looked ridiculous, a black, nylon styling cape drawn tightly around my neck, covering my clothes, my hair divided into a multitude of sections with Marcus' clips and sticking out every which way. The salon's receptionist stopped by to ask me if I wanted coffee, or maybe a glass of champagne. I had been coming to this place long enough to know the champagne was cheap and the coffee was not, so I opted for the caffeine. As she walked away I thought I noted, through the picture windows, a man in a black baseball hat standing outside across the street from the salon, staring at me. But when I turned my head to look he was walking swiftly away. I was imagining things. At least I hoped I was. It would be super embarrassing if I scared off a stalker by looking like a crazed, greying circus clown.

But there was something about the way he walked as he disappeared out of my line of sight...*why did he seem familiar to me?*

"So tell me about yesterday."

The sound of Marcus' voice startled me. I hadn't heard him approach. "Yesterday was *not* a good day," I insisted as he began to paint each hair section with a thick goo of white, then sandwich it between tinfoil.

"Uh-huh. Tell me about it anyway."

I sighed and laid out the whole story. London, his manic

warnings and fears, his collapse, his apartment, the text, the Zipcar, the business cards, Anita, Catherine, Ms. Dogz... although I left out the part about Ms. Dogz's given name.

"London," he said, thoughtfully. "I like that. We would all sound so much more sophisticated if we were named after two syllable cities. Paris, London, Florence, Milan—"

"New York?"

"Okay, maybe it's a European phenomenon." He painted another section of hair. "So you don't actually know if London's married to that woman?"

"I'm pretty sure he was. I mean, he had a wedding ring so he was married to *someone*. I tried looking her up online before I came in today, same with London but, you know, they don't exactly have uncommon names, or at least not uncommon enough. I couldn't find her daughter either although I did discover that there is a Catherine St. *in* London, so you know, there's that."

"But it was Catherine who called to give you the news, right?" he asked tapping his foot along with the Bruno Mars song that had just come on. "You have her number."

"When I call, it rings once and then goes directly to Voicemail. I tried last night and again on my way over here. I texted her too but haven't heard back."

"She's probably blocked you," he said matter-of-factly.

"You think?"

"When you block someone on your iPhone it rings once and then goes to voicemail." He painted another section of hair. "Only thing is, the person who's done the blocking never gets the voicemails, or the texts of the caller. Remember that guy I went out with, the one who lasered off his pubic hair so he could put lily and daisy tattoos on his pelvic area?"

"Flower boy!" I cried out, entertained by the memory. "You dropped him right after he gave you a glimpse of his… er…pruned garden, right?"

"Yep. And when he wouldn't stop calling, I blocked him. The bartender who introduced us told me he's been getting the one ring ever since."

"Huh. Well, I hope she *is* getting the messages because in them I pointed out once again that I only met her dad yesterday. In other words, I'm not, not, *not* his girlfriend." I paused for a moment before adding, "If she wasn't his daughter I'd be embarrassed that she didn't think I could do better."

"The state of your hair probably threw her off."

"Marcus."

"Okay, okay." He ran his gloved fingers over another section of hair. "So once again, the fates have aligned and a real life murder mystery has been dropped into your lap. What are you going to do?"

I chewed on my lower lip and rubbed the nylon fabric of my black cape between my fingers. "Nothing," I eventually answered.

Marcus shifted his weight back on his heels and met my eyes in the mirror. "Say what?"

"I'm not going to do anything," I explained. "Initially I was tempted. To you know, poke around, see if I could turn up anything suspicious. But then Anatoly weighed in. He definitely thinks pursuing this whole supposed mystery is ill advised and I have to admit he has a point." I paused as the patron next to me squealed with delight as she tossed her newly purple and blue hair. "Dena and Mary Ann think I should leave it alone too. Hell, even London's dog seems skeptical of my foul-play theories. And you know what? I'm finally grown up enough to listen to other people's opinions." I sighed and shook my head. "Plus London's daughter clearly doesn't want me anywhere near this thing. I really think I need to respect the daughter's wishes, don't you?"

Marcus went silent, allowing the chitchat and the music of the room to fill the space between us as he studied my reflection. I shifted uncomfortably in my chair. "Marcus?"

"No."

"No?" I repeated.

"*Hell* no! That child's mother might be a murderer! She may actually need your help, whether she wants it or not."

"But Occam's razor says Aaron London killed Aaron London," I protested. "I don't have any compelling reason to believe it was a homicide. Just a text and a hunch." I glanced up at Janis Joplin who was sticking her tongue out at me from a 26x38 inch Rolling Stones cover.

"Something hasn't been quite right with you lately."

"I don't know what you mean." Someone put Merry Christmas by the Ramones on in the background. It was one of the few holiday songs I could handle this early in the season.

"Yes, you do." He put his brush down with a sigh and checked the clock. "For one thing, the Sophie I know would never go days without hair products."

"Oh, come on."

"When is the last time you got any writing done?"

"Hello non sequitur," I forced a laugh. My gaze slid from the poster to my feet.

"When Sophie?"

I shrugged noncommittally and ventured a glance at Marcus' reflection. He looked firm but also concerned. Mostly he looked like he wasn't going to take a shrug for an answer. "Ok, fine," I said, throwing up my hands. "I haven't written a word since I turned in my last manuscript almost two years ago. But it's not my fault! All those years of writing Alicia Bright and now that's done and…and it's hard just coming up with something new."

"Oh, you think that's it?" he asked, flatly.

"I want it to come to me organically," I explained, self-consciously, "like it did when I came up with my Alicia Bright series."

"You came up with the Alicia Bright series while you were going through a chaotic divorce from an infuriating man," Marcus pointed out. "*That's* what motivates you."

"Divorce?"

"Craziness!" He put his hands on his hips. "Drama! Big giant messes! I have news for you, girlfriend, you are not wired like the rest of us. Throw you into a stormy sea and you'll swim like an Olympian. Drop you in a glassy lake and you'll sink like a Jimmy Hoffa."

"I am *not* sinking!"

"Really? Tell that to your follicles!" he retorted.

A large truck passed the salon making the ground rumble beneath me as I angrily gripped the armrests of my chair. "Just a few minutes ago I was telling you how great things were going for me!"

"You told me how *smooth* things were. Totally different. And I bet things don't feel quite the same between you and Anatoly these days either!"

"Don't be ridiculous! We're absolutely in love."

"Oh, go put it in a Hallmark card. Like I said, you've been off lately. But when you came in today, you seemed a little better, and *that's* because of the craziness of yesterday."

"This is ridiculous," I muttered. "*You're* ridiculous."

"Uh-huh. You once told me you and Anatoly could survive anything except decaf and boredom and you are bored out of your frizzy haired skull."

I glanced around the bustling room. No one was looking at us now which was odd because I felt like Marcus had just busted open my whole psyche and laid it on the floor. I shook my head, causing the many bits of tinfoil in my hair to brush against each other. "I guess I've been feeling kind of…empty lately." The words burned my throat, scorching me with humiliation. "I *am* happy a lot, but, I don't know, I'm missing…I guess I'm missing my spark. And things have just been weird. Every once in a while I'll think some-one's watching me, and then I look and no one's there and rather than be relieved I'm like, *disappointed* because if someone was spying on me at least that would be interesting. Which is crazy. I'm crazy."

"All the most interesting people are," Marcus countered.

"Yeah, but that's not…I mean, oh, I don't know, Marcus…I guess I'm embarrassed." I hung my head, letting the tinfoil crinkle. "I'm embarrassed that I'm struggling to fully be the person everybody knows me to be. I can't *write*, Marcus. What do I do?"

"Two things," he said, solemnly.

I looked up at him, ready to take his words as soul-saving commandments. Whatever advice came out of his mouth would be my new gospel.

"Are you ready for this?"

"I'm ready," I replied, meekly.

"All right. Number one," he held up one finger, dramatically, "deep condition."

"Oh for God's sake." I had never punched Marcus before but I was tempted.

"Two," Marcus continued, "solve a real life murder mystery…again."

"I don't get it. You've always counseled me to behave… well, reasonably. And now you want me to slip on my gumshoes in order to investigate the marginally suspicious death of a total stranger."

"Because that *is* reasonable for you." He gently swiveled my chair around so I was facing him directly. "It's not that you're a drama queen--"

"Gee, thanks."

"It's that you're a drama goddess. You have a sacred duty to follow drama wherever you see it, and you see it now. Nobody dies of pneumonia these days."

"Actually, pneumonia kills over fifty-thousand people per—"

"Don't bore me with statistics," Marcus said, theatrically. "Follow the breadcrumbs, jump in and ride the breaker. Make sense of it. It's what you *do,* Sophie."

"This is insane," I said with a laugh.

"Exactly!" Marcus replied. "Trust me, Sophie, if you let a little crazy seep back into your life and a little moisture seep back into your head your life will be the glorious mess you need it to be. And your hair," he added with a sniff, "will just be glorious."

CHAPTER
ELEVEN

"People used to call me stubborn and anal-retentive. Now that I have a few million in the bank, they call me determined and detail oriented. Too often the things we're told are flaws are the very things that we need for our success."
--Dying To Laugh

Hours later I sat in my car with beautiful hair and a troubled mind. I was still in my parking spot, five city blocks from Marcus' salon, which, in San Francisco, is considered a convenient spot (any parking spot in San Francisco that is close enough to your destination not to require hiking boots is worth celebrating). To my left and right were Victorians and Edwardians all converted into apartments and condos and in my hand was a business card. The Nolan-Volz business card that I had been carrying around with me since I found it in London's apartment last night.

In my head, I could hear Anatoly telling me to toss it. I could see Dena rolling her eyes at the very idea that there was something significant about this thing.

And I could hear Marcus' voice, *Drop you in a glassy lake*

and you'll sink like a Jimmy Hoffa.

Images of Anita sitting in the hospital waiting room, anger and fear in her eyes as she ordered me to leave. Sounds of her daughter's voice as she coolly told me her father had died, told me her mother never wanted to speak to me.

Follow the breadcrumbs, jump in and ride the breaker. Make sense of it. It's what you do, *Sophie.*

I pulled my phone out of my bag and dialed the number on the card.

"Nolan-Volz, Gundrun Volz office, may I help you?" a woman asked. She had the kind of voice that sounded sexy, bored and vexed all at the same time. I could imagine her doing phone sex for men who got off on being demeaned by hot chicks.

"Yes, um…I was hoping to reach Gundrun Volz."

"Uh-huh," she said, which was nice. She could have easily come back at me with *no shit.* "And this is pertaining to?" she pressed.

"Aaron London?" I asked uncertainly, clueless as to how to proceed. "I'm not sure--"

"He doesn't work here anymore," the voice interrupted.

I hesitated a moment. "Come again?"

"Aaron London left the company almost six months ago. He is no longer associated with Nolan-Volz."

I continued to hold the phone to my ear. I was pinching the business card so hard my fingertips had gone white. "I…okay," I tried again, but words were failing me now. What the hell could Aaron London have done for Nolan-Volz? "Could you tell me who holds his position now?"

"The position of Sr. V.P. of R and D? That would be--"

I hung up.

"Oh my God." My heart was thrumming against my chest with so much force you'd think it was being operated by a hardcore techno DJ. This whole thing was getting weirder and weirder and a *lot* more suspicious. Even Anatoly would have to see that now.

Speaking of which…

Smiling I called him up, eager to hear his voice as he realized that there really was something odd about London's death. And maybe I was just a little excited to hear him say, *wow, you were right!*

"Hey," he said. His Russian accent was a little more pronounced this afternoon, something that happened when he was irritated, turned on or not properly caffeinated.

"Hey you. Have you managed to track down Anita London yet?" I asked. "About the dog?"

"Not yet, I've been swamped. But I'm about to start working on it."

"Uh-huh." A large moth landed on my windshield, resting its little insect legs against the glass. "I just found out Aaron London was a V.P. for Nolan-Volz."

There was a long silence on the other end of the line.

"Anatoly?" I asked. "Are you still there?"

"Are you sure?" he finally asked.

"I just called the company. I'm sure."

"Why did you call the company?"

"That's what you're focused on?" The moth took off to eavesdrop on somebody else. "He was a Sr. V.P. of R and D. He left a little less than six months ago. I don't know if he was fired or if he quit but when he was going off on that company, I mean, that wasn't random. He wasn't talking out of his ass. He actually knew how they operate."

Again, there was silence on the other end of the line. He was probably in shock. "So?" I pressed when I couldn't take it any longer. "What do you think?"

I could picture him sitting in his office chair, slowly getting to his feet as he took in the implications of this news. I leaned forward, almost pressing against the steering wheel, waiting for one of his Russian curses followed by an admission that something was rotten in the state of Denmark. "I think," he finally said, drawing out the words, "that London was a disgruntled employee who had a breakdown."

So that was not the reaction I was hoping for. "But…don't you think it's possible he was a whistleblower?" I asked.

"If he was a whistleblower he would have gone to the press or a government official. He wouldn't have come to us. The man who walked into my office yesterday may have been sane six months ago, or at least sane enough to hold down a corporate job, but clearly something happened to him."

"You mean like, he was poisoned?" I didn't like the zeal that was in my voice. A woman and her three toy poodles walked past, all four of them dressed in holiday sweaters for the seventy-one degree heat. I hoped to God I didn't sound as silly as they looked.

"No, I mean like he started drinking or taking drugs, or maybe it's the reverse. Maybe he stopped taking the medication that was stabilizing him. Regardless, it's not our business."

I slumped back in my seat. "But don't you think things are kind of adding up?" I asked, my voice taking on a plaintive tone. "A woman claiming to be his wife showing up at the hospital. His neighbor saying he didn't have a wife…"

"Yes, it's adding up," Anatoly admitted. "He used to be a stable man. Then he lost his job, his wife and then, finally, he went into a downward spiral."

I stared down at the business card, the super villain name glaring back at me in bold, black ink.

"I'll try to track down Anita London this afternoon to ask her if she wants the dog," Anatoly was saying, "and…oh, I'm sorry, I have another call coming in. A client."

"Yeah, sure of course, you should take that," I said, distractedly.

"Don't overthink this, Sophie. Let this one go."

I stayed on the line long enough to hear it go dead.

And then I pulled the phone away from my ear and dialed up Gundrun Volz office once more.

"Nolan-Volz, Gundrun Volz's office, can I help you?"

"I'm sorry, we were disconnected before. My name's Sophie Katz and I'm doing a freelance piece for the San Francisco Chronicle."

"Oh, yes, do you have follow up questions for Mr. Volz?" the woman asked, still sounding bored-sexy.

Follow-up questions? What the hell was she talking about? "Yes," I said, working hard to keep the question mark out of my voice.

"If you'd like to leave your name and number I'll pass along your request."

I mechanically recited my information as I tried to figure out what exactly was going on.

"The article is running in four days, yes?" the woman asked.

"Yes," I said, deciding that sticking to the one syllable word was probably my best strategy.

"So you'll need to hear from him soon," she reasoned. "Are you requesting an in person meeting or will another phone call suffice?"

"In person is probably best," I said, a little doubtfully.

"I'll see what I can do." I thanked her, hung up, got out of my car and half walked, half ran back to the salon. I got there just as Marcus was walking out the door, a shiny, tan windbreaker pulled over his broad shoulders.

"You're back," he noted as I approached breathless and smiling.

"*If* I was going to investigate London's death," I asked, "where do you think I should start?'

Marcus' lips curled up until his smile matched my own. "Well, let's see, you claimed you weren't able to follow most of what London said to you in Anatoly's office, right? That it just sounded like the fragmented ramblings of a conspiracy theorist?"

"Yes, that's right."

"Do you think you might have understood him better if *you* were a conspiracy theorist?" he asked, slipping his hands into his jacket pocket.

"Maybe, but I'm not."

"Do you know any?"

My brow creased as I tried to come up with a name. In the distance, there was the sound of angry honking from multiple cars, above me somewhere the sound of a low flying plane.

And then it hit me. I glanced up at Marcus to see from the look on his face that he had thought of someone too.

Together we said, "Jason."

 # CHAPTER
TWELVE

"What's considered delusional today will often been seen as prophetic tomorrow."
--Dying To Laugh

Dena was not thrilled when I told her what I wanted, but Jason leaped at the opportunity to explain his conspiracy theories to a captive audience. At his request, we were to meet in Sutro Heights Park at five-thirty pm and since Marcus didn't have any more clients and Ms. Dogz needed a walk, I decided to take both of them along.

"Why are we meeting in a park again?" Marcus asked as I struggled to fit my Audi into a parallel spot relatively near our destination. In the cup-holder was a light Salted-Caramel-Mocha-Frappucino with an add shot and extra whipped cream (Marcus didn't understand why one would get a "light" beverage with extra whipped cream proving he was not properly acquainted with the complicated dance between justification and denial). Ms. Dogz was skidding from one side of the backseat to the other as she tried unsuccessfully to squeeze her muzzle through the cracked windows.

"Not enough privacy in a café," I said, reciting what Jason had told me.

"We could have met at your place," he said.

"You remember that time when someone bugged my house?" I asked as I finally got my car correctly positioned.

"That was eons ago," Marcus complained.

"I don't know what to tell you." I reached for my drink and took a long, luxurious sip of caffeinated sugar and fat. "Jason just thought the park was better."

"The wind is picking up and I just did your hair!" he snapped as I turned off the ignition.

I swiveled in my seat so I could face him. "Marcus, this meeting is about life and death." I paused to take another sip before adding, "and the blowout looks so cool when it's flowing in the breeze."

Marcus grunted his disapproval as he got out of the car. I leashed up Ms. Dogz and we trekked over to the main entrance of the park. Jason was already there, standing between the two stone lions. The looks carved into the feline faces had always struck me as both bemused and sort of judgy, expressions that seemed out of place here, in this seaside park built on the grounds of the ruined Sutro Mansion. But Jason, with his blonde goatee, camouflage pants, red flannel shirt and black printed T-shirt gave their bemused judgment a needed bit of context.

"How are you?" I asked as Jason stepped in to give me a hug. Ms. Dogz eagerly sniffed his pant leg.

"I'm as well anyone living in a corrupt Capitalist dystopia can expect to be," he answered cheerily. He gave Marcus a quick bro hug before turning back to me. "Like the hair."

"Thank you," Marcus and I said simultaneously. I let the leash slip over my wrist as I reached up to run my fingers through my newly styled locks but Marcus slapped my hand away. "Mess with it and I cut you," he growled.

Jason crouched down so he was eye-level with the dog. "So this is Sophie?"

"Wait, what?" Marcus asked, surprised. "Her name's--"

"Ms. Dogz," I snapped. "That's what we're calling her."

"Got it, sorry," Jason smiled. He started to stand again but then suddenly stopped short. "Is that my leash?"

"Wait, what?" Marcus said again.

I felt my face heating up to about a thousand degrees. "Oh, yeah," I stammered. "Um, Dena lent it to me. I'd give it back now but, well," I gestured to the dog who clearly needed to be leashed.

"No, no it's okay," Jason said, a little uncertainly. "We have more."

"You're serious?" Marcus asked. "This is serious?" I stuck my straw in my mouth and pointedly looked away.

"I did like that one though," Jason noted, taking no mind of Marcus. "It's a good length."

It was possible this was the worst conversation these lions had ever been cursed to overhear. "In all the chaos of last night, I forgot this was the leash Dena used on you," I explained. "Only a death and a stolen dog could distract me from something like that, but there it is. So now we're both just going to have to pretend that you have never *ever* been attached to this thing. It is very important to me that we both go into immediate states of denial. Can you do that?"

Jason rolled his eyes and scratched the back of his neck. "You don't have to get puritanical about it. Dena and I just have a different way of expressing sexual affection--"

"That is *not* denial!" I shouted. "I swear to God, Jason, if you say one more word about this I will throw this Frappuccino in your face--"

"Okay, okay." He laughed holding up his hands in surrender. "Come on, let's walk and talk..." he hesitated and then lowered his voice, "about what we came here to talk about."

Marcus and I gave each other looks. There was no need to speak in code or whispers. We were entering magic hour. The picnickers had all packed up. The few tourists still here were busy trying to rub away goose bumps as they made their way back to their cars. That left us and a handful of locals, identifiable by their pragmatic layered clothing and shaggy eternity scarves, milling about, sneaking in a few moments of solitude in this sanctuary that was allowed to grow over the cracked foundation of a fallen estate.

We followed Jason as he led us down the dirt path that had once been a curving driveway. "Dena filled me in on everything as soon as she got home from your break-in last night," Jason explained, kicking a small stone out of the way with his Doc Martens.

"It was *not* a break-in," I protested. Ms. Dogz was zig-zagging all over the place. First there was something she had to smell to her left, then her right. It took both attention and skill to keep from tripping on the notorious leash. "I had a key," I went on. "The neighbor let me into the building."

"Yeah, but the neighbor let you in after you lied to him, right?" Jason asked with a small smile. "Not judging. You did what needed to be done. Tell me what London was afraid of. Who or what did he think was after him?"

"Everything?" I laughed then caught myself. It was bad luck to make fun of the dead. "He was going on about the New World Order, our government and institutionalized racism or something like that. And then he was ranting about the pharmaceutical industry, I remember he mentioned Rispolex and oh, what was the other one...Thilodeen? Thiophene? I can't be sure."

"Thalidomide," Jason said, in a slightly hushed voice.

I blinked in surprise. "Yeah, that's it."

"It is?" Marcus asked, then stopped briefly to disentangle himself from the leash. "How'd you know the name of the drug, Jason?"

"There have been class action lawsuits against both the makers of Rispolex and Thalidomide," Jason explained. We passed a cluster of evergreens and the marble stones that once formed a pillar. "Both drugs caused the users to alter their bodies in really bad ways. Rispolex caused heart murmurs and sometimes caused serious damage to the heart valves of people taking the drug. And Thalidomide caused deformities in the babies of the mothers who took the drug. Rispolex was such a fuck-up the company that developed it went under."

"London didn't have any deformities," I said as I thought back to the waif of a man I had met only a day ago. "And from what I saw, I don't think London had a heart attack. Were either of those drugs made by Nolan-Volz?"

"Never heard of Nolan-Volz. Why?" Jason asked.

"It's a pharmaceutical development company. Aaron London used to be an executive there. V.P. of R&D."

Jason stopped in his tracks. "A dude who worked for a money-hungry, industrial, blood-sucking drug pusher, claims he's being poisoned, then keels over in the street and you're confused about what's going on?"

"Ooh, I see where you're going with this," Marcus chimed in. "Maybe somebody at Nolan-Volz was skimming off the top or, oh, I know! Maybe they were stealing the company drugs and dealing them to addicts! Profiting off the opioid epidemic!"

"No," Jason said sullenly. "That's not what happened."

"It could have," Marcus said, a bit defensively.

"You're not thinking big enough," Jason insisted. "It wasn't an individual at the corporation who offed him. It was the corporation itself! I bet you anything this guy's death was a corporate decision."

"You mean like they discussed it at the board meeting?" Marcus asked, dryly. "Agenda item number one, 'How to increase market share, item two, how to assassinate former employees, item three research and development—'"

"These companies are evil! They *make* poison!" Jason sputtered. "They convince parents to medicate their kids in order to fit them into a broken educational system! They push their speed on college kids using the guise of treating their supposed ADHD!"

"Speed treats ADHD?" Marcus asked, but Jason was on a roll.

"They give us heart medication that destroys our livers, liver medication that destroys our hearts, they literally inject cancer patients with artificial toxins and call it treatment. They try to squash news and research proving the benefits of homeopathic medicine, like Gaba, ox bile and medical marijuana! What this country needs is homeopathic weed, not pharmaceutical speed!"

"Ox bile?" I asked weakly. "People take, like, actual ox bile?"

"And speaking of weed," Marcus chimed in, "have you been smoking, honey? Because you're sounding a little paranoid."

"There's a difference between being paranoid and being clear eyed," Jason replied, almost petulantly. "That's why you asked to pick my brain. I'm clear eyed. And ox bile is fucking awesome. Does great things for your digestion. But you wouldn't know that because Big Pharma won't *let* you know that!"

I sipped at my drink and sent up a silent message of thanks to Big Pharma for protecting me from ox bile propaganda. Ms. Dogz was pulling me toward a different trail and I gestured for the guys to come along as I let her take the lead. The small victory seemed to cheer her and she trotted in front of us, ears flapping joyfully in the air. "London also said something about a medical ethics professor at NYU exposing some issues with pharmaceutical testing," I said, as I tried to replay my whole conversation with London in my head.

"Several years back, a professor was talking about how she found that there were a lot of companies who weren't disclosing the results of their trial studies before getting FDA approval to put new drugs on the market," Jason explained. "She went public about it, talking to anyone who would listen and sending her study out to as many publications as possible. She helped expose the issues that led to the whole Rispolex shit-show. She became a real hero to those of us who are trying to stand up to Big Pharma. But did the FDA listen to her? Do they care that they're being deceived? No.

They don't give two fucks. They did nothing to address the problems she brought to light. The guys in the FDA are just putting in their time until one of the pharmaceutical companies they're supposed to be regulating offers them a big-paycheck job in their corporate offices."

"How do you know all this stuff?" Marcus asked, articulating what I was thinking.

"Because I'm woke."

"The thing is," I jumped in before Marcus had a chance to comment on how totally awkward it was to hear a thirty-something-year-old white man who spends his nights on a leash use the word *woke*, "a lot of what London said really was pretty out there, even by…er…clear eyed standards."

"I doubt that," Jason sniffed.

"It wasn't all about pharmaceuticals," I continued. "He was freaking out about the entire medical establishment. He thought hospitals were doing unnecessary procedures on homeless people. I mean even you'd have to agree, that's nuts."

Once again, Jason came to an abrupt stop. Marcus followed suit, I *tried* to follow suit but it took a little tugging on Ms. Dogz before she agreed to let me stand still.

"Jason?" Marcus asked. "Is everything okay?"

But Jason was busy with his phone, his fingers tapping away at the screen until he found what he was looking for. He held up the phone so we could all see the archived L.A. Times article. The headline read: *3 Hospitals Accused Of Using Homeless For Fraud.*

I handed my Frappuccino off to Marcus, snatched the phone out of Jason's hand and started reading.

"Three hospitals were exposed for literally searching for

homeless people on the street," Jason summarized even as I read the words for myself. "They offered them a couple of bucks to come stay at their facilities for a few days, gave them a false medical diagnosis and then did tests and procedures on them so they could bill Medicare."

"Wait a minute, what?" Marcus put his free hand against his chest as if grasping at his heart. "That can't be true."

"It was on MSNBC," Jason continued. "Just your typical predatory, corporate, Machiavellian behavior. They managed to bilk the system for something like sixteen mil. One more reason to hate L.A., right?"

Marcus was turning a little green. "Did they…hurt anyone?"

"They didn't kill anyone but they fucked a few people up, yeah."

"I think I'm going to be sick," Marcus muttered, staring down at creamy brown remnants of my drink.

"Then you should be getting sick every day," Jason said, enthusiastically. "If we were all paying better attention it would be a non-stop vomit fest! Come on, my brother, you gotta get yourself woke!"

Marcus held up his hand in a Stop-In-The-Name-Of-Love like gesture. "Try not to get all Rachel Dolezal on me." He studied Jason for a second before adding, "I will admit, you're quite a fountain of knowledge when it comes to bizarre news stories. You never even met the man and yet you seem to be a regular Aaron London cryptographer."

"This happened," I said softly, still staring at the article. "He wasn't just making things up."

"What else did he talk about?" Jason asked eagerly.

"Um, the New World Order?" I offered. "LSD…something about Nazis. He was definitely upset about Nazis which…now that I think about it, might not be so unreasonable these days."

"MkUltra!"

I looked at him blankly as he took his phone back from me and started walking again, as if too amped to stand still. Marcus, Ms. Dogz and I dutifully followed.

"What's MkUltra?" I asked.

"The American government hired Nazi doctors," he explained, "some of whom were accused of war crimes, to help them develop chemical weapons and design ways the drugs could be tested on unsuspecting civilians. New moms who went in for postpartum depression, unsuspecting military personnel, individuals who were considered *undesirable*, those are the people that were considered fair game by our government. They dropped acid in people's drinks and fucked with their heads. And they got Nazis to help them do that. *Nazis.* You don't believe me? Google that shit. MkUltra."

"But…London *was* crazy," I said weakly as Ms. Dogz yanked me toward a spot of grass with an apparently interesting smell. "He was a mess. He was manic. He was—"

"Being poisoned," Jason said, finishing the sentence for me. "Look, you may not believe all the so-called conspiracy theories you hear about Big Pharma or the government, or corporations and modern-day robber barons plotting world domination but there's a reason so many of us do. Years ago, if someone told you the government was monitoring your emails and phone calls you'd assume they had a tinfoil hat in their closet. Now you'd just assume they read the latest New York Times article about the NSA." He pointed to my drink that Marcus was still holding. "And don't think Starbucks is so innocent. You think you're drinking a Frappuccino. But in reality, when you wrap your lips around that straw you're sucking the toxic nectar from the teat of corporate America."

Marcus immediately tossed the Frappucino in the nearest trash can.

"Okay, I get it." I stopped at a dry well house, resting my weight against the only intact structure of the crumbled estate. "What about Zipcars? Or the practice of putting invisible tracking devices on cars? Can you make sense out of all that too?"

Jason stared down at the grass, his forehead scrunched up like he was pondering a particularly difficult math equation. "Maybe…maybe not. What we really need to do is break into the apartment again," he finally said.

"Um, no. Nuh-uh!" I raised my hands in protest. "I had an excuse last time. I had to rescue this girl." I gestured to Ms. Dogz who had begun grazing on a weed. "I have no valid reason to go in there again. If I was caught, it would be very, very bad."

"Then let's not get caught!" Marcus suggested.

I looked over at him, stunned. "You can't possibly think this is a good idea."

"Well, like you said, you have the key." Marcus leaned up against the well with me and offered his most encouraging smile. "It does seem like a good place to start."

"I already started there!" I protested. "I'm not going in again! It's illegal and more importantly, I don't own a hazmat suit! Seriously, the air inside that place is…crunchy."

Marcus wrinkled up his nose in disgust. "Crunchy?"

"Yes," I said, stubbornly. "The air in there felt crunchy. Like it's so stale it has texture. I'm Not. Going. Back."

"Dena said there were papers in there," Jason said, authoritatively. "She thought they might be printouts of articles? Maybe blogs? We need to read what he was reading. We need to know what he was *researching.* Whatever it was, he was killed for it."

"Not necessarily!" I shot back.

"Yeah, it could have been the wife," Marcus said with a nod. "It's always the wife, or the husband, or the butler in the library with a candlestick. Always one of those three"

"This is serious, Marcus!" Jason said, lamentingly. "This really could be the work of The New World Order. You can't be joking about butlers."

I sighed and let them continue to argue about who the most likely suspect was as my eyes scanned the park. It was one of my favorite places in San Francisco and yet I hadn't been here in years. Why was that? What keeps us from doing the easy things that brighten our lives? I couldn't claim to be too busy. I wasn't. And are you ever really too busy to just take a half hour every week or so and…

My thoughts floated away as my eyes rested on the very outskirt of the park where there was a man, standing very still, looking in my direction.

He was wearing a black baseball cap.

Slowly, I pushed myself off the well. Marcus and Jason were too busy debating useless things to pay any attention to me. I took a step forward, in the direction of the man. Ms. Dogz looked up at me curiously and then followed my gaze as I watched him. I took another step. Then another.

The man in the hat turned and started walking away.

I *knew* him. I don't know how or even how I could know that considering that he was too far away for me to make out any of his features. Still, the very sight of him set off alarm bells that were currently clanging noisily in my head.

"Come back here," I said under my breath. Ms. Dogz looked up at me, the only one of my companions who had actually heard me.

"Come back here!" I yelled, my hand tightening its grip on Ms. Dogz' leash.

"What?" Marcus said and Jason added something along the lines of "Are you talking to me?"

There was too much distance between me and the man in the black hat for him to have possibly heard me.

And yet he broke into a jog, toward the street.

He was running away from me.

I didn't think, didn't calculate, I just started running, running after this man. I yanked Ms. Dogz after me, dragging her at first. But as soon as she understood what we were doing she quickly overtook me and started dragging me. The man was moving faster now but so was I...*too fast*. Ms. Dogz was going too fast.

"Whoa!" I cried out, grasping at the first animal command that popped into my head to absolutely no effect. And the man was still running.

I tried to pick up my pace to better match Ms. Dogz as I watched the man leave the park and turn onto the sidewalk. He was *not* going to get away. I managed to increase my speed even more. Ms. Dogz did too. The wind was blowing through my fabulous hair. The few people left in the park turned their attention to me as we raced over the grass. I was running faster than I ever had in my life! I was going to catch him!

And that's when it happened.

A squirrel.

A friggin' squirrel ran across our path toward a tree and Ms. Dogz completely Lost. Her. Mind.

With a bark, she did a ninety-degree turn to chase her new furry target. "Stop!" I cried half a second before I fell face first into the grass as Ms. Dogz yanked away from me, running to the tree trunk where the squirrel had scampered up, barking at it like she was a police dog cornering a drug dealer.

There was grass in my mouth. Dirt in my nose. My knee was stinging

"What the hell was that about?"

I looked up to see Jason, out of breath, standing over me. I turned my head to the street where the man had been. He was gone.

"What did you see?" Jason pressed

I scanned the street to the left and right. Nothing.

In my peripheral vision, I could see that Marcus had managed to get the dog back and was dragging her my way. "I saw a man." I put my hand up to my hair, wondering how badly I had managed to mess up Marcus' work. "A man in a black hat."

"As in a cowboy hat?" Marcus asked, stepping up just in time to hear my last remark. "Was he riding a horse?"

I shook my head and got to my feet, pulling a few blades of grass off my face. My jeans were torn and I could see drops of blood on my kneecap, but other than that I was fine. Ms. Dogz was wagging her tail stub, cocking her head to the side, looking deceptively innocent.

"Are you sure you're okay?" Marcus asked. I could tell the question was meant to pertain to both my physical and mental state.

I blinked at him and then looked back out at the street. "Yeah, I'm okay." I vainly tried to brush the dirt from my clothes. The man in the black hat had been watching me but he also *ran* from me. He hadn't come to hurt me. He had come to scare me...possibly to scare me away. I turned to face Jason, feeling a renewed sense of determination. "When will you be available to help me go through London's apartment?"

Jason's eyebrows jumped up into his hairline and then he gave me a slow, Cheshire Cat grin. "Hell yeah!"

CHAPTER
THIRTEEN

"A blue sky without clouds is pretty but ultimately uninteresting. Such is a life without heartache."
--Dying To Laugh

Jason had the next two days off from the medical marijuana store he worked at so he declared he would spend the first of those days casing London's apartment, seeing if anyone matching Anita or Catherine's description came in or out of there. He'd also try to gauge when the lowest traffic times were for the building and the area as a whole. Then we'd use that information to plan our entry into London's apartment the day after that.

The very term "casing," sounded so...well, criminal. Spontaneity never felt criminal. I had initially entered London's apartment on a whim. I happened to have had the key to his place and so I used it. Surely that wasn't so bad. But casing the apartment building...now I was going deep. I could get in real trouble. That should have worried me.

But as I drove home from Sutro Heights I realized, it really didn't. If anything I found the very idea of the risk... energizing.

I had just pulled into my driveway when I heard Anatoly's Harley pulling in after me. I stepped out of my car, headlights still reflecting off the closed garage door just as he was removing his helmet. His eyes widened slightly as he took in my torn, grass stained jeans and shirt. "What happened?"

I pulled Ms. Dogz out from the back seat by her leash. "There was a squirrel. Ms. Dogz doesn't like squirrels."

Anatoly's mouth twitched at the corner. "I see. Who won?"

"The squirrel gets to live another day." I looked down at my pants. "My jeans do not." My headlights switched off automatically, leaving us only the faint glow of a distant streetlight.

"Your hair looks great," he said, kindly.

"There is that," I conceded.

Ms. Dogz's stub of a tail was wiggling like crazy as she strained at her leash to get to Anatoly. He bent down to give her some love. "Need a drink?" he asked. I presumed he was talking to me even though it was the dog that seemed to have his attention.

"Desperately."

He straightened up, tucked his helmet under one arm and draped the other over my shoulder as the three of us walked up the front steps to our home.

"Any luck tracking down Anita?" I asked.

A slight flicker of concern, maybe irritation, but then Anatoly's face was smooth and happy again. "She's been quite good about protecting her privacy. I'm not finding much of anything on her online."

"Not much of anything would imply you've found a

little of something," I noted as he held the door for me. Mr. Katz strolled out of the living room to say hello. He took one look at Ms. Dogz and did a one-eighty, flicking his tail in disgust.

"All right, I didn't find anything," Anatoly admitted. "But I did track down the number for London's landlord's cell phone."

"Oh?" He wasn't able to find any information on this woman? The man was a private detective for God's sake. Something was very wrong here.

I freed Ms. Dogz from the dreaded leash and tossed it in the corner. "Has the landlord, um, been in that apartment today?"

"No, he hasn't been in there since London moved in," he said, putting his helmet down and walked through the dining room to the kitchen. I trailed after him, my concerns momentarily pushed aside by the joy of seeing him take out a chilled bottle of white. "That was nine months ago."

"But now that London's dead--" I began.

He placed the wine on the counter with a certain degree of ceremony. "He didn't know London was dead until I called."

"Anita didn't call him?"

"He's never heard of Anita," he replied with what seemed like deliberate casualness.

I sank down onto one of the stools by the kitchen island. *Never heard of her?* "He wasn't married," I said, almost more to myself than to Anatoly. "Anita London doesn't exist."

"No, I'm sure he was and I'm sure she does. You're not required to disclose marital status on a rental agreement or credit check." He took out two wine glasses and a bottle opener. "All we know is he didn't volunteer the information about Anita, and why would he?"

"But you do think it's weird, right?" I pressed. "That neither his landlord nor his neighbor knew he had a wife and kid? And that you can't find any information on her?"

"No, I don't." The splash of wine sounded lovely as it hit the bottom of the empty glasses. "As we've already determined, the two of them appear to have been separated. Anita will probably get around to calling London's landlord eventually. And the truth is, I didn't try too hard to find Anita. Just a Google search and an attempt at a very basic background check. I didn't file any requests with the records office. I didn't call in any favors with my contacts at the DMV."

"But why?" I asked, baffled. I had never known Anatoly to be half hazard about *anything*…except maybe housekeeping.

"There's no need to do more," he said simply. His tone was so nonchalant. But his shoulders seemed stiff, his jaw set. The contradictions had me completely baffled. "All we need to do was find out if she wanted this dog and make sure she doesn't charge you with breaking and entry in order to kidnap her."

"I assume you mean kidnap the dog, not Anita."

Anatoly allowed himself a small smile at the quip. "I had a good talk with the landlord," he went on. "I told him London had given you the key to the apartment and you had taken Soph…Ms. Dogz to care for her. I left him our number and gave him permission to pass it on to any of London's next of kin if they express interest in making further arrangements for his pet. So now, even if Anita finds out you were there, she won't be able to spin it as a breaking-and-entry. She will also have a way to contact us if that's what she wants to do."

I chewed on my lower lip as Anatoly handed me a filled glass. "Will the landlord be clearing out the apartment tonight then?" I asked, trying to keep my voice even. "Or will he wait until tomorrow?"

"Neither. I reached him while he was in New York. He won't be home for another three days. He'll take a look at the place then….What's that smile about?" Anatoly asked as he leaned against the kitchen island.

"Hmm?" I sipped my wine, looked away.

"You've got this mischievous smile on your face. The kind you get right before you're about to do something you know you shouldn't do."

I waved my hand dismissively. "That's silly."

"I haven't seen that smile for a while," he admitted. "Makes it all the more suspicious now."

"I'm smiling because I like the wine." I stepped forward and lifted myself on my tiptoes in order to give Anatoly a light kiss.

He pulled away and studied me for a moment, then gave me his own grin and shook his head. "I'm going to throw together dinner."

"What are you thinking?" I asked.

"Something simple…maybe lamb loin chops with Dijon and fresh herbs along with an arugula salad. Take me about twenty minutes."

I laughed and shook my head in awe. "Yeah, that sounds acceptable." Anatoly was the only one I knew who could whip together a gourmet meal in a half hour or less.

"I'm going to have to spend tomorrow night tailing a man who may or may not be faking a workplace injury in order to bilk his employer," He stepped forward and linked his finger around my belt, pulling me forward so there was only half an inch of space between us. "So let's not allow tonight to go to waste. Go upstairs, clean yourself up, put a little Neosporin on that knee and let me use the rest of the evening to take care of you."

"You're going to make me feel better?"

"To start, yes." He leaned down and touched his lips to the nape of my neck, tasting my skin, sending a little shiver through me. "I'm going to serve you a meal that will make you want to scream with pleasure. And while we eat," his hand moved to the small of my back, pulling me even closer so my body was pressed tightly against his, "you're going to tell me every detail about your day."

"Am I?" I murmured, my pulse rate rising steadily.

"You are. And then," his mouth was at my ear now, his tongue flicking at the lobe, "after our meal I'm going to make you feel more than better. I'm going to make your whole body sing." His voice, which had already gone to a low growl, slid into a whisper. "I'm going to make you lose control."

I bit down hard on my lower lip. Slowly he released me, bringing his own glass of wine to his lips as his eyes ran over me one more time until they settled on my hair. "I do like this style," he mused. "It makes me want to pull it, arching your neck back for me to kiss."

It took a second to find my voice. "Oh baby," I said, softly, "over Marcus' dead body." His eyebrows went up and

I saw the corners of his mouth twitch. "Anyway," I went on, placing my palm briefly against his chest. "there are better uses for your fingers." I turned and walked out of the kitchen, wine glass in hand, as his soft laughter followed me. I headed upstairs to our bedroom and, more importantly, to the Neosporin.

There was no doubt in my mind that Anatoly knew I was keeping things from him. The intensity of his seduction was designed to seduce my secrets from me, but perhaps also to distract himself from…something. Something he didn't want to share with me maybe?

My cell started vibrating in my purse and I pulled it out as I reached the top of the stairs. It was a number I didn't recognize. "Hello?" I answered as I made my way to my bedroom.

"Ms. Katz," said sexy-bored lady. "I have Gundrun Volz on the line for you."

I froze, right in the middle of the hallway.

"Ms. Katz, are you there?"

"Yes, um, yes of course," I managed, now talking in a hushed voice.

"I think you're fading out," the woman noted. "Am I losing you?"

"No, no," I quickly made it to my room and closed the door behind me, leaning my back against it. "I'm here," I said in a slightly louder voice now.

"Good, I'll connect you now."

I moved away from the door. I could hear Anatoly banging around in the kitchen. The sound insulation in this place was not as good as it should be.

"Ms. Katz?" A man's voice this time. I sat down on the

corner of my bed. "It's Gundrun Volz. How are you?"

"I'm…good?" I should have thought this through more thoroughly. I didn't even know what I was supposed to be interviewing him about. "Thank you so much for getting back to me so quickly."

"Of course! As I told Tereza last Friday, I'm happy to answer any additional questions you may have. Charity said you wanted to meet in person?"

"Charity…your assistant," I said, stumbling a bit as I tried to put the many pieces together. "Yes, um, that would be great if you can make the time."

"Of course!" he said again. "I must admit, I wasn't thrilled that Tereza only wanted to speak on the phone. I communicate better in person. I do have some time tomorrow if you're free."

"Um," I looked toward my closed bedroom door. Anatoly had put on some music and the sound of Bruce Springsteen became the backdrop to my conversation.

"Ms. Katz? Are you still there?"

"Yes, yes, I'm here…tomorrow's good. What time?"

"Shall we say eight am?"

I thought about all the wonderful things Anatoly might do to my body once we had finished our meal. It could be a late night. "Ten am?" I countered.

"I can move some things around for ten to work," he accommodated. "I assume Tereza will be there as well?"

"Um, I'm not sure she'll be able to make it," I hedged.

"Oh…is that…typical? This is primarily her story, yes?"

"We're working on it in tandem," I ad-libbed. "That way we can both get our own unique perspectives, compare our notes and ensure that the biases of one of us doesn't color the tone of the article. It's a Woodward and Bernstein thing." I literally had no idea what I was talking about.

"Oh, that's…an interesting approach," he said, sounding every bit as confused as I felt. "Well, whatever works for you. You'll be here at ten then? At our Caesar Chavez Street office?"

Suddenly the door to my room opened, Anatoly was there, with Ms. Dogz by his side. "What's up? You never close the door…oh, I didn't realize you were on the phone."

"Yep," I said, directing my comment to Gundrun. "Absolutely, that'll work. Bye!" I hung up and beamed a smile. "Hi."

Anatoly narrowed his eyes. "Who was that?"

"Jason."

"Dena's Jason?" Anatoly asked, skeptically. Ms. Dogz pressed past him and started sniffing around the room.

"He wants to throw Dena a surprise party and asked if I would help."

Anatoly crossed his arms over his chest. "Dena's birthday is four months away."

"Yep, he's a planner. Did you need something?"

Anatoly's eyes were still pretty narrow. He wasn't an idiot. "I'm opening a bottle of red to go with our meal and I wanted to know if you had a preference, Opus or Stag's Leap."

"Either's good. I'll just get myself cleaned up." I jumped to my feet and went into our master-bath, closing the door behind me. I held my breath until I could hear Anatoly's footsteps moving further away, down the hall. I had no doubt he was going to ply me with alcohol tonight in the hopes of loosening my lips. But it wouldn't work.

Secrets were funny things. They could destroy people and their relationships.

Unless of course you trusted your partner enough to know they would never betray you; if you know in your heart that their secrets could be both explosive and impersonal. Those were the kinds of secrets that could be more tantalizing than damaging. I hoped our secrets fit into that category because at that moment, I was enjoying the hell out of them.

# CHAPTER
FOURTEEN

"You say corporations aren't people, but they do share our character. They're nuanced, complicated and messy beings who seek our love and loyalty even as they periodically screw us over. You can't get more human than that."
--Dying to Laugh

I found Volz' sexy-bored assistant sitting behind her beige, industrial looking desk in the reception area outside his office. Her black, fitted blazer was perfectly tailored and revealing a glimpse of a white, silk camisole that complimented her brown skin. Her hair was pulled back into a messy bun that I'm not entirely sure she intended to be messy. "Ms. Katz?" She asked, her burgundy painted lips over enunciating my name.

I nodded, feeling awkward as I stood in the center of the room. In my hand was a notebook that I thought suited a reporter. In my purse I had a rape whistle just in case Gundrun Volz really was a homicidal corporate overlord (could individuals be corporate overlords? Is that how that works?). I pictured a man with Julian Assange hair and the icy blue

Jake-Gyllenhaal-like eyes. I could imagine this Julian Gyllenhaal sitting behind a desk ordering the assassination of quirky former employees who knew too much.

The receptionist picked up the phone and announced me before saying, "You can go right in, Ms. Katz."

"Thank you." I started for the door, walking slowly as the thoughts in my head starting whirling around at accelerating speed. The name Gundrun Volz did sound kind of Nazi-ish. What if he really *was* one? I'm a black Jew. Black Jews shouldn't go around having meetings with Nazis.

"By the way," the receptionist said, startling me. I stopped and turned to face her. Her gaze didn't quite meet mine. Was she nervous? Was she about to warn me about the man I was going to be alone with? It was odd that a Nazi would hire this woman, who looked biracial, as his receptionist but maybe he did it to torture her! What if this place was like a corporate version of Jordan Peele's *Get Out* and this woman was about to beg me to help her escape her existential prison! I bit down hard on my lip as she shifted her position. "I just wanted to say…" *Oh God, here it comes!* "I love your hair."

"W-what?" I said, taken off guard.

"I hope this isn't being presumptuous," she continued, "but...well, I was hoping…maybe you could give me your stylist's info on your way out?"

Oh. She wasn't meeting my eyes because she was looking at my hair. "Thank you," I managed, "yeah, of course I will." I breathed a sigh of relief. Her request gave me a needed boost of confidence. It was easier to confront possible evil on a confirmed good hair day. I put my hand on the doorknob and made my entrance, ready to face the fascist.

The fascist had a surprisingly nice office. Floor to ceiling windows flooded the room with light. Framed Ansel Adams prints decorated the walls and the couches were made of tufted brown leather. The desk itself looked like it was a polished wood, possibly redwood and the man behind it was…well, startlingly normal looking. He had salt and pepper hair with a news-anchorman cut, a broad nose, square chin, bushy brown eyebrows and big ears. His complexion was rosy, maybe a little too rosy, like he overindulged in spirits in his spare time. But sitting there, behind his desk, in a dark suit and red tie, he looked completely together and composed.

It was sort of disappointing.

"Miss Katz, so good to meet you." He walked around his desk to shake my hand. He had a firm, manly grip. "I'm so glad you're following up on Tereza's phone interview. Nolan-Volz has a lot to boast about these days. Sit, sit," he gestured to a chair in front of his desk, which I accepted. He, however, remained standing, meandering around the room as he spoke. "We've been conducting clinical trials of Sobexsol for almost a year now. It's early yet, but the results are amazing. It's going to change lives."

"That's great," I said taking notes as if I was truly impressed with whatever Sobexsol was. "And you said you guys have been working on that for just under a year?"

"They've been working on it for seven years," he said with a short laugh. "We had to figure out the science, then do the animal testing and so on before we got approval for clinical trials from the FDA." I looked up to find that he had found a semi-resting spot, casually leaning against the wall, between a framed doctoral degree from Harvard Medical school and two framed photographs, one of him shaking hands with President George W. Bush and the other with Barack Obama. "We have some of the best scientific minds in the world working here. And dedicated! We've been working with the exact same scientific team from the beginning…or close to exact. We did lose one researcher who left for a position with a company working on finding a cure for Tay-Sachs." He stopped himself, then gave me a slightly patronizing smile. "I'm sorry, sometimes I forget that most people aren't familiar with all the world's ailments. Tay-Sachs is a disease that mainly affects the Ashkenazi Jewish population—"

"I know what Tay-Sachs is. My Jewish uncle died of it while still a child."

"Oh, you're Jewish?" Gundrun asked, visibly surprised. "Forgive me, I thought you were black."

I offered him a tight-lipped smile. "I used to be black but I converted. Anyway, what were you saying about the development of your drug?"

Gundrun looked at me askance for a moment but then quickly recovered. "Right, right, of course. As I was saying, you can't rush these things," he went on. "But based on early results of our clinical trials…I tell you, sometimes I wonder if this merger wasn't a bit premature. I think the inevitable success of this new drug could put Nolan-Volz on the path of becoming a mega player, up there with Johnson & Johnson and Pfizer, even without hitching our wagon to Gilcrest & Co."

"Uh-huh." My scribbled notes were pretty close to illegible but that seemed appropriate since the odds of my ever wanting to re-read Volz's comments about his favorite pharmaceutical seemed pretty slight.

"May I ask what other individuals were instrumental in bringing…um…Sobexsol to market?"

"As you know, it's really been our only project. So everyone here has been instrumental. My co-founder, David Nolan, provided us the funds to get off the ground. Matthew Reynolds has been the scientist leading the research studies, V.P. Lori Casey has helped us get the grants and additional funding we need--"

"What about Aaron London? Was he intricately involved?"

It's not just that Gundrun Volz went quiet, it's that he practically stopped breathing. I looked up from my notepad to see his eyes had doubled in size, his mouth gone slightly slack.

"Aaron London," he repeated.

"Yeah, I spoke with him the other day. He had a lot to say about your research and development methodology."

"Aaron London doesn't work for the company anymore," Gundrun said, his voice still completely even, his eyes still looking wild.

"I'm aware of that,"

He hesitated a moment and then offered me another smile, this one almost apologetic. "I'm afraid that if you've used Aaron London as a source you might have gotten some misinformation. He's bipolar and he stopped taking his medication a while back. It's really a shame. He used to be such a good employee."

London was bipolar? I was hit with a small flicker of doubt. Could it be that my first instinct was right? That London was completely delusional? "He sounded pretty stable last we spoke." My toes curled as I tried to sell the lie.

"I find that…surprising." He pushed himself off the wall and started meandering again, this time in my general direction. "What exactly did he say?"

Oh, that you're part of the New World Order and are working with the government and mainstream medical establishment to kill us all. "He said a lot," I said out loud. "His perspective on your industry was…insightful and unique."

Gundrun Volz took several steps more in my direction before stopping a few feet away. I didn't get the sense he was trying to come across as threatening exactly but the effect was that he was looming over me, establishing a dynamic that definitely was *not* designed to make me feel at ease.

"Why don't you sit down?" I asked, in a pointedly polite tone. "If you don't mind. It'll be easier on my neck."

He hesitated a moment, perhaps surprised at my hubris, before, somewhat theatrically, taking his seat behind his desk. He held his arms out to each side as if to say, *look at what I'm doing for you.* "I want to assure you the company was unaware that Mr. London had stopped taking his medication while he was here." He picked up a plastic blue pen from his desk and started toying with it. "I didn't even know London was bipolar until he started to fall apart. It's illegal of course to demand that kind of information from your employees. Still, we here at Nolan-Volz would never knowingly allow someone with a severe, diagnosed psychiatric disorder to work here untreated. We pride ourselves on the professionalism of our staff, and their rationalism. We are a company based on science after all." He then added with another apologetic smile, "I'm sorry he wasted your time with his rantings."

I watched the pen rotate between his fingers. This interview was getting interesting. "Why are you so sure he didn't say something good?"

"Excuse me?" Volz cocked his head to the side, the pen momentarily stilled.

"I didn't say London was bad mouthing your company. Why are you assuming he did?"

Volz's smile broadened. For the first time I noticed that his teeth were whiter than any teeth I had ever seen. It didn't suit him. One shouldn't have a Crest Whitestrip smile and an aging statesman face. "I suppose I simply found it logical that he would continue his erratic behavior once he left. But perhaps he *did* get help?" His Paper Mate was on the move again. "You said he seemed…normal? Yes? Or something like that."

"I said he seemed cogent," I corrected although I think what I had actually said was that he seemed stable. Lies were tricky to keep track of. "He expressed some concerns about your methodology in developing your pharmaceuticals… and…and about how you addressed unexpected side effects of drugs still in development," I improvised. God, I was taking a risk here.

"That's still rather vague," he rightfully pointed out. "As I was just alluding to, developing a new pharmaceutical is a laborious and drawn out process. We don't test it on human subjects until we're damn sure it's safe. Nothing happens unless the FDA signs off on it. By the time we're asking people to participate in drug trials our main question is whether or not the drug is as effective as it needs to be."

"But there *are* unintended side effects occasionally," I

said. "You read about it all the time."

"I promise you, we *always* proceed with caution. If there are issues we disclose them...like some drugs don't mix well with others or, on rare occasions, you have to avoid certain foods while taking a particular pharmaceutical. Like with Rispedal, not ours by the way, you have to avoid eating grapefruit while on that particular drug."

"Rispolex?" I asked, looking up from my pad.

Gundrun's eyes went from wide to very, very narrow. "That's *not* what I said. I said, *Rispedal*," he snapped.

It had been an honest mistake on my part, I had simply misheard him. His tone was needlessly defensive...which meant I was close to something here. but I had no idea what. "Your company doesn't make Rispolex?"

"I just told you, Sobexsol is the only drug we've been working on. Are you not listening or are you playing some kind of game?"

I chewed on my lower lip, trying to make sense of this. "What kind of game would I be playing?"

"I have no idea, Ms. Katz," he said curtly. "What's important is that Nolan-Volz always takes every precaution necessary, not just those legally required of us and there's a lot legally required of us. Despite popular opinion, pharmaceutical companies aren't like other corporations. Ethics frequently come before profits for us. When doctors make mistakes and prescribe our medications in ways they weren't intended, it hurts our industry. Not just our bottom line, but our sense of decency."

With effort, I managed not to burst out laughing. "Do you always publish the results of your clinical trials?" I asked, recalling what Jason had told me about that NYU professor.

"As I noted, we just started clinical trials but we've been very open about them," Gundrun said immediately, his eyes falling to his desk and his pen wiggling furiously between his fingers.

"There's a professor at NYU who did a study on how the results of clinical drug trials weren't disclosed--"

"That was a flawed study." He cocked his head to the side, glaring at me now. "Is that what London spoke to you about? It's much ado about nothing. We are members of one of the most highly regulated industries in the United States. There's no room for shenanigans."

The use of the word *shenanigans* in an actual conversation almost made me like this guy. But not quite. "London would disagree," I said, assuredly. "He thought you were cutting corners. He thought you were doing tests the FDA doesn't know about. If he's truly crazy than the details of the accusations aren't really important, but that's the gist."

Gundrun lost control of the pen. It went flying across the room. He stared at it for a moment as if shocked by the consequences of what was clearly a nervous tick. Then he laughed, perhaps a bit too loudly. "I've never been able to have a conversation without keeping my hands busy. Perhaps I should invest in one of those fidget gadgets." He tightly clasped his hands together on his desk, forcing them to be still. "Nobody gets anything past the FDA. Certainly not someone as bad at keeping secrets as me. If Aaron was in his right mind he'd scoff at the very things he suggests." His smile slipped from his lips as he leaned back into his chair. "I believe it was the whole thing with his wife that pushed him into a manic state," he added, quietly. "Lost love can push anyone over the edge, can't it?"

"Wait, what whole thing with his wife?" I scooted a little forward in my seat.

"Well, I could tell that losing…damn, what was her name?" he shifted in his chair as he turned his focus to the office window. "Something with an A."

"Anita?"

He paused for a beat. "That might have been it," he said, uncertainly. "I could tell losing Anita was difficult for him, although he never talked about it. His condition makes it difficult for him to regulate his emotions. And he is not a man who is comfortable being single. Men like London need the stabilizing force of a good woman."

Well hello, 1955. "Do you know what went wrong?" I asked, "With his wife that is?"

"I was his boss, not his therapist or confidant," he said, the edge creeping back into his voice. "Anita had problems. I don't know the exact nature of them, depression, anxiety, whatever. And London couldn't be an easy man to live with. I suppose it became too much for her. But that's just random speculation."

"You don't remember London's wife's name and yet you know she suffered from depression and anxiety?"

"I met her at company events. Christmas parties and the like. She came across as jittery and withdrawn. But you're right, I don't *know* that was indicative of anything, I'm guessing. Would you like me to go on the record with a guess?"

"Well, you never said we were off the record sooo…" I smiled and shrugged. "Did you ever meet his daughter?"

He looked at me blankly for a moment and then let out a

short, startled laugh. "I didn't know he had one."

I blinked at him, surprised.

"As you must have gleaned by now, we didn't socialize outside of work. Perhaps if we did I would have seen the signs that he was falling apart much earlier than I did." He loosened his grip on his hands enough to steeple his fingers in a way that revived my ideas about his super-villain identity. "Sophie…may I call you Sophie?"

"Of course Gundrun," I replied without missing a beat. "Speaking of names, Gundrun Volz it's…unusual."

He smirked and shook his head. "I know, everybody wants to know what kind of parents would give their son a girl's name."

"I'm…sorry?'

"Gundrun. It's a girl's name, but you obviously already figured that out. My friends and colleagues spare me the embarrassment of it by just calling me Gun."

Gun? I don't care how unassuming this man looks, he is definitely a super villain.

"Sophie," he went on, "I'm a little baffled by this interview. Are we here to talk about Sobexsol, the Gilcrest merger, what Aaron London said or are we here to talk about who Aaron London is? And if it's the latter, why?"

Shit. I took in a deep breath as I decided how to best handle the question. "I'm just trying to get a sense of who my source was."

Gun arched his bushy brown eyebrows, causing the lines across his forehead to deepen into trenches. "Was?"

"Oh, you don't know?" I readjusted myself in my seat, all the while carefully watching Gun's expression. "Aaron London is dead."

Three seconds.

Three seconds is all it took for Gun to react exactly as any decent human being would. He verbally conveyed his shock and horror. He asked all the right questions. Was I sure? How did it happen? Had he been sick? And this daughter of his, does she know? Is she okay?

Yes, they were all the right questions. His reaction was on point...except for those first two seconds that preceded the third.

In those first two seconds, he had seemed disturbingly happy.

CHAPTER
FIFTEEN

"The problem with conspiracy theories is only one of them has to be proven to be true for people to start believing all of them."
--Dying To Laugh

"I've spent the entire day reading up on Gundrun Volz but outside of his starting up Nolan-Volz and a *lot* about his philanthropy, there just isn't much interesting out there. " I was sitting on my sofa, my feet crisscrossed in front of me. Mary Ann was in the armchair to my right, Dena lounging in my window seat, a glass of red in her hand. The two of them had agreed to do another girls night with me (but only after I promised them this one wouldn't include a break-in). Our original plan had been to watch old movies like we used to do on a weekly basis, but we had started talking and drinking and talking some more. The television and Blu-ray remained untouched and neglected. Ms. Dogz had turned her body into a big, black comma at my feet and Mr. Katz was snuggled up against my side, purring like he was an only child again. "He doesn't seem to have a criminal record. He's been married for sixteen years, worked in pharmaceuticals his whole adult life, lived in the Bay Area for even longer than that. But there's more to read, more to go through. I know he's guilty of something. Something really bad."

"I still can't get over his name being Gun!" Mary Ann exclaimed as she readjusted the position of her bra strap. "You can't be a real humanitarian if your name is Gun, right?"

"At the very least it would make pacifism a challenge," Dena agreed, her eyes on the darkened world outside my window. "Gun's for disarmament just sounds weird. But as for the rest of it," she shrugged and sipped her wine, "it doesn't seem all that suspicious to me, Sophie."

"Now you sound like Anatoly," I complained. "The more I look into this thing the weirder it gets."

"But if he was bipolar…"

"Even if he was, that doesn't mean he didn't know what he was talking about," I said. "It just means people would be less likely to believe him. And Gun got *so* defensive the minute I brought up London's name. And I'm telling you, he was *relieved* to hear London was dead."

"If he found out he was dead from you, that would mean he didn't kill him," Dena reasoned.

"Not necessarily. Not if London was being slowly poisoned. He could have hired someone to do that. The evidence pointing to this being a homicide keeps piling up."

"Jason agrees with you," Dena noted.

"Well there you go then," I said, satisfied.

"You know that's not a good thing, right?" Dena asked before taking another sip.

"Oh come on, it's not a *bad* thing," I pressed. "I mean, yeah, when I first met Jason I thought he was out of his mind. But you're the one who's always argued that he just has a different take on things. He sees the world a little differently than the rest of us but that doesn't necessarily mean it's an overly distorted view." I leaned forward. "Those are *your* words. You must have said them to me a hundred times over."

"Yeah, well maybe I'm changing my mind about all that," Dena countered, still evading eye contact. "Maybe I'm thinking of breaking up with Jason."

Both Mary Ann and I did a double take.

"You're *not!*" Mary Ann exclaimed while at the exact same time I said, "Again?" Dena and Jason had broken up before. He was the only guy she had ever taken back after ditching. I thought that implied he was somehow different than the others. I wanted this to work for them.

Also, girlfriend-code would require that I have nothing to do with Jason if the two of them split and selfishly, I *really* didn't want to cut off communication with him before he helped me figure out exactly what London was trying to tell me.

Dena finally turned her face toward the room, eyeing Mary Ann, then me. "I've always liked that Jason is different," she said, evenly. "He's an incredibly smart man, his ability to memorize facts and dates is impressive and I know he'd kill on a debate team. But people overlook his intellect because they mistake his obsession with conspiracy theories as stupidity."

Now it was my turn to look away. I had been one of those people who thought Jason was a bit of a moron, at least at first. Once again my first impression had been way off, just as it had been with London. There's very little correlation between crazy and stupid.

"But I always recognized his obsessions as evidence of a sharp, deviant mind," she persisted, "one that looks for different angles and can see connections others can't, even if he does allow himself to draw misguided conclusions from those connections. His ideas were crazy, but not ludicrous and that made him...entertaining."

The way she said the word *entertaining* implied she thought of him as a mere amusement. But I knew better.

"You don't think it's entertaining anymore?" Mary Ann asked, although by her tone it was clear she was really asking, *Don't you love him anymore?*

Dena shrugged as if slightly embarrassed by the whole thing. "A moment ago you said Jason has a view of the world that is different than the rest of ours. That used to be true. He was into conspiracy theories before they were cool."

I giggled then stopped abruptly when I realized she wasn't joking.

"Don't fool yourself," she said, sharply. "Conspiracy theories are *definitely* in right now. Believing in conspiracy theories almost makes you basic."

"That's what this is about?" I asked, laughing again. "Well, I guess that makes sense." I turned to Mary Ann. "Remember how she almost gave up S&M after Fifty Shades came out because she was afraid of being mistaken as a bandwagon-dominatrix?"

"And then, when I read that book I realized it has nothing to do with BDSM," Dena shot back. "It was an insult to the entire master and servant community."

"I really liked that book," Mary Ann said, meekly.

Dena looked like she *really* wanted to reply to that but

she seemed to stop herself, pressing her lips together and shaking her head. "It's true that I was worried Fifty Shades might make my *weird* look *normal*, but that's not what I'm talking about here. I'm not worried that the increasing normalization of conspiratorial thinking will make Jason's correlating world view seem boring. I'm worried that the normalization of conspiratorial thinking could destroy us."

"Destroy who?" Mary Ann asked. "The three of us?"

"The entire country. Maybe the entire Western World."

I laughed despite myself. "And they say *I'm* dramatic."

"Sophie, I'm serious." Ms. Dogz immediately woke up and lifted her face toward Dena, checking to see if she was being called. "It doesn't matter what end of the political spectrum you're on. Almost everyone, and I mean a good eighty-five percent of the general goddamned public, buys into these crazy theories that aren't based on any kind of logic, just fear and paranoia. So no." She exhaled loudly as a siren went off miles away and looked pointedly at Mary Ann. "It's not entertaining anymore. It's…scary."

"But you're not scared of anything," Mary Ann said. She sounded like a little girl who had just discovered the fallibility of her parents.

Dena stared down into her wine. "I'm scared of a society that rejects reason because they don't find facts to be as compelling as fiction."

"But I *write* fiction," I blurted out.

"How is that in any way relevant?" Dena asked.

"It's relevant because…because as an expert on fiction I'm attracted to the truth that resembles it. I relate to it. Maybe I even need it. Maybe we all do." I scooted forward on the couch cushion, disturbing Mr. Katz who fixed me with an aggrieved stare. "Come on, anyone who has been paying attention to the news now knows that crazy things happen all the time. London's death was kind of crazy. If he was murdered, like he *thought he would be*, that would be crazier still. But I'm good with crazy, Dena. I may not be as seeped in the paranoid mindset as Jason but still, I *understand* crazy."

"We're having two totally different conversations," Dena said before throwing back some more wine.

"Are we?" I asked. Why was I getting irritated? I had no idea, and yet not indulging the emotion didn't feel like an option. "I'm talking about the murder of an innocent man. What are you talking about?"

"I'm talking about how my best friend co-opted my boyfriend in order to share in and exacerbate his dysfunction," she retorted. "My boyfriend is an addict. He's addicted to something that is destroying more lives in this country than opioids. He's addicted to paranoia. To conspiracies that reaffirm his whacked out world view. And what do you do? You supply him with more of his drug of choice. You're making him worse, Sophie. This stupid *case*," she used air quotes around the last word, "is making us all *worse*."

Mary Ann was hugging her knees to her chest looking both uncomfortable and worried. "Whatever it is we're doing right now, right here," she said, making a broad gesture with her hand as if trying to encompass our entire antagonistic exchange, "I don't think we want to be doing it."

I looked from Dena to Mary Ann, then back again. "Look," I said, quietly, "I didn't know you and Jason were having problems. I certainly didn't mean to exacerbate them."

Dena silently sipped her wine.

"I'll call him," I offered. "I'll tell him he can't go into London's apartment with me."

Dena scoffed but I could tell she was listening. "I'm the one with the key," I continued. "I decide who accompanies me. I was speaking with him before you arrived, he thinks the best time to go over there is in the middle of the after-noon, like three o'clock. I'll call him back, thank him and tell him his part in this is done. I won't consult him anymore. I won't drag him further into this. I won't *let* him insert himself into this. It'll be my problem, not his, not yours."

"But it's not your problem either, Sophie," Dena said with a sigh. "It's Anita London's problem. It's her kid's problem. I don't know, maybe it's even the dog's problem. But this has nothing to do with you."

"I can't let it go, Dena," I said, softly. "I...I need this."

Dena looked at me quizzically. I waited for her to push me to divulge my recent inner turmoil in the way Marcus had. But instead she just brought her wine glass to her lips once again. "Whatever. If you want to be self-destructive on your own I can't stop you. Just cut Jason loose." She looked away again and we all sat in silence for at least two excruci-ating minutes. Finally Dena let out a deep sigh and forced a small smile. "Is it too late for us to watch a movie?"

It was a little after two am. Dena and Mary Ann had left less than two hours earlier. I was snuggled under the covers, hovering in that space between sleep and consciousness. Images of Dena scowling at me kept floating against my closed eyelids, her warnings echoing inside my head until they began to just sound like jumbled and meaningless admonitions. I saw Images of London too. I saw him collapsing on to the street, his glasses cracking beneath him. And standing in the corner of my mind was Gun, flashing his frighteningly white teeth.

I wasn't pulled back into wakefulness until I felt Anatoly climb into bed next to me, exhausted, warm, perfect. It was hardly his first stakeout. I had become accustomed to them, only waking long enough to know he was there before falling asleep again. But this time was different. I don't know why, but having him creep into my bed in the middle of the night, even though he slept in this particular bed *every* night, seemed sort of…well, thrilling.

I made a mumbling sound like I was fast asleep while allowing my hand to sort of flop onto his abs, rock hard as always. How does one maintain a six-pack without spending every second of their life in a gym and how did I luck into snagging one of the few men who could do it?

Still pretending to sleep, I slid my hand a little lower, then lower still until I was sure that his abs weren't the only thing that was hard. My hand curled around my prize, moving up, then down.

"Why Ms. Katz," he said in a low, slightly sleepy voice, "you're in a mood tonight."

"You have no idea," I murmured. I rose, climbing on top of him without another word, looking at his face that had been made featureless by the dark. His hands pushed up my nightshirt as I straddled him, only my legs touching him now, my knees on either side of his waist.

His hands moved to my hips and slowly but firmly he pulled me down, guiding me as he pushed inside my walls in a slow, smooth gesture. And then, just before he filled me completely he lifted me up, just a little, denying me full satisfaction while at the same time making me long for it even more than before.

"I need you," I whispered

He responded by pulling me down again, this time with speed and force, making me gasp as I felt every inch of him fill me. We started moving to a rhythm that was completely organic and totally ours. Anatoly's hands sliding to my waist, then my stomach until finally they were cupping my breasts as I continued to ride him. Dear God, did I love this man's hands. They were big, strong and just a little bit rough. I felt the slight hint of a callus on the padding of his right thumb as he ran it over my hardening nipple. He then lifted me with those hands, pulling me off him only to pull me back down again, setting off a new series of explosions. I reached forward and gripped his shoulder, digging in my nails, unable to restrain myself, too far gone to be careful with him.

He flipped me over so my back was pressed against the firm mattress, our connection never broken. So strong, so powerful and yet so very gentle. A series of luscious contradictions. He stilled for a moment, bringing his face only inches from mine. "Sophie," he whispered, "are you sure I can't run my fingers through your hair?"

"Fuck," I gasped, "you."

"That's exactly what you're doing." And then he took away my ability to speak as one of his perfect hands found a key pressure point, sending me into a delicious frenzy. I wrapped my legs around his hips as if it was possible to force him further inside me, I was shuddering, wondering how I could have ever believed we were losing something. This passion was every bit as overwhelming as it was the first time he touched me. Back then there had been so many secrets.

And what was this energy between us now? Was it fueled by secrets once more? Or by love?

"You're beautiful." The words were breathed against my skin, tickling me, ensuring that the warmth in my heart matched the fire of my body.

"But you can't see me," I said. "It's too dark."

"Sophie," his accent had become thick, making my name sound exotic and mysterious, "I know every detail of you. I *see* you."

And just for a moment, that brought me out of my ecstasy, and put my brain into play. Why hadn't this man, with whom I shared so many intimacies, been the one to guess that I hadn't been writing? Anatoly, the man who claimed to be able to truly see me?

But one well-placed kiss drove those thoughts straight out of my head. His hands were on the small of my back now, even as I arched to press myself against him even more tightly, to absorb him more deeply as he increased his pace, making me cry out, my nails scratching at his back.

Spontaneous, intense, explosive, everything we used to be and everything we were becoming again.

I felt him climax inside me at the exact same time I reach my peak. The orgasm rolled through my body, shaking me to my core.

The weight of him as he collapsed on top of me was deliciously satisfying, adding the final punctuation mark to our lovemaking. I ran my fingers over the broad, defined muscles along his back, feeling the beads of sweat, basking in the afterglow and feeling almost, *almost*, perfect.

CHAPTER
SIXTEEN

"The fact that there are so many pornos featuring average looking pizza delivery boys proves that most pornos are for men. If they were for women the guy on the doorstep would be hotter and delivering a package from Sephora. "
--Dying To Laugh

I parked my car half a block from London's place at two fifty-six pm. I was feeling a little nauseous. Whether that nausea was due to fear (I was breaking into the apartment by myself this time, Marcus was working and I had disinvited Jason) or anticipation of the unique odious fragrance of London's home, was hard to say. I looked over at my passenger seat. I had an impressive stack of empty paper bags that I could use to stuff the articles on the wall in and a small box of latex gloves that would prevent me from having to touch anything.

"I can do this, I can do this, I can do this," I whispered as I made eye contact with myself via my rearview mirror. It was perfectly reasonable to assume there was a clue in that apartment, that at least *one* of the countless paragraphs

London had printed out and hung up would point to something other than a deteriorating mind. If I was really going to see this thing through this was the logical next step.

"I can do this," I said one more time before grabbing the bags and the gloves and getting out of the car. London's keys were jingling in the pocket of my light wool jacket. They probably weighed a tenth of an ounce but they felt heavy there as if they had been mystically infused with the weight of their purpose.

When I had arrived at London's apartment building with Dena and Mary Ann in tow, I had thought it had an air of mystery about it. I couldn't fully picture what was inside its walls, what people, what secrets or even what dogs. Today it looked different to me. It looked like a challenge, its sharp Edwardian lines and rectangular shape resembling nothing more than a puzzle that needed to be taken apart and put back together in a way that made more sense.

I reached for the keys as soon as I got to the front entrance, nervous but ready. There was no one in the lobby when I opened the door. No one on the stairs as I crept up to the infamous apartment. I put my gloves on and unlocked London's apartment door. Just as it had last time, the first thing that hit me was the smell. I flipped on the lights.

Light made everything so much worse. Now I could see the blobs of dried red sauce on the discarded paper plates littered across the floor, the mold spores floating on the surface of old, half-filled cups of coffee, the two flies perched on the edge of the dog bowl and so on and so on. In the far left corner was another door, this one cracked open to reveal a sliver of what I guessed to be a bedroom. Based on my limited view, it would seem that room was in a similar state of disarray. I tugged on the edges of my gloves, making sure they were covering as much skin as possible. Just looking at the place made me feel like I needed an extra dose of the Hepatitis C vaccine.

I skirted around a few dirty socks and stepped up to the *Wall Of Words* (as I had come to think of it). The first headline my eyes landed on read: *Are Pesticides Causing Autism*?? from some site called *Live Organic Or Die.* Not promising. But the next article was titled *What Big Pharma Doesn't Want You To Know About Clinical Trials.* The source was Newsweek. It was about that NYU professor Jason had told me about. Funny how she kept coming up. Next to it was a printout from the BMJ Journals (whatever that was) that seemed to have her official analysis and conclusion of the study she had conducted. I pulled the article off the wall and folded it up neatly before putting it in my purse. I looked over at an end table placed by the window and noted a discarded apple core that was in the process of being devoured by a small swarm of ants. I curled in my lips and then started ripping articles off the wall with a lot less ceremony, tearing them from tacks and tape that had fastened them to the plaster and stuffing them into my paper bags. There were so many papers, so much *stuff.* And the stench! As the minutes dragged on and my bags filled up, my eyes began to water from exposure to the putrid haze. There could be a dead body rotting in the broom closet and I wouldn't even be able to smell it under the stench of the dirty socks and moldy pizza boxes.

Eventually, I worked up the courage to check the bedroom. That wasn't an easy task. A dog bed along with books and discarded clothes, all left on the floor, made it impossible to open the bedroom door more than halfway. The light switch was easy enough to find, revealing the layers of dirty laundry, crumpled papers and bits of trash that covered every inch of the wall-to-wall carpeting. The sheets on the bed were pulled back and dingy. The fitted sheet had come off one corner revealing a torn, stained mattress.

"Okay, I can do this," I whispered to myself although honestly, I should have thought to invest in a gas mask. I grabbed some of the papers on the ground and put them in bags. Some of those papers appeared to hold hand-written notes but I didn't take the time to read them. *Fill up your bags and get out*, was the mantra I was silently chanting as I held my nausea at bay.

London had a dresser, the drawers too filled to fully close. On top of it was a bunch of old, plastic water bottles and two cases for his glasses along with more papers. Oh and there was a greeting card…wait…it was an *anniversary* card! The front featured the black silhouette of a couple in a loving embrace set against the background of a giant white heart. *Happy Anniversary To The Love Of My Life* was written in bold Hallmark font. I slipped it into my purse, vowing to read it first…after I got out of there.

There was another open door on the other side of the bedroom, this one leading to a bathroom. I tread over paper that crinkled under my feet. What was more disturbing was the dirty clothes that sort of crunched when you stepped on them. Clothes should never, ever crunch.

The bathroom was almost claustrophobic. On top of the toilet basin was a comb, a half empty box of Band-Aids, a box of Kleenex, a roll of toilet paper and a razor. It was the only shelf space in the whole room. On the floor were empty razor cartridges while crumpled up Kleenex were overflowing from the wastebasket. There was blood on some of the Kleenex. I gagged and looked away. "I can't take this," I muttered and started to leave. But then I stopped myself as I looked back at the mirrored medicine cabinet above the sink. What drugs would be in the bathroom of a former pharmaceutical executive who had turned against pharmaceuticals?

I reached forward and opened it, not knowing what to expect.

My lack of expectation did not mitigate the shock I felt when I saw what was actually in there:

Nothing.

Just one solitary, half empty tube of toothpaste. That was it.

My eyes darted back to all the things jammed on top of the toilet basin. Every inch of this place was filled with stuff, but he had kept his medicine cabinet empty.

Or someone had emptied it.

Little goose bumps formed over my arms. Had someone else been here? I walked back out, through the bedroom and into the living room. I glanced at the coffee table. London's ring was right where I left it. There certainly wasn't any evidence that someone had come in here and straightened up. I looked over at the pile of laundry on the couch…hadn't there been a scarf on top of that pile? But perhaps not…there certainly wasn't one there now.

"I think I'm done here," I said aloud. I had a bag in both hands. I had seven more lined up on the floor, all filled to the rim. I couldn't carry them all down together. It would take two trips.

My phone started vibrating in my purse. When I checked

the screen I groaned. Jason.

"Jason," I said upon picking up, "if this is about the case--"

"I'm outside," he interrupted.

I hesitated a moment. "Outside where?"

"The apartment building! I'm here!"

"But, but you're not *supposed* to be here." I started to sit down on the armrest of the sofa then quickly remembered where I was and stood back up again. "Go home."

"Yeah, I've been thinking about that," he said. "And the more I think the more I know, I *have* to be here. You need me."

"Oh stop being such a guy about this," I snapped. "I don't *need* you. I'm perfectly capable of taking care of this on my own."

"Do you know what you're looking for?" He asked.

I glanced over at the bags on the floor filled with papers I had completely randomly selected. "I'm looking for clues," I said, stupidly.

"Right. And those clues are going to be coded in the language of conspiracy theorists. You'll have no idea what here is relevant and what's not. But I will. I *breathe* this stuff. From what you've told me, your man London and I probably hit up the same news sources. I can tell you if there are patterns you need to follow up on just by reading the first paragraph of each article. I can find the connective string."

"Jason," I said, firmly, "I'm not going to break my word to Dena, period."

"Dena's not my keeper," he said, stubbornly. He then paused before adding, "well, sexually, she is in a way but only--"

"This conversation is over," I said, effectively cutting him off. "Go home."

I hung up and grabbed as many bags as I could manage, four total. I'd come back for the rest. If Jason was out there I'd shove one of the crumpled up articles in his mouth and give him a swift kick in the ass.

My phone rang again and *again* it was Jason's name on the screen.

"Wow," I said upon picking up. "You are really not getting this, are you? I do not need your help. I will not take your help. You are *not* helping."

"They're *heeeere*," he sang.

I looked over at the darkened television in the corner, half expecting to see it filled with staticky poltergeist. "Who's here?"

"A woman with a blonde bob and a teenager a few inches shorter, with long, thick blonde hair."

"Anita and Catherine," I whispered. So much worse than poltergeist. *Shit!*

"They're parked kitty-corner to the building," Jason continued, "and they're getting boxes out of their trunk."

"Do you think I can slip out the front door without their noticing?"

"I'd say there's less than a fifty percent chance of that."

"Shit!" I said, aloud this time. I looked around the apartment. The thought of trying to hide in a closet or worse, under a bed in here literally made me gag. "What do I do?"

"They know you, they don't know me. Grab as many bags as you can and bring them to the lobby, *quickly* Sophie. I'll go to the front door. When you go out, I'll go in and grab the bags and act like I'm going to one of the other apartments. I'll wait…I don't know, five or ten minutes and then head out with the bags. I'll go through the articles at home and tell you what I've found."

"*I'm* going to be the one who goes through these articles!"

"Do you want my help or not?" he asked.

"*Shit!*" I pulled the phone away from my ear and pressed it to my chest. I had no time to negotiate or argue. I swore again under my breath and brought the phone back to my ear. "I'm coming down with the bags now. You better be at the door when I get there." I hung up and stared at the bags that remained on the floor. I couldn't just leave them sitting there. That would make it obvious someone had been here. I put down the four bags in my hand, grabbed the other bags and opened the hall closet with the intention of jamming them in there. Bad idea. It was all I could do to slam it closed fast enough to prevent the junk already piled up in there from tumbling out and burying me in an avalanche. "Maybe the kitchen," I said to myself as I took the bags in that direction.

One look at the kitchen and there was bile in my throat. There was a tin of what looked like homemade cookies rotting on the counter and dead ants and roaches on the grimy floor. "Not going in the kitchen." I took the bags and dumped their contents all over the living room carpet. Not surprisingly, the floor didn't look that different than it had before. I scattered the bags around the room before grabbing the four I could carry and rushing out the door. I ran down the steps but when I neared the bottom, I slowed, pressing myself against the wall and peering into the lobby to see if the coast was clear. It was, and I could see Jason on the other side of the glass door. *Thank God.* I put the bags down by the step and went to him, opening the door. He acknowledged me with an impersonal nod, the kind you might give to a stranger who offered to hold the door for you and walked past me. I could hear him picking up the bags as the door closed behind me.

It was only when I was a few steps out that I saw them. They were just a little further down the block. They were walking toward the building, their heads turned toward each other as they conversed. They didn't see me. Not yet.

I started to walk down the front steps, determined to make it to the sidewalk and just walk the opposite direction as quickly as possible.

And it was then that Anita looked over her shoulder and saw me.

CHAPTER
SEVENTEEN

*"The most valuable thing you can give a person is trust.
It's also the gift most likely to be treated cheaply by
those fortunate enough to receive it."*
--Dying To Laugh

My breath caught in my throat. Cat followed her mother's gaze. She was wearing an outfit not unlike Jason's, plaid flannel shirt worn over a T-shirt and jeans, a sharp contrast to her mother's cream silk shirt tucked neatly into elegant black slacks. My heart ached for Catherine. She was here to get her father's things, to try to make sense of the mess he had made out of his life and deal with her own grief and instead she was going to have to deal with me, her father's supposed mistress, clearly exiting his place. I was an awful, awful person.

Unless of course, they were imposters.

Or, as Marcus suggested, Anita was a murderer and Catherine needed me whether she thought she did or not.

As I tried to think it all through Anita remained exactly where she was, stock still and glaring. You would have thought she had laid eyes on Medusa.

Well, here goes nothing. I straightened up and stretched my mouth into a smile as I walked up to the pair. When I was about five feet from them I stopped, stuck my hands in my pocket and shifted my weight back on my heels. "Hi," I began but Anita immediately cut me off by turning toward her daughter.

"Go wait in the car."

Catherine met my gaze. I thought I detected a moment of hesitation from the girl as Anita put her empty boxes down by her feet. But then Catherine simply nodded obligingly and slowly walked away.

Anita waited until she had gotten into a grey Mercedes before sharply turning her attention back to me. "I spoke to the landlord this morning. You had no right to be inside that apartment, let alone remove anything from it. I could have you arrested."

"Do *you* have that right?" I asked, keeping my tone level, even friendly. "It's not as if you and Aaron London were a couple by the time he died."

Anita drew herself up, her shoulders rigid. She didn't say a word for a few dozen, incredibly awkward seconds. The wind picked up her hair as if desperate to force some movement.

"Yeah, I know about your separation," I finally said when she continued to silently stare. "I also know a few other things about what was going on with London, things that I'd really like to share with you if you'd just let me."

Anita finally graced me with a response, a short, humorless and somewhat chilling laugh. Why must every villain have an evil laugh? "Why are you here, *again*?" she asked.

"Um, do you want his dog back?" I replied, settling on

deflection as a response. Although as soon as the question came out of my mouth I regretted it. I did *not* want to give Ms. Dogz to this woman.

"She's not my dog."

I feigned a cough and covered my mouth to better hide my smile.

"When did you figure out that Aaron and I were separated?" she asked. "Did you know when we met in the hospital?"

"Oh, no, not at all." A car in desperate need of a new muffler groaned down the street giving us both a welcome but all too brief excuse to look away from one another. "You seemed so angry about my being there...I mean, not that you should have been under any circumstances. Like I said, Aaron London and I absolutely were *not* involved. Still, based on your reaction I had assumed you two were still a thing."

"We were more than a *thing*," she retorted. "He was my husband."

"Yes, that's what I meant," I acknowledged. A seagull landed on the sidewalk a few steps behind Anita, snapped up a half-filled, discarded bag of Fritos and took off again. It was everything I could do to keep from calling out, *take me too!*

"We're still married...I mean we were before...this."

I nodded and allowed myself a quick glance at her left hand. No wedding ring, no tan line.

"I loved him," she continued, quietly. "And then he lost his mind."

"How...or when...I mean, tell me how he got the way he did? I know he used to hold a good job at Nolan-Volz.

What happened to him?"

Anita let out another rough laugh. "Why should I tell you anything?"

"Because I'm really, *really* not his girlfriend."

Anita wrapped her arms around herself as if trying to keep warm. "If you weren't involved with my husband, why do you have the key to his apartment?"

I hesitated a moment too long. Anita took the pause as an admission. "Well neither one of us has him now, do we? I have to say, you're not his type. Aaron always preferred blondes. I've certainly never known him to have an exotic fixation…but I suppose all men go through their phases."

"Okay, so you're grieving, and I feel bad about that, so I won't punch you," I said, in my most conciliatory tone. "What I'd really like for you to understand is that your husband came to me and my partner. My partner is also my *boyfriend.* His name's Anatoly and he's a P.I. London came to us for help."

"That still doesn't explain how you ended up with the key to his apartment," she correctly noted.

"I did try to get in touch with you," I continued, desperately trying to evade. My phone dinged and I glanced down at my bag. It was then that, from the corner of my eye I noted Jason coming out of the building with the bags. Had it been five minutes? I made a little show of searching my purse for my phone while casually side stepping a little more toward the street, bringing Anita's focus away from the building. "I wanted to talk to you about the dog," I said as I pulled my phone out, "and about everything London told me and Anatoly. Your husband thought…" for a moment I let my voice trail off as I noted my new text message.

It was from Catherine.

"…he thought he was being poisoned," I continued, trying to maintain a poker face. Catherine's text read:

I want to talk, but my mom can't know
Maybe we can meet?

"If you're trying to tell me that Aaron could be paranoid, I'm very much aware," Anita was saying. "And if you're trying to come up with some elaborate story to hide the true nature of your relationship with my husband, you're wasting your breath. The only one poisoning Aaron was Aaron. He died because of congestive heart failure. But let's be honest, he really died of personal neglect and substance abuse. The man had more pharmaceuticals in him than a Walmart pharmacy."

"London was abusing pharmaceuticals?" I asked, honestly aghast. That wasn't possible. Not London who thought all pharmaceuticals were instruments of the devil.

Anita scoffed. "He told me he stopped the Abilify, which admittedly would've been bad."

"Abilify…to treat bipolar disorder, correct?"

"Yes! Although I'll tell you this, he didn't need it when he was with me. He was stable when he was with *me*."

The way she said *me* made it clear that she was blaming London's next fling for his instability…and apparently I was supposed to be the next thing. I pressed my lips together. There were only so many times I was willing to protest my innocence.

When I didn't take the bait, she sniffed and looked away. "Anyway, he didn't stop taking the Abilify. The doctor told me it was in his blood stream along with everything else you could think of. They couldn't even identify it all it was so mixed up. They said he was even taking prescription strength allergy medication. The man didn't have allergies! He was a mess. Maybe you thought you could save him? Perhaps you see yourself as a modern day Florence Nightingale? Well, you're not. He's dead. You helped kill him if you did anything at all."

"I barely knew your husband," I hissed. Apparently, I *did* have it in me to protest my innocence one last time. "I sure as hell didn't help kill him. But..." I hesitated, and then continued in a softer tone, "I didn't help him either. When will they be able to identify the...well, the drugs in his bloodstream they weren't able to immediately identify? When will the autopsy be?" On my phone I texted back to Catherine:

Of course! Any time.

"There isn't going to be an autopsy."

I jerked my head up from my screen. "But...there has to be!"

Anita gave me a withering look. "This isn't a suspicious death. He's not a celebrity. I don't have to request an autopsy. I don't have to stand here and waste my time talking to you either." She bent down and picked her boxes up again. "My daughter and I need to see his apartment and find out what kind of disaster he's left us."

"So you really haven't been in there yet?" I asked. If that was true she was in for a brutal surprise. I almost wanted to pull out a pair of latex gloves from my purse and offer them up...but to Cat, not to Anita. Anita was a bitch.

"You may be a regular visitor here," Anita retorted, "but

his wife and daughter haven't had the chance to even step through the door yet. And by the way? If I find you've taken anything of value out of there I *will* call the police." Anita lifted her chin and shook her hair out of her face before turning her back to me and marching off to her car. As she did I saw Jason drive by, presumably with the bags of articles that *I* compiled in his car. Jerk.

A few seconds later Anita was coming back toward me, Catherine by her side. Nothing about that woman resembled an innocent grieving widow. Anita had a story and I could sense it was a dark one.

As the two walked past me toward the apartment building Catherine hung back by half a step from her mother for just the briefest of moments. Just long enough to mouth the words *"I'll text."*

I smiled to myself as they went inside the building. I didn't have to feel guilty anymore. Now I could fully be all in.

CHAPTER
EIGHTEEN

"I miss the monsters of my childhood, the creatures that hid under my bed and came alive in the best told ghost stories. The monsters of my adulthood are both less interesting and a lot more terrifying."
--Dying To Laugh

There were no more texts from Catherine. For the rest of the afternoon and well into the evening, I kept my phone clutched in my hand. But the only time it vibrated was for Facebook, Twitter, email notifications and one text from Anatoly apologetically informing me he was going to have to tail the workers-comp scammer again tonight. There was nothing from Catherine at all. I did try texting *her* but got no reply. I was willing to cut Catherine a lot of slack because of her grief but she was beginning to bug me.

On the other hand, reaching Jason was no problem, for all the good it did me. He refused to relinquish the papers, at least not yet. He clung to his argument that his knowledge base made him more qualified to figure out how they were relevant.

Dena was going to kill me.

I decided to use the time before my inevitable murder to read over the few things I had been able to stuff into my purse. The BMJ piece written by the NYU professor was packed with facts but dry as hell. I had to re-read several of the sentences over again because my mind kept wandering. The professor's main point was that *Trial disclosures remain below legal and ethical standards* (her words). She named off several companies who were the worst offenders, most of whom I had never heard of: Gilphar, Orvex, Alson-Richter and a few others. She was particularly critical of Orvex. But Nolan-Volz wasn't mentioned which made me think the article might just be further evidence of London's broad paranoia than of the reasons behind his specific demise.

The anniversary card was a *lot* more interesting.

The personal note written inside read:

> *My love,*
> *Ours was a forbidden love, too powerful to deny. Seven years later I still feel the power of our love every day. I know how much you've sacrificed for me and I know I'm not always the easiest person to live with, but never doubt how grateful I am to have you in my life.*
> *Yours Always and Forever,*

Anita signed her name with a scrawl so that all you could read was the A and the beginning of the N that flowed into a wavy line.

Something about the note felt wrong to me but I couldn't put my finger on what it was. Maybe it was the forbidden love thing? How was their love forbidden? Had they been with other people at the time? Then again maybe it was just the overkill of clichés and overall cheesiness. *Ours was a forbidden love, too powerful to deny? Really?* Did she steal that from Hallmark's movie of the week?

It wasn't until 8pm and after a consultation session with my favorite therapist, Smirnoff, that I finally got around to calling Dena.

"Hey," she said upon picking up. "Good timing, I just got home."

"Oh?" I settled into the armchair in my living room, sitting cross-legged like a girl ready for kindergarten circle time. "Are you going to be seeing Jason tonight?"

"No, I need some me time," she confessed. "I'm going to curl up with two inches of scotch and *The Handmaid's Tale*."

"The book? I haven't read it," I admitted.

"It's dark and it's fucking with my head but I'm really digging it."

I smiled and then took a deep breath. "Dena...I saw Jason today."

She went quiet for a moment before asking, "You asked him to meet?"

"No," I replied quickly. "He just...showed up. At London's apartment. I told him not to come. He came anyway." Ugh, my words sounded so halting and awkward.

"And then you sent him away?" she asked, warily.

"Yes!" I immediately confirmed then winced as I forced myself to tell her the rest of the truth, speaking so fast the words rushed together into one rambling run-on sentence. "The thing is he didn't leave and then Anita showed up and everything kind of got mixed up and Jason offered to help me get the articles out of the apartment building without her noticing and I didn't really have any choice but to say yes, because I really needed help but now he won't give them back because he says he can read the articles faster than me and make sense of them faster than me because, well, this is the kind of stuff he reads and I *did* argue with him but…" I finally paused for a breath before admitting, "in the end I let him take the articles home to read."

"Uh-huh."

I winced again. Dena's *uh-huhs* were never a precursor to anything good.

"I'm sorry," I said, softly. Ms. Dogz wandered into the room and then turned her body into a comma as she lay down by the coffee table. "I screwed up."

"You did," Dena agreed, her voice even, "but not as badly as I have."

"You?" Mr. Katz entered the room. He must have sensed that the conversation was about to get interesting.

"When you first wanted to talk to Jason about…well about whatever this thing is that you're wasting your time with, you didn't call him, at least not at first. You called me."

"I did," I confirmed, "and you were less than thrilled. Rather than respect your feelings I pushed it and called him anyway."

"Yeah, that's true. But I didn't tell you *why* I wasn't thrilled about it and I didn't explicitly tell you no. Anyone who knows me knows that I don't have a problem saying *no* or shutting things down if it suits me. So when I didn't say no…I can't blame you for taking that as a reluctant yes. So some of the blame is mine, and the majority of the rest is Jason's for not taking no for an answer…and for being crazy. He's responsible for his crazy. I shouldn't have projected my frustration with him onto you."

I exhaled loudly. My friendship with Dena was one of... possibly *the* most important friendship of my life. I wouldn't have been able to forgive myself if I had damaged it. "Sooo, are you going to take this out on Jason?" I asked. "What are you going to do? Smack him upside the head?"

"No, that's foreplay," she replied, dryly. "I'm going to talk to him and then I'm going to think about our relationship."

That sounded ominous.

"He loves you," I said softly. "You know that right? I mean he really, really loves you."

"Yeah, and there are a thousand subcategories of love," she noted, "most of which don't come with lifetime guarantees. I don't know what category Jason and I fit into." She hesitated a moment before asking, "What about you and Anatoly? What kind of love do you have going for you? Lifetime guarantee?"

"Yes," I said automatically...although...were there *any* guarantees in life? "We're in the soulmates-who-have-tons-of-amazing-sex subcategory," I clarified.

"Not bad." I could hear the smile in her voice. "I'm going to call Jason now, okay? Oh and for the record? I still think this London thing is stupid."

"I know you do. Be gentle with Jason."

"Gentle's not my thing," she quipped before hanging up.

That night, long after I had given up on hearing from Catherine and after I had settled into bed, I found myself in a rather unpleasant dream. I dreamt that I needed to write, but the words I needed were scattered around London's apartment, hiding under crusty paper plates and crinkly newspapers that I couldn't bring myself to touch. My own squeamishness and reticence were insurmountable obstacles. I wanted to cry but I found I couldn't even do that. I was just…lost.

I don't know exactly what woke me up from that nightmare. I checked the clock by the bed. Three seventeen am. I started to pull my feet out from underneath Mr. Katz as was my habit when I woke in the middle of the night. But Mr. Katz wasn't there. I gently kicked my legs around, searching for the weight of my favorite fur ball. But no, nothing.

With a yawn, I propped myself up with one arm and scanned the room. Ah, there he was. I could make out the dark silhouette of my Mr. Katz sitting on the floor, staring at the open bedroom door. That was the joy of not having kids. When you only lived with your lover you never had to close the door.

What *was* odd was the way Mr. Katz was sitting up, not curled up the way he would normally be at this time. I looked down to Ms. Dogz's makeshift bed. Ms. Dogz wasn't there.

"Huh," I said, quietly. I got out of bed, found my robe draped over a chair and slipped into it. Still groggy I made my way down the hall, my cat followed closely behind me.

It probably wasn't a problem that Ms. Dogz had chosen to sleep in another room. She appeared to be fully housebroken. But then again, I had known this animal for just over seventy-two hours and if she was a chewer of furniture or a late night carpet pisser…well, that just wasn't something I wanted to discover in the morning.

At the top of the stairs, I hesitated. The light in my stairwell didn't work. That usually wasn't a problem for me because the hall light upstairs was bright enough that I could make out each step. But I couldn't see anything in the living room beneath me. I loved my home more than any other place I had ever lived, but in the wee hours of the morning, when there was no street noise to be heard, and rooms full of darkness, it really could be a little creepy. When I first moved in people told me it was haunted. And every once in a rare while, I found myself wondering if those people were right.

But I was being silly. The only thing in here that was going to go bump in the night was Ms. Dogz who might knock over the kitchen wastebasket at any moment.

I made my way down the stairs, only then turning on a small lamp to cast light into the living room. "Ms. Dogz?" I called. Nothing.

"Sophie?" I tried again, silently cursing myself for giving in so easily to using her previous name.

She did respond though. She responded with a growl.

It stopped me in my tracks. She wasn't in the living room. But she was close.

She growled again. It was a deep, frightening sound, one that didn't match the sweet tempered mutt I had welcomed into my home. I hesitated, suddenly unsure of myself.

"Sophie?" I said again, a little softer. It was disconcerting, calling out my own name into an empty room.

I moved toward the front of the house. Mr. Katz didn't follow me this time.

It was in the foyer that I found the dog. I turned on the light to see her clearly. She was facing the window that stood along side the front door. Her hair was up, her ears back.

"Sophie?" I said again, nervously this time.

Again she growled, still staring out into the night. She was growling *at* something…or someone.

Anything can hide in the dark.

Almost of its own accord, my hand reached out and I flipped on the porch lights, then I jumped back, half expecting to see the man with the baseball cap illuminated on the other side of the window.

But there was no one there. I stepped forward, cupped my hands against the glass.

Nothing.

I looked down at Ms. Dogz who looked up at me, her eyes silently pleading with me to believe her. *I'm not* crazy, *I really saw something!*

She reminded me of London.

I went to the laundry room. There was a gun safe right next to the keypad for the house alarm (the code for which I could never remember). But I remembered the code to the safe. In less than a minute I had my loaded gun firmly in hand. Quietly I walked back to the front of the door. *Breathe in, breathe out, breathe in, breathe out.* I tried unsuccessfully to steady my heartbeat. After inhaling deeply one more time I flung open the door and stepped outside, gun tight in my grip, trusting that there was indeed something to confront.

Except there wasn't.

I took another step, then another and another. Ms. Dogz

remained in the doorway, wary, on guard. I walked as far as the first of the two steps of my front porch. Not a single car on the street. I turned toward a rustling in the bushes, then the trees. Just the wind.

I turned around to face Ms. Dogz. "There's no--" I cut myself off as I noticed my front door. There was a small piece of paper taped to it, a little bigger than a business card. As I stepped closer, I could see it was the kind of card you would expect to see in a bouquet of flowers.

My hand was shaking as I peeled it off of the finished wood and brought it close enough to read the words scrawled across it in black pen:

Be careful, Sophie.

Slowly, I slipped the card into the pocket of my robe and turned back to the night. "Is anyone there?" I called out. I hated the tremor to my voice. The little shiver in my body that had nothing to do with the cold.

I locked the door as soon as I stepped back inside. I wished to God I could remember the alarm code for the house. I wanted to be alerted, loudly, if anyone tried to get in. I walked back into the laundry room and studied the keypad. Anatoly always set it to some WWII date, which didn't help me. It wasn't the beginning or the end of WWII I knew that. It might have been the end date of some battle? Was that it?

And then I heard it. Footsteps.

Oh.

I lifted my gun. Ms. Dogz was still out there. Why wasn't she barking? What kind of dog would let someone slip inside her territory without going into a barking frenzy?

Unless my stalker had just entered now and had done something to Ms. Dogz.

The thought gave me the anger I needed to push me to action. I stepped out of the laundry room, gun outstretched in front of me. Slowly, carefully I walked toward the dining room.

I saw the shadow of a man.

"Freeze!" I screamed, my hand shaking now. But the shadow moved.

I had killed before, I could kill again.

But I really, really, *really* didn't want to kill again.

"I said freeze!" I screamed.

And it was at that moment that the man stepped into the threshold of my kitchen. Anatoly.

He looked from my gun to my face and then back to my gun which I was now lowering, my hand still trembling. "Jesus," he said, in a quiet voice. "What happened?"

I looked to his left to see that Ms. Dogz was standing a few feet behind him, seemingly relaxed now. No acknowledgment at all of the doggie messaging she had been sending me a few minutes ago. My eyes darted back up to Anatoly.

"Sophie, what is it? Why do you have the gun?"

Ms. Dogz trotted up to his side, once again responding to her name of choice.

This dog and this man, these were my protectors. But over the last few days, only one had been my confidant, and it wasn't the bipedal one.

Anatoly was still staring at me, his concern seeming to intensify by the second.

"I think," I said, softly, pausing a second to place my gun on the kitchen island, "I think I may be in danger."

 # CHAPTER
NINETEEN

"Interesting how an ugly dress can be considered avant-garde if you price it high enough. Perspective can be bought."
--Dying To Laugh

Anatoly sat across from me at the dining table, wearing jeans and a hooded sweatshirt. The bottom of his shoes undoubtedly still damp from traipsing around our property in the misty night looking for signs of our intruder. He had found none. His shoulders were slumped like a man who was on the verge of falling asleep (which he probably was), his head bent as he read and re-read the card that was sitting before him. *Be Careful, Sophie.*

I fidgeted in my seat. I had told him about the man in the black baseball cap, the second trip to London's apartment, the trip to Nolan-Volz, everything. Now that someone was coming to our home I could no longer deny his right to know.

"What are you thinking?" I asked, quietly.

Anatoly used his finger to slowly rotate the card, looking at the words from every angle as if there was a clue hiding in the specific slant of the B, the careless curves of the S. "This," he said, tapping the stiff, white piece of stationary against the table, "is serious."

I exhaled as I was hit with an unexpected wave of relief. He finally understood London's death was not as simple as it first appeared.

Again Anatoly rotated the card. Ms. Dogz was sleeping under the table and I ran the sole of my barefoot across her back.

"The person who left this for you," Anatoly said, finally looking up at me with eyes bloodshot from exhaustion, "it's unlikely he or she has anything to do with Aaron London."

My mouth dropped open. Had I heard him correctly?

"Have you had arguments or conflicts with anyone recently? Any that you haven't told me about?"

"Are you *kidding me*?" I finally managed to sputter. Mr. Katz, who had been sleeping in the corner, briefly lifted his head then quickly settled back down for more sleep.

Anatoly's shoulders straightened, stiffening. "Sophie--"

"How much evidence can you ignore? This started happening right after London died! Of *course* they're connected!"

"This," Anatoly said, lifting the card and gently waving it in the air, "didn't *start* happening. It's one incident. It happened."

"It's one incident out of many!" I protested. "It's probably the guy in the black baseball cap!"

"That's a strong possibility," he admitted, putting the card down again. "But you need to remember, there are a lot of men who wear baseball caps. You don't even know if it was the same man."

"*What?*"

"The man you saw outside the salon may be different than the man you saw at Sutro Heights."

"I just told you, I saw him looking up into your office too! I've seen him *three* times!"

"No one can look into my office from a standing position on the street. At best they can see a small section of the ceiling from that vantage point," Anatoly leaned back in his chair, fixing me with those tired eyes. "I know that because I checked before I leased the space. I needed to ensure my clients would have all the anonymity they desired. If people could see into my office from the street, I would have the drapes drawn at all times. But they can't."

That threw me for a second. "I hadn't noticed that." I linked my fingers together, resting my forearms on the table. "Your office has drapes? Not blinds, but drapes?"

"Yes," he said, cautiously.

"That's so cute!" I allowed myself the small spark of satisfaction that came from the sight of his jaw setting. "Listen to me, Anatoly," I continued, making my tone serious again, "the man I saw at Sutro Heights, he was spying on me and he got spooked when he realized he had been spotted. I tried to approach and he just took off."

"From your description of events," Anatoly said evenly, "you ran after him. Generally speaking, when a stranger starts to chase you, you run."

"If a woman ran in your direction you'd run away?" I asked, dryly.

"No," he admitted, "not if she looked like you."

The compliment fell flat. It was after four in the morning and I had come this close to accidentally shooting my boyfriend. Flirting was not in the cards. "I'm certain it was the same man wearing the same cap all three times," I insisted. "I'm certain that Gundrun Volz is hiding something from me. I'm *certain* Anita is not exactly who she wants me to think she is. I'm certain London had reason to be afraid. And most of all," I paused to take a deep breath, "I'm certain that the note left on our doorstep tonight was directly tied to all of that. It's a threat. Someone is threatening me because I'm going around the city asking questions about Aaron London."

Anatoly shook his head and leaned back in his chair. "That scenario would seem more plausible if the questions you've been asking were any good."

I felt Ms. Dogz stir beneath my foot. She was undoubtedly as insulted as I was.

"What have you discovered, exactly?" Anatoly challenged. "A bunch of blog posts London saw fit to print out and pin to his wall while in a manic state? That he was bitter after being fired from his last job? That his first marriage was on the rocks? That he didn't make good use of his medicine cabinet? You think someone took a three am trip to leave you a written warning for *that*?" He tapped his fingers against the card, hard this time. "This appears to be a real threat. It's directed at *you*. That's what we have to deal with, not some John Grisham fantasy in which corporations try to assassinate their detractors. *This* is real."

"It's not a fantasy," I said, stubbornly.

"Right now, we have to focus on keeping you safe," he continued as if I hadn't spoken. "Do you have plans tomorrow?"

"I'm meeting up with Mary Ann, why?"

He nodded his approval. For some reason, the gesture irked me. "So you won't be alone. Good. Try to stay in public, high traffic places. Keep your cell phone ready and your mace. The person who left you this," he lifted the note again, "may be someone from your past with a grudge to bear. God knows you've pissed off enough people."

"The person who left me this is pissed because he thinks I'm getting closer to figuring out who and what killed Aaron London!" I slammed my fist on the table, startling Ms. Dogz. "God, why can't you see that! What is wrong with you?"

"What is wrong with *you*?" he countered, raising his voice for the first time. There was virulence in his tone. It almost made me gasp.

"Anatoly," I whispered.

He grimaced and got out of his chair. Without another word he walked out of the dining room and into the kitchen. If he had stormed out, I would have known how to react. But his calm silence threw me. After a moment I withdrew my foot from Ms. Dogz's back and followed him. I found him at the sink, pouring himself a glass of water. "If you hadn't found the note tonight," he said, turning around to face me once more, "would you have told me about any of this?"

"I…" I hesitated and bit down on my lip. "I should have," I finally admitted. "It's just…you were so against this whole thing."

"And why do you think that is?" he asked, with just the slightest trace of derision. "I took pains to make sure you were in good standing with the property manager of London's apartment building. The more you go back, the more you use that key that you have no right to have, the harder it will be to protect you from the illegality of your own foolishness."

"I wasn't being foolish," I snapped.

"You knew I wouldn't want you to go back there," he continued. "Even more than the whole meeting with Gundrun Volz, you must have known that going back into Aaron London's apartment was one thing I absolutely would not have agreed to."

"I don't have to ask your permission for...well, for anything," I said, coolly. Mr. Katz strode into the room and took his place by my side, making it clear which parent he stood with.

"No, you don't," Anatoly admitted. "What bothers me is not that you're not deferring to me. It's that you seem intent on antagonizing me. Knowing I don't want you to take these risks not only doesn't bother you, it *pleases* you. You're looking for a fight." He took a sip of his water and put it down on the counter. "Tell me I'm wrong," he challenged.

I blanched and looked away. I *wanted to* tell him he was wrong. But that was one lie I couldn't pull off. And the truth that he had just called me out on, was sort of awful.

"I'm not...looking for a fight," I attempted. "Not *exactly.* But Anatoly," I turned back to him, confused, almost pleading, "when have you and I ever gone out of our way to avoid conflict? We have never been peacemakers. I thought we both understood that. I thought that was why we fit."

"It's one thing not to avoid it, it's another thing to covet it." He stepped forward, tucking his thumbs into the pockets of his jeans, staring straight into my eyes with an intensity that made me feel both vulnerable and teary. "What's going on with you, Sophie?" Ms. Dogz rushed to his side, but for once, he ignored her. "What is it about your life, *our* life that has left you unsatisfied? What hole are you trying to patch up with far-fetched theories and dead-end investigations?"

I stilled my trembling hand by crossing my arms in front of my chest. "First, let me say that I don't think my theories are far fetched or that my investigation is a dead-end. That note on the door...the *only* way anyone could come to the conclusion that it isn't connected to what's going on is if they're in severe denial."

Anatoly muttered something in Russian. I decided not to ask for the translation.

"But you are right about one thing," I continued. "I am trying to patch something up. Maybe I'm going about it the wrong way. Maybe I'm not being as communicative as I should be. But Anatoly, I think you *know* that things have been different with us lately. And I think...I hope, you've noticed that I haven't been fully myself in quite some time. I hope you can see that despite our arguments and disagreements, the last few days I've been more...more *me.* And we've been more *us.* You do see, that, right? You do *like* that, don't you?" Was I about to cry? God, how pathetic. I self-consciously swiped at my eyes with the back of my hand. "Conflict, fights, passionate lovemaking, is that not what you want anymore? And if it's not..." my voice faded off.

If not what's left of us? Where do we go from here? But those were questions I didn't ask aloud. I simply didn't have the emotional courage or the fortitude.

Anatoly looked stricken. He opened his mouth as if to say something but then shook his head and looked down at Ms. Dogz who responded by looking up at him with a heartbreakingly forlorn stare. For a long time, we remained silent. From outside I could hear the faint sound of birds chirping, trying to beat the sun to the day. The only window here looked out into my tiny backyard. I couldn't see the street at all. But I imagined it being filled with Zipcars.

"You should go back to bed," he said, quietly. "You must be exhausted."

"And you're not?" I asked with a humorless laugh.

"I'm fine," he lied. "I'm going to search the property again."

"No one's out there," I protested, wiping away another tear. "He dropped a note and took off."

"Go to bed, Sophie."

"Or what?" I snapped as Ms. Dogz's ears perked up.

Anatoly finally looked up to meet my eyes and the look on his face…oh he was riled up again. We were going to have a real fight now. I rolled my shoulders back and tilted up my chin, my hands clenched into fists by my side.

He studied me for what felt like a five-minute stretch but was probably mere seconds. And then he just shook his head and looked to the back door. "Go to bed," he repeated, his voice softer this time, less a command than a surrender.

And that surrender, somehow that hurt more than being hit with harsh or biting accusations and insults. It felt like he was surrendering on us. I shifted my weight from one foot to the other, not immediately sure of what to do. But when he didn't say more, I found myself also surrendering, stepping away from him, turning my back, heading up the stairs, Ms. Dogz at my heels, Mr. Katz staying exactly where he was. As I reached the top, I heard the front door open and close as Anatoly went out to search for a stalker that was no longer there.

 # CHAPTER
TWENTY

"The only thing about life that isn't complicated is death.
Death is very simple."
--Dying To Laugh

A vague buzzing, like a really annoying bee. That's the sound that woke me up. "Make it stop," I grumbled, hoping whatever it was Anatoly could just kill it. But when I blinked my eyes open Anatoly's side of the bed was empty and the buzzing wasn't coming from a bee but from my phone, vibrating against my nightstand. There was a pit in my stomach that I couldn't explain. Why was I waking up worried? Disoriented I reached for my phone. It was ten-fifty am and Jason was calling me.

"Jason," I said, sleepily into my cell. I looked over at Anatoly's side of the bed again. Oh. The events of last night were seeping back into my consciousness. I now had an explanation for the pit.

"Nolan-Volz is poisoning people," Jason said in lieu of hello.

"You mean someone at Nolan-Volz poisoned Aaron London," I corrected. Mr. Katz wasn't in the room, which meant Anatoly had probably already fed him. Were Anatoly and I having a fight? Was that how we left it the night before?

"No, no," Jason corrected. "They're poisoning lots of people. I'm sure of it. That's what London was trying to tell you. These articles we found in his apartment? They're just story after story of how pharmaceutical companies screw up and poison people and then they do these huge cover-ups. This London dude understood the game."

"Uh-huh," I propped myself up on one elbow. Ms. Dogz was relaxing on her bed, a little bit of drying dog food clinging to her nose. Anatoly's shoes that he wore the day before were not on the floor. That could mean one of two things. One, he put them away in the closet (not likely). Or two, he had put them on and walked out the door. "Were there any articles about Nolan-Volz specifically?" I asked.

"No. But have you seen today's Chronicle?"

"Um, no…it's probably in my driveway…unless Anatoly took it with him." I sat up and tried to do some math in my head. I had gotten two hours of sleep between the time I went to bed and woke up due to the ominous intruder…well, not intruder, ominous note-dropper. Then I had gotten back to sleep at…five? No, I had lain awake for at least…

"There's a whole article about Nolan-Volz and your friend Gun in today's Chronicle."

"Oh…that's the article he thought I was working on," I exclaimed, my focus now back with Jason. "Was it critical? Complimentary?" I got to my feet and headed down to the living room, Ms. Dogz trotted after me. No sign of Anatoly.

"The latter," Jason said, sounding disgusted. "But check this out, Gundrun Volz used to be a top executive at Orvex.

Sophie, this is some seriously sinister shit."

"Why?" I asked. I stopped in the center of the living room to rub away some sleep sand still in my eye. My yawn stretched my face until I felt a tightening around my cheekbones. Mornings before caffeine? *That* was sinister shit. But God bless Anatoly, I smelled coffee. "What's Orv…oh, wait a minute."

"Yeah, that's right. You know what Orvex was," Jason said, sounding rather proud of himself.

"They made Rispolex," I whispered. "Gun was involved in a company that…that…"

"That poisoned people," Jason finished for me.

That was, if not an oversimplification, certainly a poor framing of the facts. Orvex didn't exactly poison people, not intentionally. But according to that Newsweek article, they did cut corners they weren't legally allowed to cut and their product did cause serious health issues.

"In the article, he claims to have learned a lot from the mistakes made at Orvex," Jason scoffed. "He says he's been very clear with his scientists about how important it is to follow all the protocols and eschew shortcuts. You see what he's doing, right? He's deflecting blame onto the scientists. Like he didn't tell them to take those shortcuts. But I'm sure he did. And while the company did go out of business, did a single Orvex executive face criminal charges? No. No, they didn't. And now he's killing people over at Nolan-Volz. That's how this bullshit works."

"Okay, slow down." I sat on the armrest of the couch. Ms. Dogz sat next to me, her expression expectant. "His having worked at Orvex…it's odd. Maybe even suspicious but we don't want to jump to conclusions."

"Jump to conclusions? Rispolex caused heart murmurs! Aaron London had fluid around his heart! These drugs are hurting our hearts! How's that for a metaphor for corporate America?"

This was way too many hysterics for me to handle this early in the day. "I'll read the article, okay?" I assured him as I pushed myself back to my feet and headed for the front door.

"I'm coming over tonight so we can go over everything," Jason volunteered.

I hesitated, my hand on the knob of my front door. Anatoly's face from last night flashed before me.... that look of rage, then surrender. We were in dangerous territory. We had things we absolutely had to work out and if I valued my relationship, it really shouldn't wait until tomorrow.

"Tonight's not good," I said. "Anatoly and I need some alone time."

"People are dying!" he whined. "Have alone time tomorrow. We need to meet tonight."

"Jason," I sighed as I started to open the front door. "I--"

I was interrupted by a screeching siren alarm. *Our alarm*, the one we never used. Ms. Dogz freaked out. She started running around the foyer and then sprinted outside into the front yard only to turn around and sprint back inside. And the alarm was still going. *Shit!*

"Jason, hold on," I yelled into the phone as I ran through the house, to the laundry room where the alarm keypad was. "Umm..." what was the code? Oh God, what date did he use for this one? The siren was still going. Would the police come?

"Fuck, fuck, fuck, fuck!" I brought my phone back to

my ear. "Jason," I yelled, "I have to hang up. I have to…oh, oh, I remember!"

"Remember what? What the hell's that noise? Oh Jesus, are they coming for you?"

"What? No, I don't know what you're talking about. I need to call you back so I can look up the date when the battle of Stalingrad ended." The police would be here any second. No police before coffee!

"You don't know the end date of Stalingrad? I know the end date of Stalingrad."

"What is it?" I shouted.

"If I tell you can I come over tonight so we can figure this shit out?"

"*Jason!*" If I could have reached through the phone to strangle him, I would have done it.

"February 2nd , 1943," Jason replied, proudly.

"Great." I hung up the phone and put 02021943 into the keypad. The alarm stopped. "Oh." I stood there in the silence, the wailing still echoing in my ears.

I tightened my robe and fell back against the washing machine. Everything was a mess. My relationship was getting rockier by the minute, someone…or someones…possibly corporate America, was leaving threatening notes on my front door and…

…The sound of approaching sirens captured my attention. The police charged for false alarms, didn't they? I gave Ms. Dogz a look. "Everything's a mess."

Ms. Dogz bashfully looked away as if she didn't want to see me in such a pathetic state. I stepped out of the laundry room and found my eyes were drawn to the coffee maker. On it was a bright yellow post it: a note from Anatoly telling

KYRA DAVIS

me he had set the alarm and reminding me of what the code was. That could have been helpful.

I sighed and went to the front door, catching a quick look at my reflection in the glass of the dining room display cabinets. I was wearing a knee length plush white robe with colorful polka dots all over it. Obviously the perfect armor for dealing with the fallout of the battle of Stalingrad.

I put Ms. Dogz on her S&M leash and opened the door anticipating the police would be there soon. Ms. Dogz and I listened as the sirens got closer and then the black and whites came into view. "Play it cool with the policemen, Ms. Dogz," I counseled. "At the moment you're undocumented."

The cars sped to the house...and then past the house. They just drove right by. "Oh," I said surprised. "Sooo... they're not coming to check on me?" Did that make me feel more or less safe? I waited a moment to see if maybe they just missed their stop. Did police ever do that? Just accidentally pass up the house they're rushing to because their GPS messed up? It did seem a bit unlikely.

But they didn't circle back. I was on my own. Maybe I was *always* on my own. Maybe all the trappings of security and protection meant nothing in the unpredictable and unstable world of 2017.

Maybe there really were no impediments that could keep my stalker from hurting me.

The Chronicle was still in my driveway. If Anatoly was irritated with me, he would have taken it. He knew I liked to read it over coffee.

On the other hand, if he was deeply angry he wouldn't stoop to pettiness. So either he wasn't all that upset with me anymore or we were on the verge of (another) breakup. I tread out, barefoot to the driveway and fetched the paper, all the while scanning for unwanted notes.

The minute I got back into the foyer I found the article on Nolan-Volz. The headline read:

Gilcrest & Co. To Acquire Nolan-Volz After Promising Early Results of Anti-Addiction Drug

The byline read Tereza Calvan. This was the Chronicle article Gundrun Volz thought I was interviewing him for. I quickly read the paragraph that had made the first page and then flipped to the page where the article continued. The pending acquisition was announced less than a week ago and the stock market was salivating over it. Apparently, Nolan-Volz had gone through a few bumpy years half a decade ago when they struggled to win federal approval to begin clinical testing for Sobexsol. It had gotten to the point where there had been speculation that they would have to fold. But eventually they did get that approval and the early results had been stunning. Sobexsol was a drug aimed at curbing people's addictive tendencies. For those who were biologically prone to addiction Sobexol targeted the part of the brain that was responsible for the addictive cravings and significantly dulled them. It was considered a huge breakthrough in neuropharmacology. And at a time when more people in America died of opioid overdoses than car crashes, the prospects of massive sales were huge.

And of course, Gundrun Volz was quoted quite extensively. The article made him look like a visionary.

"So now he's a lauded public figure," I whispered to myself. That would make it harder for me to convince others that he was dangerous. I thought about last night's note again. God, things had gotten totally out of control. Part of me was tempted to find a way out or at least make myself a very strong Bloody Mary.

But instead, I found myself walking through the living room, dropping the paper onto the coffee table and then heading into my office. I was almost in a trance as I sat down at my computer. Listening to the familiar chime as it powered on. And then… I clicked onto Word.

I stared at my empty document. I slide my fingers over the keys, reacquainting myself with them, feeling their smooth edges, the way they petted and scratched my fingertips. I hadn't really felt the keys like this in well over a year. The keyboard was a little like an old lover. You knew what it could do, you just had to remind yourself where and how to touch it, which pressure points to hit, how to make it sing.

Slowly, I began to type.

In the center of her palm was a spot of crusted blood, just to the left of her lifeline, right on top of the line of fate. It wasn't her blood. But it was definitely her indictment, the consequences of which were crouched behind some shadowy corner, ready to jump out and strike her down.

I kept writing, my fingers picking up speed until they were flying creating a living breathing woman out of nothing, giving her a burden and a history that was unimaginable…except I *was* imagining it.

I was writing.

Writer's block, GONE! I was cured!

The cure lasted for exactly six and a half pages.

My cursor was impatiently blinking at me again as my hands hovered uselessly in the air. The letters on the keys suddenly seemed random. I couldn't think of a good way to string them together.

I sat there like that for a full ten minutes, occasionally writing a few words before immediately deleting them, my creativity rolling further away with every tick of the clock. Whatever had boiled up in me had now boiled away to nothing.

"Fuck," I whispered. But unlike Anatoly, my keyboard didn't have a sexy-clever come-back. My words were just... gone.

I sat back and stared at my screen. Perhaps the question shouldn't be why did I lose my creative spark so quickly but what had sparked it to begin with. Had my subconscious found the words I needed tucked under the moldy pizza boxes of London's apartment? Had inspiration been woven through the words of that menacing note?

I got up and went back to the newspaper. Maybe there was something in the article that I missed...something so horrible and terrifying I would be inspired to finish the chapter.

But when I picked up the paper I noted a headline on the front page that I had missed before:

Unidentified Man Found Strangled To Death in Presidio Park

But it wasn't the headline that bothered me. It was the fact that someone had underlined it. As in, underlined it with a fine point pen.

I dropped the paper.

Why would someone underline a headline about a local murder...unless they were trying to make a point. To threaten me. Again.

I swallowed hard, picked the paper back up and found my way back to the laundry room, activating the alarm once again, using a little piece of bloody history as the passcode.

"I'm fine. Everything is fine," I whispered to myself.

I was a liar.

I found Ms. Dogz waiting for me in the kitchen, looking up at me expectantly. With unsteady hands, I put the paper down on the island and started to read.

I read the article over four times. But it told me nothing. A tatted up white dude, about six-feet tall, had been found dead in the bushes of Presidio Park. He had been strangled with a metal cord. He had no ID on him. No wallet but the police weren't saying if it was a suspected robbery or something else. It was an ongoing investigation.

So two dead. London and this other guy. I lifted my hand to my neck, imagining what it must be like to have something as harsh as soft steel deprive you of the air you needed to breathe.

I was going to get so much writing done today.

# CHAPTER
TWENTY-ONE

"If someone gives you a sugar pill, tells you it will cure your physical ailments and you really believe it, there's a decent chance the pill will work. If a man tells you he can fix all your problems and you really believe him, there's a good chance he will drive you insane and completely dismantle your life. When it comes to our relationships, we need to check our magical thinking at the door."
--Dying To Laugh

I almost canceled on Mary Ann. I had written a full twenty pages and walking away from my computer felt physically painful. But in all the years I had known her, Mary Ann had never flaked on me. Not one single time. And so I simply couldn't bring myself to flake on her, although I did tell her ahead of time that I might be a bit distracted.

Also, how long could I be home alone before the man in the black baseball cap showed up?

So perhaps a little time with the sweet and ever amiable Mary Ann really was the best option for the afternoon. Still, I couldn't quite believe what it was we were about to do. I sat in my car, now parked in the covered parking lot, Mary Ann by my side, shaking my head. "How did you talk me into this?"

"It's exciting, isn't it?"

I gave her a bewildered look. "But...we don't belong here."

"I do!" She got out of the car, happily slamming her door behind her.

I followed her with considerably less enthusiasm.

"This," she insisted, linking her arm with mine as she led me to the warehouse style building, "is a pragmatic thing to do. I'm being very mature and pragmatic."

Yesterday Mary Ann had downloaded a new app that gave her a word-of-the-day. Today was *pragmatic*. I bit back my reply and managed a forced, tight-lipped smile as we walked through the automatic doors of Babies R Us.

She half skipped, half ran over to where the shopping carts were. "Should we get two carts? This is a big sale and I do want to take full advantage of it."

"But you don't have a kid," I pointed out for the umpteenth time.

"But I'm *going* to have a kid," she explained as she settled on getting just one shopping cart and gleefully wheeled it toward the shelves.

"But you don't know *when* you're going to have a kid," I tried again.

"Of course I do! I'll have my first little one in almost exactly nine months!" she leaned over and whispered con-spiratorially, "We've had sex for the last two nights in a row *without* condoms!"

"Yeah, but that doesn't mean--"

"Oh! Look at this!" She grabbed a Björn baby carrier from a shelf and held it out, with straight arms, to admire it. "Everyone tells me Baby Björn is the best. It's not on sale, but it's probably unwise to skimp on something like this, don't you think? Or do you think it's better to get one of those swing things. Lots of the attachment-parenting people swear by the swing things."

I had no idea what she was talking about. The only *swing-things* I had ever heard about were the sex swings Dena carried in her shop.

"Oh!" Mary Ann laughed and reached for another box. "I meant sling. Sling things! Gosh, there's so much to learn in such little time!"

"You know, it's possible you're not pregnant yet," I said, as if repetition was the clearest route to sanity.

"Oh no, I'm sure I am." She reached for my hand and placed it firmly on her flat stomach. "You feel that? It's like it's almost...oh, I don't know...like it's bloated or something."

"Yeah, but maybe you're bloated or something," I suggested although if this was bloated I needed to get my ass to a Weight Watchers meeting immediately.

Mary Ann laughed and released my hand. "Don't be silly." She turned back to the shelves. The Chipmunks Christmas song started playing in the background, solidifying my suspicion that this place was one of the circles of hell. "The slings are on sale but they look kind of complicated. I think I'll stick with the Björn. The Swedish always raise their children to be so nice and talented and tall. Just look how well Alexander Skarsgård turned out. I bet his mother carried him around in a Baby Björn."

"Yeah, that would explain why he's so tall," I said, dryly.

"You never know," she placed the Björn in the basket and moved us toward the car seats, "maybe they stretch out in there. Anyway, why didn't you think you'd be good company today? What's going on?"

"Oh, just the London thing. You know I tried to talk to Anatoly about it but he's being every bit as stubborn as Dena is. Maybe even more so. He's mad at me for looking into it at all, which doesn't make sense. More's happened since I've last talked to you about this. And that means there's more reason than ever to think London was murdered."

"London was murdered," she repeated, thoughtfully. "That sounds wrong. Like you're talking about a sporting team or something. Like America just murdered London on the soccer field."

"Okay, except America's a country and London's a city and that's not really an expression, but aside from that I see your point."

"*Right*?!" she said as if I had just stated my full agreement. But then, her attention really was elsewhere. "Do you think it's okay to get a discounted car seat?" She studied a large box featuring a happy, safe, car-riding baby. Next to the box was a sign with the words twenty-five percent off in glaring red print.

"Probably? At the very least it should be secure enough for *theoretical* children."

"You're probably right," Mary Ann agreed, missing my sarcasm. "So why do you think Anatoly's so freaked out about your looking into the London thing? Does he have the same concern as Dena? That you're giving into paranoia?"

"Yeah," I admitted as I helped Mary Ann heft the car seat into the cart. "I don't really understand the argument. It's not like I'm building a bunker underneath the house. I'm just investigating a suspicious death."

"Maybe he's upset about something else and he's, um, what-do-you-call it…projectiling."

"Projecti…I think you mean projecting," I corrected. A mother dragging a screaming toddler behind her, scooted past us down the aisle.

"Yes, that's it, projecting," Mary Ann agreed. "Did you see how darling that little boy was?"

"The one with the red face?"

"First, that's kind of racist Sophie," Mary Ann scoffed as she moved us toward bedding. "Second, I don't even think he was Native American. Latino maybe? Or Armenian? Whatever, he was just *adorable!*"

"Are you serious? Okay, you're serious."

But Mary Ann didn't seem to hear me. "If Anatoly seems mad about something that it doesn't make sense to be mad about, he may *really* be mad at himself."

"You think?" I asked.

"Didn't you tell me Anatoly refused to listen to London or take him seriously? Maybe he's mad at himself about that and you're looking into it just reminds him of it."

I blinked in surprise. That was the thing about Mary Ann. She could say something that was incomprehensibly… well, stupid and then turn around and say something surprisingly insightful and wise. "If you're right," I said hesitantly, "how do I deal with that? How do I even get him to talk about it?"

"If it were me, I'd start by getting him into a calm, happy mood before I talked to him about anything," she said as she zeroed in on a Winnie The Pooh baby blanket. "Get him to a place where he thinks you're catering to him, maybe even spoiling him a little. Pour him a small drink...Russians like cognac, right? Pour him a little cognac, give him a nice shoulder rub, bake him some cupcakes and then when he's feeling relaxed and receptive, *that's* when you bring up the whole murder and mayhem stuff."

"I'm not sure that will work."

"Trust me," Mary Ann said as her eyes moved over a row of mobiles. "And I have a great chocolate cupcake recipe I could give you."

"I don't think a cupcake can solve this," I said, doubtfully.

"Sophie," Mary Ann turned to me and fixed me with a stare, "have you ever seen an angry man with a cupcake in his hand?"

I opened my mouth to reply then thought about it for a second. "Okay, I'll give you that. Still, if you offer someone a cupcake and then tell them you want to talk about poison..." my phone rang and I shut up and fished it out quietly hoping it was Catherine. I didn't recognize the number on my cell, but then maybe she was calling me from her home number. I gestured to Mary Ann to hold on for a moment and picked up. "Hello?"

"Sophie!" Gundrun boomed.

My heart dropped a little. Had he figured out I wasn't who I said I was? "Hi Gun...drun," I said, unsure if I was still invited to use his nickname. "How are you? Did...did you like the article?"

"It's absolutely fantastic! As I said to you before, I

didn't think the first interview was nearly in depth enough but I could see your hand in this, a lot of things I spoke specifically to you about made it in. I appreciate that."

"Well, it was my pleasure Gun." I suppressed a loud sigh of relief. Obviously, the reporter had been able to get information about Gundrun and Nolan-Volz without asking him directly about it. That's what reporters do. But if he wanted to attribute the information to me, I'd happily take the credit.

Mary Ann gave me a funny look and made a symbol of a gun with her hand while mouthing *boss man*? *Yes,* I mouthed back as I also made a gun symbol with my hand…which I then held up to my head.

"Still, they wronged you by not giving you credit. Only Tereza's name was listed as the byline. What kind of nonsense is that?"

"Well, I really worked as more of a research assistant on this one," I hedged. "Tereza did all the writing and the vast majority of the work."

"I still say you were robbed. But I want you to know, I for one am damned grateful for your work on this."

His tone and speech patterns were different than the last time I had spoken to him. Perhaps this is what he sounded like when he was truly happy?

"Please let me show you my appreciation. Come to my home for dinner tomorrow night. My wife cooks a mean eggplant parm."

"Oh." Another shopper stepped up to the shelves beside us, her baby was strapped into a seat that seemed specially designed to fit into her shopping cart. "Thank you, but I don't think that would be appropriate." The baby smelled awful.

"Why's that? The article has been completed and published. I can't influence it anymore. Beside, this would be a business dinner. You clearly had more questions about pharmaceutical development and the other concerns of Aaron London. I'm afraid I was a little brusque on those points. But after that article? The least I can do is give you the information you want and set you up well for your next piece...which I do hope will have your name on it. Seriously, Sophie. I owe you."

Oh. Well when he put it like that...

"When were you thinking?" I asked.

# CHAPTER
TWENTY-TWO

"My husband and I have a communication problem in that he always wants to communicate. There's a lot to be said for just shutting up every once in a while."
--Dying To Laugh

When I came home I found Anatoly standing outside the house, helmet tucked under one arm and staring up at the second story windows. I pulled into our driveway, behind his motorcycle and came out to join him. "What are you looking at?" I asked.

"I'm trying to figure out if there's a way to climb up there." He graced me with a cursory glance and a nod before looking back up at the window. "The locks on those windows aren't as secure as they should be."

"Our house is in full view of the street," I pointed out with a forced laugh. "No one's going to scale it in order to climb in a second story window."

Anatoly grimaced, keeping his eyes on the house. "Your problem is you're too paranoid about highly unlikely dangers and not nearly paranoid enough about the more plausible ones. I'll fix the locks on the windows tomorrow." He finally brought his eyes down to me and then gestured toward the front door. "Shall we?"

He waited for me to walk up to the door first, the perfect gentleman if not the perfect partner at the moment. We entered our home single file. I sat down on the couch next to my feline feeling awkward. Anatoly had dropped off his helmet by the door and was occupied with scratching Ms. Dogz's belly. "You saw my note about the alarm?" he asked once he finally joined me in the living room.

"Yes, I saw it…a little late. Isn't our alarm system connected to a security patrol service or the police department so that when it goes off something…you know, happens? Like, someone responds or something."

"It's not," Anatoly admitted taking a seat in the armchair. So very far away. "However if it goes off for four minutes straight without one of us entering the code the alarm company will check in."

He was focused on me. I had his attention if I wanted it. But I didn't know how much else I had. His heart? Yes, I was sure I still had his heart. But his understanding? His support? Certainly not his patience.

"Anything interesting happen today?" he asked. His tone was casual but I could sense the edge in the question.

"Mary Ann's looking for baby items even though she doesn't have a baby. She's absolutely sure she's one, maybe even two days pregnant."

"Anything else?"

I thought about the call from Jason, then from Gun and of course, the underlined headline. "That's all."

Anatoly's jaw set. "You can't be honest with me."

My lips curved into a small, sad smile. "It would be

easier if you actually wanted the truth."

The flash of anger in Anatoly's eyes was unmistakable. "I have never been one to stick my head in the sand."

"No," I agreed. "You've also never been one to turn your back on a man in need. And yet we both did that this time. And now you're following one unfortunate first with another."

"Damn it, Soph--"

"It seems outlandish," I said, cutting him off, "but also heartbreaking that a man could come to us for help only to have us dismiss him as a lunatic." Anatoly's jaw was so tense I thought it might crack and shatter to the floor. I really should have done this after making him a cupcake, but it was too late for that now. "It seems ludicrously, perhaps unrealis-tically Machiavellian that someone could slowly poison a man until he lost his senses and thereby the credibility he would need in order to get help." I glanced over at Mr. Katz, he had fallen asleep, but I decided that the position of his body was kitty language for *You tell him, Sister.* "But some-times the truth is ludicrous," I said, bringing my eyes back to Anatoly. "And I'll admit, dismissing one oddly suspicious event as coincidence is rational. Dismissing a string of them? That's denial. You're in denial."

Anatoly looked stricken. "I didn't misjudge the situation. London was destroying himself. I couldn't help him with that."

And I heard it, the undercurrent note of angst hidden under layers of bravado and cultivated frustration. Anatoly couldn't admit that he might have failed in a life or death situation. And his failure wasn't that he hadn't saved London because in truth London came to us too late for that. The failure had been in our judgment. Anatoly prided himself on his good judgment. Perhaps we all did. But the thing is, the one universal human sin is that occasionally, we all exercise grievous misjudgment.

"Anatoly," I said, leaning forward, "you really need to consider the possibility--" the doorbell rang, interrupting me.

Anatoly sat up a little straighter. "Are you expecting anyone?"

I shook my head. "But if it was, like a stalker…he wouldn't ring the bell, right?" I whispered.

"That depends on whether he wanted you to come to the door or not," he answered before slowly getting to his feet. "Wait here," he instructed.

I stayed in my seat as Anatoly disappeared into the foyer. It was fine. Everything was fine. I looked over at Mr. Katz who twitched his ears. That's kitty language for *it might not be fine.*

And then I heard the door open and a voice. Not Anatoly's voice but a voice I certainly recognized.

"Hey man, is Sophie here? She's expecting me."

In seconds Jason was standing in my living room, wearing an Atari T-shirt under a Western-style suede leather shirt and on top of black baggy jeans. There was a stack of manila folders in his arms. Anatoly was steps behind him looking confused, although whether Jason's presence or his outfit was the thing confusing him was anyone's guess.

"You are going to love what I found," Jason said, beaming down at me.

"Jason, I told you tonight wasn't a good time." I looked over at Anatoly. "I did tell him not to come."

Jason's face fell. "But…you owe me for Stalingrad!"

"I don't know what that means and I don't care," Anatoly growled. "Sophie and I were in the middle of a private conversation. We don't want company."

"He's right. We can discuss all…that," I waved at the files as I got up from the sofa, "on another day. Here, I'll walk you out."

"He left notes," Jason said as I tried to lead him to the door.

I stopped. "Who left notes?"

"London! I have personal notes in here! He typed them up but they're definitely his thoughts. They're clues, Sophie."

I hesitated. I could feel Anatoly staring at me, waiting for me to make my decision. And I knew what he wanted that decision to be. But I couldn't help myself. I turned to Anatoly. "We'll just be, like, ten minutes, okay? Fifteen tops."

Anatoly stared at me, his expression completely unreadable. I offered him an awkward smile then took Jason's arm and brought him into the dining room. "Let me see the notes," I said eagerly.

"Are there any electronics in here," he asked, still holding tight to the files.

"Electronics?" I repeated. "Why?"

"You know how easy it is to turn your laptop into a listening device? Your TV? Your refrigerator?"

"Our refrigerator is very good at keeping secrets," I assured him. "Where are the notes?"

"You have way too much faith in the integrity of your appliances," he replied with a completely straight face. "Before you look at the notes, take a look at this." He dropped a file on the table. "These are details about, like, two dozen different class action cases involving pharmaceuticals, going back fifty, sixty years. And all different companies. I told you, they're *all* corrupt. The Christian Scientists got this one right. The medical establishment can Not. Be. Trusted. We all think we're the rugged-individualist protagonists in some kind of glorified Ayn Rand novel. But the truth is we're the complacent, weak-willed followers you find in the books of Orwell! You hear what I'm saying?"

"Jason, just show me London's personal notes."

"The case he has the most information on was Orvex," he went on, ignoring my request. "Man, your friend Gun is lucky he got away with his career intact. If this Sobexsol thing doesn't fly I think he's done. This is his chance to prove to the world that he can do something right in pharmaceuticals ooor…that he can't."

"And you think he can't?" I asked, flipping through the file.

"Nobody can do anything right in pharmaceuticals," Jason insisted as he hugged the rest of the files to his chest protectively. "I keep telling you, Big Pharma is evil."

"Yeah, okay, whatever. Show me the personal notes." I closed the file feeling more than a little impatient now. "Please."

Jason graced me with something very close to a pout. But he did give me the file with all of London's notes. A few were written by hand but most were typed just as neatly as the blog posts and the articles. But unlike those other documents, the notes felt fragmented. Slices of thought, sprinkles of emotion, a dab of fatalism here, a smidgen of heartbreak there.

The first note read like a stream-of-consciousness chapter of a Faulkner novel:

She's withdrawn. I see her look away. Always, always away. I was helping. She knows what I've done. So many risks! But it's all worth it. It should be worth it. She just needs to stop looking away.

I put the note down and picked up the next one:

To love honor and protect. I've done that, haven't I? I've been a husband to her in every way that matters. This must just be the transition. She is better. Slurred speech? Gone. Red eyes? Clear. She still trembles, maybe even more so now. But that's to be expected. And she has a cold. Her immune system may be out of whack. But that's to be expected too. She's angry. But that's probably normal. She's better, because of me. I've taken care of her the way a man should take care of his wife. When she's stabilized she'll see me as a hero.

"Is this a chronicle of the end of his marriage?" I mumbled, more to myself than to Jason. I had only collected a fraction of the papers that were in that apartment. Had I missed anything that would clarify the meaning of this? I picked up another note. But that one was completely different than the other two. It read:

Eight months in: Subject had half a glass of wine and then stopped, without wanting more. Can stand among smokers without wanting a cigarette. Minor hair loss, but that seems to be tapering off.

"I think this is from his work," I noted, pushing it aside.

"Sophie," Jason took a step closer as Ms. Dogz trotted into the room to see who was calling out to her. I had never met a dog more responsive to her name than this one. "There's a pattern…or at least there is with the blog posts he collected. Over eighty percent of the articles are about faulty, unethical drug trials or about approved drugs making patients sick. And Nolan-Volz is on the cusp of introducing a new drug to market."

I finally turned back to Jason, putting London's notes down. "But the early results of the Sobexsol trials are great," I reminded him. "That's what's being reported."

"You can't trust what the media tells you," Jason said, stubbornly. "They're just reciting corporate talking points." He leaned in a little closer. "London's establishing a pattern of behavior here, not his, *theirs*. Some of these stories are about things that are confirmed to be true. The MKUltra stuff, there are some articles here about syphilis experiments they did on African American men, that's documented and absolutely true, as is the stuff about Thalidomide." He shuffled through the papers to show me a few more of the articles. "Some of it is a little more controversial," he admitted, "like the whole thing about vaccinations causing autism or there's a story about how a certain over-the-counter antihistamine may result in infertility. Admittedly, there isn't a lot of documented evidence to back any of that up. But what matters here is not what's true and what's false. What's important is the pattern of behavior of corporations and our government!"

I shifted my weight back on my heels, taken aback and a little appalled by what I had just heard. "Jason," I said quietly once I found my voice, "it always matters what's true and what's false. That's *always* the important part."

"Okay, yeah, I feel you but--"

"Where's Anatoly?" I looked past him for the first time fully noting his absence.

"Huh? Oh, I don't know. I thought I heard him leave a few minutes ago."

"You heard him *leave*?" I asked, incredulously. I rushed past Jason to the living room. It was empty save for Mr. Katz. Anatoly's keys were no longer on the coffee table. I rushed to the front door and threw it open. His motorcycle was gone. I stared at the empty space for a moment, only turning my eyes away from the spot as I heard another car start up and pull away from the curb.

The car didn't have its headlights on which was odd enough. But the street lights did afford me just enough light to make out some of its minor details as it accelerated past my house.

It was a Zipcar.

"Sophie." I turned to see Jason, Ms. Dogz at his side. "Is everything okay?"

No. Everything is not okay. I mutely walked back into the house, my mind jumping from the Zipcar to Anatoly's quiet exit then back again. I wasn't sure which one scared me more. "I have to call him," I whispered to myself.

"What?" Jason asked. "I didn't catch that."

I went into the living room for my purse and dug out my cell phone. "Go home, Jason," I said, a little louder this time. "Leave the files. I'll look over them tonight on my own."

"I really think I can help you with this," Jason protested.

"You *have* helped me," I acknowledged. "But you and I…we're both on thin ice with Dena." *And with Anatoly.* "You may not really get that but…trust me," I continued. "Go see her. Tell her you're not going to help me anymore with this whole London thing."

"But--"

"Do you love her?" I asked, cutting him off.

"Yeah, yes, of course I love her," he sputtered.

"Then sacrifice for her."

He blinked. Then looked back at the dining room where he had left the files. "I'm really into this," he said, plaintively. When I didn't reply he exhaled loudly, his shoulders sagging. "You really think she'll be *that* upset if I keep helping you?"

"I really think so."

"I don't want to upset her."

"I know," I said. Mr. Katz stood up on the couch and swished his tail, clearly moved by the emotional moment.

Jason looked back in the direction of the files again. "Okay," he said, quietly. "Okay."

I escorted him to the door and when I opened it I scanned the street. I didn't see any Zipcars this time. Whoever had been parked in front of my house was gone.

"So you're going to read the files now?" he asked. "Or are you going to sacrifice for Anatoly?"

"I'm going to *call* Anatoly," I said with a smile. "I'm going to ask him to come home." *And I'm going to tell him I'm frightened.* I didn't trust Jason to protect me from evil Zipcar drivers. I needed Anatoly for that. More importantly, I needed Anatoly to talk to me. Like *really* talk.

"Good luck," Jason said. He sounded like he meant it. I watched him walk out to the street before closing and locking the door. I started to make the call to Anatoly when my phone rang. An anonymous caller.

"Hello?" I said, cautiously into the phone.

"Hi."

I fell back, putting all my weight against the wall behind me. That was Catherine London's voice.

"I wasn't sure you'd call." Ms. Dogz settled into the corner across from me, putting her head on her paws as she settled in for a late-night nap.

"Yeah, I almost didn't. My mom doesn't want me to have anything to do with you."

"I get that." Mr. Katz entered the room and rubbed up against my legs. "I think right now what matters is what you want."

There was a long silence on the other end of the line.

"Catherine, are you still there?" I asked, a little desperately.

"Nobody calls me Catherine," she said coldly. "Except my mom when she's pissed. I go by Cat."

"Right, sorry," I looked down at Mr. Katz with a smile. Perhaps my little beast would like this girl.

"My dad sometimes calls me Catherine too," she said, almost begrudgingly. "I played Catherine of Aragon in a school play and since then he's been calling me Queen Catherine." She paused before adding, "It's stupid. Catherine of Aragon was torn away from her daughter, abandoned by her husband and died alone. Who would *want* to be Queen Catherine?"

She was smart. I also noticed that she was referring to

her father in the present tense. I did that a lot after I lost my father, forgetting, or at the very least not fully accepting, that he was gone. "Were you and your dad close?"

Another pause, followed by a sigh heavier than any girl Cat's age had the right to. "We were," she admitted, switching tenses again. "I used to look up to him. When I was little I thought he was the smartest man on earth…and the most loyal." She punctuated her sentence with a sad little laugh. "Now he's gone and…I don't know. I knew how sick he was but…I really didn't believe he would die. It's…I don't know…it's, like, unreal. It's just unreal."

"Yeah," I said, remembering how life had taken on a surreal quality once my father had died too. I had been nineteen at the time, a few years older than Cat. I had done everything I could to avoid facing the reality of life without my father or facing reality at all. Instead I had run off to Vegas with a superficially charming asshole and married him in a wedding officiated by an Elvis impersonator in a Denny's parking lot. Heavy drinking and drug use would have been less self-destructive.

"My dad never mentioned you," Cat continued. "I mean, you guys couldn't have been together for that long, right? If you hooked up after he was single again. Like, she…she ended it all ten months ago so it had to be more recent than that. Unless he was cheating on her, which I guess shouldn't surprise me."

"I met your dad the day he died," I said, almost pleading with her to believe me.

"Yeah, okay," she said in a voice that implied she didn't believe me at all. "Anyway, I have questions. I was hoping maybe you'd be cool with answering a few of them."

"Of course. To the best of my ability." Mr. Katz settled onto my foot, his subtle way of telling me I was saying all the right things.

"Yeah, okay. But this has to be on the down-low, okay? If my mom found out I was talking to you she'd freak, like big-time. We can't meet in public."

"Got it, we'll keep it on the down-low," I promised. "Do you want to come here, to my home? That way we can keep it quiet."

"Yeah, I guess that'd be good," Cat said, a little doubt-fully. "I'm not going to be able to get away today. My mom's taken some time off of work to be with me while we, you know, process. And it's not like a problem for her company. They're a start-up and let her bring the stuff they're working on home all the time to test it out or whatever. She could work from home for a full *month* and I'll barely be able to get away from her for more than ten minutes at a time. But I think she's going into the office for a meeting in two days. Maybe we can get together then? I'll text a time when I have it?"

"Yes, absolutely, I'll do whatever I need to do to make it work."

"Yeah, okay...I'll call or text or something," she said and then the line went dead.

I pulled the phone away from my ear and stared at it for a moment. Ms. Dogz had woken up and was staring at me with those black eyes. "Do you miss your old family?"

Ms. Dogz tilted her head to the side. I didn't understand doggie language well enough to know what that meant.

"Did you even know Catherine London?" I tried again. Ms. Dogz simply stared at me.

"Do you identify more as black or as a dog," I asked. Ms. Dogz tilted her head to the other side.

So tilting the head to the side obviously meant, *Are you kidding me?*

I could only hope that sussing out the meanings of Catherine's gestures and words would be as easy.

# CHAPTER
TWENTY-THREE

"Anyone can live without love, but no one can thrive."
--Dying To Laugh

I sat at the dining room table looking at the notes and articles long after Jason left. But I wasn't reading them or even thinking about them. I wasn't even thinking about Orvex or Gun or Zipcars or global conspiracies. I was thinking about Anatoly. I imagined Anatoly riding down Highway 1, the roar of his bike intermingling with the roar of the dark ocean. Maybe it would clear his head and he would come back to me happy, ready to do a little more talking, or a lot more lovemaking. I would be happy with either.

But he hadn't answered when I called. He didn't want to hear from me.

So I let the minutes, then the hours tick away as I blindly shuffled through those blog posts, all filled with exclamation marks and italicized words. Ms. Dogz made herself comfortable on the area rug in the living room leaving me in solitude in the dining room. Eventually, I started Googling. About a quarter of the findings in the articles London had hung on his wall seemed to be well supported and widely accepted. The rest, not so much.

Mr. Katz strolled into the dining room and took a seat in the corner, slowly blinking his eyes at me. "You're right," I replied to my cat after I interpreted his blink. "We do live in a time when a growing portion of the population thinks the world is flat. So in comparison, believing GMOs are part of a government conspiracy to lower the cognitive abilities of the mass public isn't all that outrageous."

I put aside the printed article that claimed exactly that and pulled out my phone as if just looking at it could make Anatoly call me. My fingers hovered over the screen as I considered trying him one more time but then thought better of it. The fear I had felt earlier in the evening had subsided. Now I just felt mildly anxious and…sad. I was sad.

But feeling a little sad was a significant improvement on feeling a little empty.

I looked over again at Mr. Katz. His eyes were closed now even as his tail twitched. I thought about Cat London. Was she sleeping well these days? I wondered if she would text or call me tomorrow to firm up the details of our meeting. But she was a teenager so it seemed more likely she would wait until the last minute before thinking to set up any meeting details. And as was the case with Anatoly, I knew that pushing her to communicate on my preferred time schedule would simply end up pushing her further away.

By midnight I found myself in our bed alone, again. He came home not long after that and I held my breath as I waited for him to join me. I quickly crafted a fantasy of a repeat of two nights before…with him sneaking beneath the sheets and my hand sneaking beneath his pajama pants. But although I waited with baited breath and all, he never even entered the room. It was only after listening to a few specific doors open and close and a bathroom sink turn on and off that I realized he was setting up camp in the guest room.

He had never done that before.

I considered barging in there, demanding that we talk about what was going on with us. But what was I supposed to say at this point? And I still hadn't told him about the newspaper with the underlined headline or the invitation I had received to have dinner with Gundrun Volz and his wife. I suppose he'd accuse me of holding out on him again, keeping a secret. But I knew that what really upset him was not that I was keeping secrets but that I had these particular secrets to keep.

And once again he left the next morning before I had even woken up. A few days earlier Anatoly and I had been fine, I hadn't had a stalker, no one had been threatening me and I didn't have an opinion about Zip Cars. I had made a mess of everything.

Except I was writing.

That day I wrote twenty-seven pages. Twenty-seven *good* pages.

I was beginning to wonder if my creative spirit was somehow tied to the spirits of Hell. At this rate, I'd have to actually burn the house down just to find the motivation to finish the first three chapters.

CHAPTER
TWENTY-FOUR

"If someone tells you they're doing something for the greater good what they're really telling you is they're about to do something very bad. Good deeds don't have to be justified."
--Dying To Laugh

I chose white. White was the perfect color to wear for my meeting with the Volzs at their Pacific Heights home. So I put on a white, long sleeved jumper that I almost never wore with a wide wrap belt. My intent was to look both professional and innocent. Like *way* too innocent to set up an interview with a corporate CEO on false pretenses. I decided the perfect accessory to my professional-innocent look was a butcher's knife, discreetly hidden underneath my wallet, cell phone, charger and other items that I regularly kept in my handbag. On the one hand, the idea that I would have to knife fight my way out of the eight million dollar home of a pharmaceutical CEO, seemed rather implausible.

On the other hand, Implausible might as well be the title of my autobiography.

I had to park a full three city blocks away from where

Gun lived and every time a car rode by or a wind picked up I worried that specks of dirt would come flying at me, and add unwanted patterns to my pristine white clothes.

Still, I was in reasonably good shape when I reached the double doors to Gun's Victorian mini-mansion. He greeted me in jeans and a sports coat. I was relieved and gratified to see his wife was there, as promised. She was standing a little behind him in her own pair of jeans and a pink, oversized scoop neck top that slid around every time she moved.

"The lady of the hour!" Gun said, shaking my hand vigorously. I smiled but kept my feet firmly planted on the opposite side of the threshold. I had already promised myself that I wouldn't enter the house unless his wife was there as promised. I was reckless but not stupid.

As if reading my mind, a woman entered the foyer and stood a few paces behind Gun "Allow me to introduce you to the lady of my life," Gun said as I finally stepped into the house, "Cara."

Cara was not what I expected. Everything about her screamed *kindness* and a complete lack of pretension. From her blonde hair pulled back into a careless ponytail, to her lack of makeup and her slightly crooked toothed grin. "I've heard so much about you, please come in!" She gushed as she clasped my hand in both of hers.

She ushered us into the living area. On the coffee table was a tray with assorted vegetables surrounding what might or might not have been a homemade dip. There was also a bottle of white chilling in a bucket and two wine glasses out and ready. "That was such a flattering portrait you painted of my man," she said with a laugh as she poured me a glass of wine. "I have to say, it made me want to take another look at him, remind myself of what I have!"

"Well, that was mostly Tereza," I said, carefully. "I just helped a little bit with some of the research on Nolan-Volz."

"You're too modest," Gun insisted as he also accepted a glass from his wife. The room smelled faintly of potpourri mingled with Cara's floral perfume. What I didn't smell was food. Shouldn't the smell of freshly baked eggplant Parmesan be detectable to the nose? Or did they have a smell proof kitchen, the perfect accommodation for every incompetent chef.

"Do you not drink?" I asked as Cara reached for a celery stick.

"Oh, I do, sometimes," she said with a smile as she sat down next to her husband. "Now, Gun tells me you're a novelist too?"

I looked over at Gun. I hadn't told him that.

"Forgive me, I Googled you," Gun explained.

"Oh," I held my wine between both hands. I still hadn't taken a sip. "I recently decided I needed to mix things up and try my hand at journalism. I do so much research for my novels anyway, you know? But yeah, normally I just write books."

"*Just?*" Cara said with a laugh. "Oh, you really are too modest. I would love to read your novels. Gun, will you get the titles for me? I'll order them from Amazon first thing tomorrow. You can get them on Amazon, yes?"

"Um, yes…" I brought the wine a little closer to my body, trying to internalize the mellow chill of the glass. "I could just give the titles directly to you if you like?" I said with what I hoped was a discernible amount of humor.

"Oh, of course," she laughed. "But as I'm sure Gun told

you, I can't stay very long. Our daughter is at a party in Daly City. Can you believe they have parties in Daly City?" She laughed. "I thought the only thing that city had to offer was fog and free parking! Anywho, I promised to pick her up. I actually should get going now if I want to make it on time. You know how traffic is. It seems to get worse by the day! By the minute!"

"You're...leaving us alone?" I asked, a tiny bit of panic creeping into my voice.

"Oh, don't worry, I'm not the jealous type," she said in what seemed to be an odd non sequitur. She leaned over and gave Gun a kiss on the cheek. "I married one of the rarest species of man. You know, the trustworthy breed." She laughed merrily at her own joke before getting back up to her feet. "Besides," she added as she reached for one last celery stick, "I would just be in the way of this follow-up interview. He's the star, not me."

I looked over at Gun. He was smiling benignly at me. "There's no need for her to be here for the second interview, is there? Or is this the third? Seeing that both you and your byline stealing partner have interviewed me in the last week, I suppose this will be the third interview, yes?"

"Oh, don't be so mean," Cara said, cheerily. "I'm sure Sophie and Tereza...is that her name? Tereza? I'm sure Sophie and Tereza have some kind of perfectly equitable arrangement worked out, don't you, Sophie? Or maybe not?" She added as she took in the concerned look on my face. "Maybe we *should* be bad-mouthing Tereza? I'm perfectly happy to call her an evil bitch if that's helpful. I try to be very accommodating of my guests."

"No, no. No need to bad mouth Tereza." I swallowed

and looked down at my wine glass. "You know, I probably shouldn't have agreed to an interview at this time, after work and all when you should be unwinding." I gave Gun a weak smile. "It would be better if we rescheduled for sometime during the work day, wouldn't it?"

"Not at all, Sophie. As I told you on the phone, this is the best time. You'll excuse me for a moment as I walk my wife out?" He got up and placed a hand on her waist. His tone was light and he was still smiling at me but the smile had turned a little sinister. I thought about the butcher knife in my purse. I should have brought the gun despite not having a concealed carry permit. A gun for Gun. A nervous giggle escaped my lips, causing Cara to give me an odd look as she allowed her husband to escort her to the front door.

I kept my seat and listened to the two of them exchange a few more pleasantries while in the foyer. There was the sound of the door opening and then closing again. In seconds Gundrun was back, but his smile was gone.

"So," he said as he reclaimed his seat.

"So," I said, quietly.

He reached for his wine and took a long sip. So the wine hadn't been poisoned. That was somewhat reassuring. He leaned further back in his chair but kept his posture stiff. "The Chronicle has never heard of you."

Shit. "Well, that's not really fair," I hedged. "They've reviewed my work twice. Interviewed me for their lifestyle section once--"

"That's not what I mean and you know it."

"Yeah," I lifted my chin, trying to look poised and defiant. "I know it."

"Why did you want to talk to me about London? Who

was he to you?"

"He was…a friend."

Gun's nostrils flared. I had never really seen someone's nostrils flare before but Gundrun had class A raging-bull-like flaring nostrils. "If you're trying to convince me you were his mistress, I don't buy it."

Thank *God.* At least one person didn't think I looked quite that hard up.

"He never got over *Anita,*" Gun explained, adding an almost sarcastic emphasis to the name. "He wouldn't have given you a second look."

"Oh," I shifted uncomfortably in my seat. "Well, he also wasn't really my type. My boyfriend's actually really hot. Just so you know. He's Russian and he served in the Russian and the Israeli army. He's still in fantastic shape. So."

Gun just stared at me as if he was trying to assess if I was devious and trying to create a conversational diversion or just cognitively impaired. "What did Aaron tell you?" he finally asked.

If I knew what London had been trying to tell me I wouldn't have to be here. "He thought you were doing things at Nolan-Volz that weren't quite kosher. Particularly when it came to research and development," I improvised. But of course there was *one* thing London had been extremely clear on. I took my wine glass and pushed it a little further away from me. "He also thought that you were poisoning him."

Gun looked at me for ten, twenty, almost thirty excruciating seconds and then he just burst out laughing.

Again, with the villainous laughing. Both Gun and Anita were doing a disservice to their kind with such stereotypical behavior. The only difference between the two laughs was that Anita's sounded a little superior and judgmental. Gun's laugh sounded manic.

I tried to slyly look around the room. *Was* there an actual gun in this place? What were the odds it would be on his person now? I had faced down people with guns before. The last time had been in Vegas with Alex. Alex had been sort of charming about it in a I'm-Not-Really-Going-To-Hurt-You-But-I've-Got-A-Rep-To-Uphold kind of way.

There was nothing charming about Gundrun Volz.

"Nolan-Volz means a lot to me," he said, his laughter subsiding and his face settling back into a scowl. "I have worked my entire career trying to develop drugs that will help people. I want to *help* people. You…you think we're all a bunch of Martin Shkrelis trying to bilk sick, needy people for all their worth. That's not what we're about. That's not what *I'm* about."

"I hadn't even thought of Martin Shkreli," I said, coolly. "Funny that you did."

"You think you're the first outsider who has tried to expose the minor mistakes of my industry and use that to paint us as the enemy of those we serve?" he snapped. "You think that you'll make a name for yourself that way? Rack up a few thousand more Twitter followers? I've dealt with people like you before. I won't allow you to take your fifteen minutes at my expense."

"That NYU professor, the one who exposed the mistakes you made at Orvex, she got a little more than fifteen minutes, didn't she?"

"Those were not my mistakes!" he yelled. "I am not Orvex. She ruined them, *not* me. I co-founded Nolan-Volz because I wanted to show the world that I was *better* than the organizations I used to work for. I'm doing this for the *people*."

"For the people," I repeated, pointedly looking around at our opulent surroundings. "You're like Gandhi in an Armani suit."

"I make a good living, that's true," he leaned forward, fixing me with his glare. "I send my daughter to a top-notch private school. My wife gets to drive her Tesla and take a yearly spiritual journey with the Sherpas of Nepal. I've become a success by helping sick people. Do you have a problem with that?"

"No." I scooted further back in my seat, ready for the lecture on the compassionate nature of the free market. It would be nice if he was working his way up to a confession, but I couldn't imagine he'd make things that easy for me.

"I'm sorry things went wrong for London. That wasn't my fault." I noted little beads of sweat breaking out along Gun's frown lines. "That was *his* fault. I did nothing but support him. When he asked for my help I gave it. That's all." He stood up. For the second time in our brief acquaintance, he purposely loomed over me. "If you think you're going to swoop in here like his avenging angel," he growled, "trying to take me down, trying to take *Nolan-Volz* down, you are not only misguided but also stupid. There is nothing to avenge."

"Aaron London said--"

"I don't give a shit if he told you differently," he interrupted although I had no idea what he thought I was going to say. "Aaron made his own fate. His wife made hers. And I'm making mine now. It would be wise if you chose not to try to stand in the way of that."

"I'm not sure anyone can stand in the way of another's fate," I said, with a wisp of a smile. "Destiny maybe."

"You're not as cute as you think you are."

"That's becoming more obvious to me every day."

"If you walk away from this now, no one will suffer," he said, his voice was low, gravelly with the slightest tremble, a cross between a plea and a growl.

I glanced at my still full glass of wine. "What happens if I don't walk away?"

He didn't respond but I could see him tensing, leaning forward, further into my space.

But he was not very good at this looming thing. His increasingly shiny forehead and the wild look in his eyes undercut his attempt at a threatening demeanor. He looked scared.

But then, people often commit desperate, violent acts when they're scared.

I pushed myself up to my feet. That in itself took some maneuvering since Gundrun didn't budge from where he stood. My hand was firmly on my purse ready to pull out my knife at a moment's notice. There was no more than a foot between Gun and I now. He was about five inches taller than me so even standing I had to lift my chin to meet his eyes. "I hear you, Gun. There's just one problem." I said, managing to keep my voice even and my gaze steady. "The suffering's already begun. Just ask London."

I waited for Gun to reply but he just stared at me, his fists clenching and unclenching. I turned to leave, but he grabbed my arm, hard. My free hand slipped further into my purse and I grasped the handle of the knife. This was it. I would have to defend myself.

But then he let go. I looked over my shoulder as he took a small step back, his face a mess of anger and anxiety. "All you can do is destroy," he said, quietly. "Destroy the people and things I care about. Or you could give it up. The path leading away from this thing could be prosperous, Sophie. Do you understand what I'm saying?"

"I...I'm not sure that I do." I shook my head, confused. "Are you offering me a bribe?"

Gun managed a smile that implied I had interpreted his meaning correctly. "You can do what I do," he went on, "work to help people who need it while profiting in that pursuit. Except for you, there will be no actual work involved. Just... walk away."

I hesitated. I so desperately wanted to know what he was talking about. If we were in the offices of Nolan-Volz I'd stay and try to manipulate the conversation a little more and try to figure all this out. But being here alone with this man in this house...the risks were simply too great. I had to leave quickly.

"Please tell your wife I enjoyed meeting her," I managed before turning and heading for the front door. Gun didn't stop me this time and I left without looking back, wondering if my last words had inadvertently sounded like a threat. And if they had, would Gun respond with one of his own? Or would he skip the threats and just take action?

I walked briskly down the sidewalk, replaying the events of the evening, every once in a while glancing over my shoulder to see if Gun was following me. I was going to have to tell Anatoly about this but...oh God that conversation was *not* going to go well. London was involved in some serious shit. Gun wanted to shut him up and now he wanted to shut *me* up.

I looked over my shoulder again. The streets were unusually quiet. It wasn't very late but this area of Pacific Heights didn't have a lot of night traffic. No pedestrians in sight, only the occasional car going by. The advantage of that was that if Gun *was* following me I'd be able to spot him on the otherwise empty sidewalks. He wasn't following me.

I carefully stuck my hand in my bag, feeling the steel of the blade that was there before carefully taking out my cell. I could see my car now, just a little ways ahead, parked on the other side of the street. I was safe. I dialed up Mary Ann.

"Sophie?" her voice chirped. "What's up?"

"Hey, I think I need to have another real talk with Anatoly and I was just wondering," I said as I started to cross the street, "do you think you could get me that cupcake recipe? I may need it after all."

And that's when a Zipcar came racing around the corner. I screamed, my phone went flying as I leaped out of the way of a car that was clearly aiming for me. I landed between two parked cars, just in time. The first thing to hit the pavement was my forearm, my elbow next, banging against the unforgiving surface. For a second I didn't feel anything, didn't *hear* anything but an odd ringing. And then in one rush, all my senses came back. I could hear the car, way down the street now, then gone. I could feel the pain shooting up my arm and less so the side of my leg that had hit the concrete. I could hear the faint screams of Mary Ann from afar, through my phone as she desperately tried to figure out what was going on. I crawled toward her voice, a good ten feet away.

"Mary Ann," I said, in a strained voice. "I gotta go. I think a Zipcar driving racist may be trying to kill me."

# CHAPTER
TWENTY-FIVE

*"I just want a man who listens to me as intently as my
Amazon Echo."
--Dying To Laugh*

As I walked down the street toward Anatoly's office I attracted my fair share of concerned looks. White had been an incredibly bad idea. My jumpsuit was torn and filthy, complete with bloodstains around the areas where I had skinned my elbow, arm and leg. A few people coming out of the restaurants and bars in the area asked if I needed help. I suppose that was considerate of them, but all I could manage was a scowl and to dismiss them with a few clipped words.

When I did arrive at Anatoly's office, I looked up at it from the street. The lights were on in there, but he had been right about the privacy that was afforded him. From the street, all one could see of his office was the ceiling.

But that didn't mean the man in the baseball cap hadn't been there. It didn't mean there wasn't some evil, mysterious Big-Pharma henchman ready to poison whistleblowers and run down questioners in some sort of capitalistic, homicidal ride-sharing scam.

I crossed the street and climbed the flight of stairs, feeling nothing other than pain, anger and a sense of complete intolerance. Intolerance for any more bullshit. I flung open the door to Anatoly's office without knocking and found him behind his desk staring at his computer. He looked up surprised. Then his eyes went over my fucked up ensemble. "Another squirrel?" he asked.

"Aaron London was murdered." I slammed the door behind me for emphasis.

Anatoly let out a loud sigh. "I won't have this conversation with you again."

I walked across the office and shoved my bruised, scraped up arm in his face. "Aaron London was murdered," I repeated. "And the person who did it just tried to murder me."

Anatoly stared at my arm and then looked up at me. "They tried to kill you just now?" he asked, a little too skeptically for my taste.

"They tried to run me down in the street!" I snapped.

Anatoly's expression cycled through skeptical to shock to darkly angry. "Someone tried to run you over with their car?" he asked in the tone you would expect from a man on the verge of morphing into the Hulk. "Did you get a look at the driver? Do you know who it was?"

"I didn't see the driver and before you ask, no, I didn't get a look at the plates. But I did get a look at the car."

Anatoly stood up and took my arm gently in his hands, examining my wounds. "What kind of car was it?"

"It was a Zipcar."

He abruptly looked up, meeting my eyes, checking to see if I was serious. But *oh my God*, was I serious.

"I went to see Gundrun Volz. I told you I had posed as a reporter before. Well, he wanted to meet again so I went. Maybe I shouldn't have, but I did."

"You met him at Nolan-Volz...just now?" he asked, looking up at the wall clock. "At this time?"

"I met him at his house."

Anatoly's eyes zoomed back to me. Then he cursed in Russian and let go of my arm before walking to the window and staring down at the well lit, bustling street. "You know how irresponsible that was, don't you?"

"Yeah, well, I was feeling a little desperate. I needed information and my P.I. boyfriend wouldn't help me get it."

Anatoly turned back around and gave me a warning look.

"Okay, fine, that, was unfair," I grumbled. "I know it was stupid. But his wife was there, at least for part of the meeting and then she left and *then* he told me that I needed to walk away from this or people would suffer."

"Walk away from what?" Anatoly asked

"Are you fucking kidding me right now?" I shouted, not even trying to restrain my frustration. "You know damn well what he wants me to walk away from! I've been telling you about this for days but you won't listen!"

"Okay," Anatoly said, holding up his hands in a request for patience. But my patience had run out.

"Less than ten minutes after I left Gun's house someone was trying to turn me into road kill! This asshole with his super villain name and overly bleached teeth thinks London gave me information that could mess him up. I think it has something to do with Nolan-Volz...probably with the drug they're testing now, this Sobexsol thing. But really, who the hell knows? What's clear is Aaron London wasn't as crazy as we thought he was. His death was not simple or straight-forward. He came to us for help because he *actually needed help!*"

Anatoly stood there, stock still as he took this in. Then he slowly pivoted back to the window. I stood there, cradling my arm, waiting, breathing a little too hard as I tried to resist the temptation to go into full tantrum mode. Yes, I had put myself into a ridiculously dangerous situation and maybe I had overestimated what I could handle but I would *not* stand here and let Anatoly deny the obvious for another second!

The lights of the street flicked and danced, making the window a little lighter one moment then darker the next. Anatoly remained unmoving, a statue against the backdrop of the low-budget light show. The sound insulation in here was good but I could still hear the dim noise of the cars in the area, the occasional honk, the faint peal of drunken laughter.

As Anatoly remained silent and still my frustration start-ed to wane. I looked around the office, uncertainly. "Anatoly, what are you thinking?"

He said something in Russian.

"English please." I switched the position of my arm, holding it over my head, hoping that elevation would blunt the pain.

"I made a mistake," he explained simply. "He came in here, ill, possibly suffering from the effects of poison, some-thing I, having lived in Russia and having been associated with the Russian mafia, should have recognized. He asked for my help. He told me he was dying and I…simply sent him away. I sent him away to die."

The admission, one that I had thought I had come to terms with on my own days ago, knocked the wind out of me. "Anatoly…" I began, but for once I didn't know what to say.

He pivoted toward me and he looked…well… devastated. I'm not sure I had ever actually seen Anatoly look devastated before. "You were right," he said. "I was in denial."

I bit down on my lip and studied my shoes. "I'm sorry," I mumbled. "I've always been a big fan of denial. Maybe I shouldn't have taken that away from you."

"His story didn't seem to add up. On the face of it, it didn't make sense." He looked past me, seeing something I couldn't, a memory perhaps, maybe even the memory of London, how he had looked standing in that doorway, weak, sick, hopeful. "But I've heard more outrageous stories that had a lot of truth to them."

"We couldn't have saved his life," I said, with begrudging tenderness. Now that he was facing up to things I wanted to tend to the wound not pour salt in it.

"I'm a good judge of character. That's always been true. I don't make these kinds of mistakes…at least I didn't until now."

"Well, to be fair," I said, shuffling my feet a bit, "when we first met you did think I might be a serial killer."

"That was different," Anatoly said, waving off the reminder.

"Why?"

"Because," he paused as he tried to come up with an excuse for that one. After a moment he just shook his head. "There were extenuating circumstances, that's all. And you thought I was a serial killer too," he reminded me.

"Yeah, I did. I occasionally make bad judgment calls, just like you." I sat down in the chair before his desk, still keeping my arm raised above my head. "I mean, come on, you gotta know that *everybody* thinks they're a great judge of character, right? Everybody who used to like Bill Cosby thought they were a great judge of character."

Anatoly didn't respond but I thought I saw a wisp of a smile pulling gently at the corners of his mouth. "From what I can tell, the only truly good judges of character are dogs," I continued. "If we all listened to our dogs more we'd be able to consistently make solid judgment calls about the people we meet in our day to day life."

"What about cats?" he asked. His smile, while small, was now clearly visible.

"Cats will throw you under the bus for sneezing the wrong way. If we listened to cats, we'd hate everybody."

Anatoly pulled out the chair behind his desk and sat across from me. "I didn't believe you," he said. "I wasn't listening."

"To be fair, I was kind of acting like a crazy person," I countered.

"Things are going to change now," he assured me, leaning forward in his seat. "I'm going to get the information on Anita London and Gundrun Volz. I'm going to figure out what they did to London, if anything, and why."

"Thank God."

"And that means," he continued, "you can now back off from this whole thing."

"Right...wait, what?" I cocked my head to the side so that it rested just below my raised, sore elbow.

Anatoly eyed my arm. I must have looked like a child desperate to be called on by her teacher. "Let's see what we can do about that." He opened the bottom drawer of his desk and pulled out a first aid kit before walking around and gently taking my arm in his hand again to examine it. "You can move your fingers, right?"

I wiggled my fingers in a little demonstration of their considerable abilities.

He smiled and leaning back against his desk before swiping an alcohol pad he had retrieved from his kit against my scrapes and scratches.

"Ow, God! That stings!" I hissed through gritted teeth.

"But you're tough," he reminded me.

"The toughest," I agreed, wincing again. "What were you trying to say before?"

"I'm going to investigate London's death." He tossed the wipe into the trash. "You don't need to anymore. Leave it to me and I won't let you down this time."

"Oh, okay, sure," I said with a giggle. It was kind of nice that Anatoly could joke about all this.

"It's obviously gotten too dangerous." He pulled out the Neosporin. "But I promise, I will figure out exactly what happened to Aaron London. You don't have to do anything."

I studied his face for a moment. There was sincerity, concern, but no humor in it. I immediately pulled away and got up from my chair. "You're serious? You really think I put myself through this hell just so I could let a big strong man step in and finish the job for me?"

"Sophie, you were almost killed today." He dropped the Neosporin back into the kit. "Someone delivered a threatening message to our front door and that message wasn't directed at us, it was directed at *you*. You're the one in danger now. You're the one who needs protecting. And I *will* protect you. But you have to help me by taking a very big step back."

"The only place I'm stepping is up!" I put my hands on my hip. God, my arm really stung but I didn't allow myself to grimace. I was improving on my tough act by the second. "When London first walked into this office you were pissed at me for inserting myself into the case. But then you *tossed* the case. *I'm* the one who picked it up. It's mine now. I'm inviting you to help out--"

"Inviting me?" Anatoly asked, incredulously. "You've been insisting on it for days."

"I've been *insisting* that you acknowledge that I'm not crazy."

Anatoly lifted his eyebrows.

"I mean that I'm not crazy for thinking London was murdered," I clarified. "And now that you've finally figured that out you're welcome to help me navigate this thing. But it's my ass in the driver's seat. And you do not fuck with the driver while she is driving. Got it?"

"You're suggesting I sit back and let you put yourself in harm's way?" He shook his head and cut a large strip of gauze from the roll he had in his kit. "You know me better." He tore off two pieces of medical tape, stepped forward and grabbed my arm, yanking it in front of me.

"Damn it, Anatoly, that hurts!"

He pressed the gauze against my wound and impatiently taped it down. "You got lucky tonight. We're not going to rely on luck. We're going to be practical."

"I'm sorry, have we met?" I snarked. "My name is Sophie Katz and I am not a practical person. I'm an *interesting* person. I'm a person who gets things done, the things that boring, practical people refuse to do!"

The gauze and tape were now firmly in place but he didn't let go of my arm. "If I have to lock you in our room, I'll do it. You are not going to get yourself killed."

Patronizing. The very word makes me feel violent and being on the receiving end of it makes me close to homicidal. But I checked myself, preserving my dignity as I stood up a little straighter. I rolled my shoulders back and looked directly into his eyes. "You're not the boss of me."

"I'm not the…" Anatoly blinked a few times in disbelief. "Are you twelve?"

"Do I *look* twelve?" I snapped.

"No." He stared at me, his eyes moving over my messed up outfit, my still fabulous, but undoubtedly tussled hair… and then to my lips.

It took about two seconds for us to move from the middle of the room to his desk, where papers and the first aid kit were immediately shoved to the floor, a small tube of Neosporin rolled along the bleached hardwood surface. My stinging arm wrapped around his neck, his hands moved up and down my back, one moved under my shirt, grasping my waist, the other placing delicious pressure against my upper thigh.

"Wait, wait, wait," I put my hand up between us and Anatoly pulled back, confused and concerned. The golden lighting of the room gave his jet-black hair an almost supernatural dark glow.

"What is it?" he asked. His Russian accent was now every bit as thick as the low hanging San Francisco fog.

"Did I hurt you?"

"No, I just…" I reached out and held his face in my hands and stared deep into those big brown eyes, searching for the courage to ask the crucial question. "Do you think… I'm as cute as I think I am?"

For a moment he fell silent. The only detectable sound was the low humming song of the street. Cars, people, distant sirens, all a backdrop to our quiet breathing. And then, finally, he spoke. "Is that a serious question?" He pulled back another inch so he could better examine my expression. "Your charm is that you are even cuter than you are infuriating. And Sophie," his voice dropped to a seductive murmur, "you can't begin to fathom how infuriating you are."

I gave a curt, satisfied nod. "Okay, let's have sex now."

And with that his mouth was pressed up against mine again, his tongue tasting me as his fingers deftly unfastened the button on my jeans. I leaned back as he pulled them off then drew me to him so there wasn't a centimeter of space between us. I felt his desire pressing up against my thigh and I couldn't help but smile. Dena's dildos had nothing on this guy.

His hand moved up my back. When I felt his fingers moving through my hair I gasped. "That's forbidden!"

"Marcus will never know," he murmured as his other hand slipped under the elastic of my panties. And then he had me gasping for another reason. I couldn't catch my breath, I didn't *want* to. All the chaos and frustration and tension of the last few days seemed to be bundled up in this one encounter and I wanted nothing more than the delicious release he offered. His lips found my neck and his fingers found my core and I gently bit down on his shoulder to keep myself from crying out. And just when I thought I couldn't take it anymore he unfastened his own jeans and in an instant, he was inside of me, joined with me. And we were Sophie and Anatoly again. Crazy, passionate, argumentative and absolutely fantastic: that was us, that was now, that was everything. I arched my back and allowed him to support me as he pressed into me again and again. I absorbed his desire for me, his need.

And when he called out my name even as I murmured his in a gasp, that's when I knew he must be right. I was *so* much cuter than I thought I was.

 # CHAPTER
TWENTY-SIX

*"Sex and marriage is like a 7-11. There's not as much
variety as you would find in a bigger store, but if you get
hungry at two in the morning, it's there."*
--Dying To Laugh

Sex is a funny thing. People diminish its importance with
words like, "It's *just* sex." But when sex is *great*, it's monu-
mentally important. People don't forget *great* sex. Once
you've had it your standard for what you expect out of a
relationship completely changes. I've yet to meet anyone
who has ever walked away from a partner with whom they
have *great* sex. I've met people who have left relationships
in which the sex *used* to be great, those troubled alliances in
which the betrayals and irritations has made intimacy an
unfortunate chore rather than an act of desire. But you do not
walk away from a person who can turn your bed into your
own, personal disco inferno.

Where the cynics have it right is that sex doesn't actually
solve problems within relationships. In those moments when
the chemistry feels perfect, the entire relationship feels
perfect. And given the choice between a long, painful con-

versation and a quick intense orgasm the latter will always be the winner. Or at least it will until the problems become more intense than the orgasms. And then what do you do?

Fortunately, sex was not the solitary basis of my relationship with Anatoly. I was reminded of that now as he accompanied me on the long walk back to my car, holding my hand firmly in his, his proximity simultaneously exciting and comforting. No, if anything our foundation was made out of something a little more rare--passion. Heated arguments, hotter sex, a lust for adventure, fiery convictions...it was fantastic. I had once told Anatoly that living with him was like living in Hawai'i Volcanoes National Park. It was beautiful, exciting, primal, smoldering and yes, dangerous.

The most beautiful things in the world are always at least a little out of our control.

We finally reached my car and Anatoly stopped, looking left, then right, scanning the street for Zipcars and men in black hats. "If you're being followed they're being very discreet about it," he noted, speaking the first words since he had button his pants and I had refastened my bra.

The prospect of a discreet stalker wasn't exactly reassuring. But aloud I said, "I'm sure it's fine. I seriously doubt we're being watched."

That was a lie. Not only did I not seriously doubt it, I suspected it. But the truth seemed unwelcome at that moment, as it so often is.

Anatoly smiled wryly. "It's best if you wait here in your car for a little while. Give me time to get to my bike and get home first, just in case there's someone waiting for you there."

"Why don't you call me the minute you get to your bike

and then we can arrive home together," I replied, glancing up at the charcoal grey sky.

He hesitated and then leaned over and gave me a sweet, lingering kiss. "A compromise I can live with." When he pulled away I let myself into my Audi, taking my place behind the wheel.

"You'll wait for my text?" Anatoly asked, insisting on assurance. "I had to park quite a ways from here."

"I'll wait." I watched as he closed my driver's-side door and strode off purposefully down the sidewalk.

I leaned back against my seat and closed my eyes. I wasn't going to step away from this case. I was absolutely sure Anatoly knew that. But I was equally sure he was going to push back against it and make it difficult for me.

My phone vibrated in my bag and I fumbled for it, reluctantly opening my eyes again. The number on the screen was unfamiliar. "Hello?"

"Sophie Katz?" asked the bored, sexy voice of Gundrun Volz's assistant.

Breathe in, breathe out, breathe in, breathe out. "Speaking," I confirmed. I sounded so calm. Like I had no problem being called by the assistant of the man who may have tried to kill me a few hours earlier. As if I didn't have to remind myself on how to breathe while I waited for her to put her dreaded boss on the line.

"Hi," she said, suddenly sounding unsure of herself. "This is Mr. Volz's assistant, Charity. You, um…never gave me that information--"

"Exactly what information does Gun think he's entitled to?" I interrupted.

"Oh no, not Mr. Volz. *Me,*" she corrected. "I was hoping

you might be able to share your hairstylist's information?"

I blinked, taken a bit off guard. "That's...why you're calling?"

"I'm sorry, is it a bad time?" she sounded genuinely apologetic. "I know I'm being pushy. It's not as if you know me. But since I moved here I've been to four different hair-stylists and none of them have really improved my situation."

"Uh-huh." I was still feeling a little disoriented. Tonight I had confronted a potential murderer, been forced to dodge a speeding car, had a knock-down-drag-out with my boyfriend followed by some amazing problem-avoidance-sex and now I was talking about hair. The night was on a weird trajectory.

"My hair's a little different," she was saying. "Not everyone knows how to deal with it. The hair toward the front of my head has these loose, defined curls but the hair on the crown of my head is a frizzy mess and the rest of my hair is so out of control I don't know what it's doing. I...I need help."

She was singing the curly-haired girl's anthem. "Yeah, of course, I get it," I assured her. "Should I just text you..." but I cut myself off. I was being handed a huge opportunity here. This was my chance to talk to this woman about her boss, Dr. Evil. "The thing about my hairstylist," I said, beginning again, "is he's very...in demand. Everyone wants to see him but he obviously can't see everyone."

"Oh." For once her voice sounded more disappointed-sexy than bored-sexy. "I mean, if I have to wait a long time for an appointment, I could do that," she offered.

"Four months?" I asked. "Because that's the average

wait."

"Oh."

"Actually average isn't really right." A couple of giggling teens walked by, adding a muted laugh track to my conversation. "Five months is more like the average." That was probably a stretch but she didn't need to know that.

"Oh.". Each *oh* got a little lower in tone and a little more tragic in inflection.

"You know," I pushed my seat back, stretched out my legs, "I might be able to speed things up for you a bit."

"Really?" She asked. The sound of hope in her voice was the sound of my hook catching.

"Yeah, let me call him. He's a really close friend of mine and we have plans to hang out tomorrow night." That was another fib. "But maybe I could just hang out with him in the salon while he does your hair?"

"Wait…do you mean you think you can get me in to see him tomorrow night?" she asked, excited now.

"Would that work for you?"

The answer was a clear and definitive yes. Less than one minute after getting off the phone with her I called Marcus.

"I can't help you," he said emphatically as soon as I explained the situation.

"Yes you can." My phone made a little buzzing sound and I pulled it away to see I had a text from Anatoly telling me I should wait another five minutes before heading home. *How far away had the man parked?* I could have been curled up on my couch by now.

"Sophie, I'm not just booked, I'm overbooked," Marcus explained. "Everybody wants to get their hair done for their holiday parties. And I'm not going to stay late into the night to tame some stranger's curls. I have a life."

"Marcus, you are the one who pushed me into looking into London's death," I pointed out, banging my palm against the steering wheel. "It's because I took your advice that Anatoly and I have been arguing non-stop."

"In that case you should be thanking me. I know how much you like your make-up sex."

"And it's because I've been investigating this thing," I continued, ignoring his snark, "that I was almost killed tonight."

There was a long silence on the phone as a bicyclist zipped past my car. "You want to run that one by me again?" Marcus finally asked.

"Today I went to Gundrun Volz's home--" I began.

"I'm sorry, you *what*?"

"He invited me there," I explained. "He wanted to thank me for the article I did about him in the Chronicle."

"But you didn't do an article on him for the Chronicle... did you?" he asked, sounding really confused now.

"No, I didn't but he didn't necessarily know that and he said he thought I did and I didn't realize that he knew I didn't until I got to his house which he invited me to in order to thank me for writing the article."

"Wait--"

"And then ten minutes after I *left* his house," I went on, thoroughly done with waiting, "a car, a *Zipcar* no less, tried to run me down. Seriously, it turned the corner, aimed and then barreled right toward me. It was pure luck that I was able to get out of the way in time."

"Oh my God," he whispered. I relaxed a little bit. *Oh my God* was the right reaction. He would help me now.

"So that's why I'm asking you to see Gun's assistant after hours," I explained as I pulled onto the street. "I need you to clip her hair so I can pick her brain. Is your answer still no? Say it's not."

"It's not," Marcus said, definitively.

I sighed in relief.

"It's *hell* no," Marcus finished.

"*What*?" The brake lights of the car in front of me flashed, blinking a red warning.

"Honey, I know I'm the one who told you to pursue this thing but that's when I thought you were being crazy. I simply couldn't picture a homicidal, Macbeth quoting, maniac signing up for a Zipcar account."

"You thought I was being *crazy*?"

"Zipcars are just adorable. They should be driven by adorable people!" he explained. "Murderers drive BMWs, Mercedes and Toyota Corollas. That's just the way of the world, or at least it should be."

I gripped the steering wheel a little more tightly. This conversation was *not* going the way I had planned.

"But now that some motherfucking Zipcar enthusiast is trying to commit vehicular homicide…Sophie this thing may actually be *real*."

"*Of course it's real!*" I shouted, banging my palm against the wheel again. "I can't believe you went all motivational-speaker on me without actually believing in the cause you were advocating for!"

"You needed an adventure!" Marcus protested. "I thought this would be a good one, a *safe* one for you! But girlfriend, this London Bridge is falling down so you need to do a U-turn and find a different route to happiness."

"If someone wants me dead I have to stop him." I came to an abrupt stop at an intersection, making my brakes squeal in protest. "You showed me the way into this mess now you're going to help me find the way out. That starts with figuring out what the fuck we can do with this woman's schizophrenic curls. You understand me? You *will* make time for her and you *will* let me sit with you two so I can extract the information I need. And what the hell does Macbeth have to do with any of this?"

"Are you serious? *Confusion hath now made his masterpiece.* It's what that hero guy in Macbeth says when he finds the king dead."

"Oh," I said, taken off guard. "Wow. You're right, that's where that quote comes from. That's just…wow."

"Is that meaningful?" Marcus asked, now sounding more curious than angry.

"Yes," I said, solemnly. "It means you would kill in Shakespearian trivial pursuit and it means you have to agree to see Charity tomorrow night."

"Why does it mean that?"

"It just does!" I insisted. "You now owe me and if you don't come through I will *not* forgive you."

Marcus didn't respond immediately. I waited as I stepped on the gas and accelerated toward home. Finally, when he didn't speak up, I pressed him. "You still there?"

"Yes," he said, irritably. "I'm still here."

"Well then?"

He sighed audibly. "Tell her I don't do relaxers anymore, so if she wants to play it straight I'll introduce her to my friend Supersilk. And no weaves or braids without a regular appointment. I don't have time for that."

"So you're saying…" I waited, holding my breath.

"Yes, fine, I'll see her. I should be done with my last client by six pm tomorrow. You two can come in at seven-thirty. No earlier, I need to make time to feed my body and nourish my soul."

"Oh my God, yes! Thank you, thank you, thank you!"

"Shush, don't thank me for something you strong-armed me into," he said dryly. "And by the way? Even if I didn't agree to this you'd have to forgive me by *your* next hair appointment. It's not like your curls don't suffer from bouts of their own psychosis."

"I love you, Marcus."

"Goodbye, Sophie," he said irritably and hung up.

I was only hundred feet away from my house now. Ana-toly's Harley was already in the driveway and the lights inside the house were on. I parked behind it and then got out to examine it, placing my hand gently on the shimmering black metal. It was cool to the touch. I found myself smiling despite myself. I found him inside, in the living room. A martini had already been made for me and was sitting on the coffee table. He was sitting in the armchair with a beer in his hand and a dog at his feet. Mr. Katz had claimed the entire couch for himself, stretching his back legs over one cushion and his torso over another.

"You've been home awhile," I noted. "If you had called me when you reached your bike, like you said you would, we would have arrived near the same time."

Anatoly smiled and leaned back in his chair, looking a bit like the lord of the manor. "Infuriating, cute and obser-vant. That's a lethal combination."

I situated myself on the far corner of the couch, allowing

Mr. Katz to hold claim to the lion's share. "I assume you walked the perimeters, checked the street for suspicious vehicles, the front step for more notes, checked under our bed for monsters?"

"If there are monsters under our bed I don't think I want to know about it," he demurred then took a swig of his beer. "To the rest of it, I plead guilty."

I thought about that for a moment, turning my face toward the dark window. I could feel Anatoly's eyes on me, sense him tensing, waiting for another fight. I shook my head. "I'm not mad. I can take care of myself. I *will* take care of myself, but it's sweet of you to want to protect me."

"You're the most important person on earth to me," he said quietly. "I'll be damned if anyone keeps me from protecting you, not even *you*."

I turned my eyes back to him. I could tell him again that I wasn't going to step back from the chaos of London's death. I could tell him about Charity. But instead I simply relaxed back into the cushions. "I'm just glad you didn't find anymore secret messages on our doorstep. Cryptic notes, underlined headlines, it's creepy."

"Underlined headlines?" Anatoly asked.

Oh, oops. I glanced down at Mr. Katz, silently asking him why he didn't remind me of what I had and had not yet told Anatoly. "I guess I have something to show you."

Anatoly cocked an eyebrow and took another swig of beer. I walked over to the kitchen where I had left the newspaper and brought it back for Anatoly. I tapped the headline that was underlined. "I just opened up the newspaper and there it was."

Anatoly put the beer bottle down on the end table and

took the newspaper from me. His eyes narrowed as he scanned the article. "But this has nothing to do with London."

"I know that's what it looks like on the surface," I admitted. "But there must be something we're missing. Or maybe it's a coded message? I don't know. I was planning on going back to his apartment to see if I could find anything that would link this story to London but three break-ins to the same place…I'd be pushing my luck." I dropped back down on the couch, startling Mr. Katz. "Everything has gotten so complicated." Anatoly remained quiet, his eyes still running over the length of the article. I reached over and started petting Mr. Katz. "What are you thinking?" I asked.

"I'm thinking that something about this doesn't smell right," he murmured. He shifted slightly in his seat his eyes never leaving the words on the page. I waited for him to further explain but finally he just put the paper down on his knees and shook his head. "I'll look into this tomorrow too. I do have some clients I need to deal with as well. I'll make it another long day. I'll get answers."

"Thank you," I said, simply.

"Sophie I know you don't want to hear this," he leaned forward, keeping firm eye contact, "but I need you to stay home tomorrow. The dog can use the backyard when she needs to go out. I know you feel a sense of ownership over this thing, but you have to lay low until I can figure out what we're dealing with. I won't shut you out," he said with a smile, selling the lie, "but you do have to work with me here."

"You really think that's the only way to go? For me to stay housebound?"

"Only for a day or two. We'll set the alarm, you'll keep your cell on you at all times, you'll be safe. And when I do have a better sense of things you can help me bring it all to a close."

I could *help* him bring it to a close? I started petting Mr. Katz a little more forcefully. But when I spoke my voice was calm, even pleasant. "All right then, Anatoly. Just this once, I'll play it your way."

As if.

CHAPTER
TWENTY-SEVEN

*"I love my curls because they're a reflection of me. I
hate them because I'm an unpredictably temperamental
person."*
--Dying To Laugh

Marcus' salon felt different after hours. Empty, the chairs
around us took on the air of antiques standing along side the
posters of long dead stars. Charity looked different tonight
too, softer and maybe a bit more vulnerable. She sat in Marcus' chair, the apron drawn close around her neck as drips of
water from her hair slowly trickled down along the right side
of her face. Her eyeliner had become slightly smudged and
her lipstick faded. Marcus, on the other hand, looked as
modern and polished as ever as he clipped away at her locks
with his gleaming silver scissors.

"So," Charity said, continuing the conversation we had
been having, "you just left journalism? Not the Chronicle,
but journalism all together?"

"Yeah, the article about Nolan-Volz, that was really
more of an experiment. I didn't even let the reporter I
worked on the piece with add my name to the byline."

This time Marcus actually scoffed. It was a little scoff though and I'm pretty sure Charity took it more as a tsk.

"I write fiction," I went on, distracting her from the scoffing and tsking. "Books mostly. What about you? Do you like working at Nolan-Volz?"

"It's fine," she said, vaguely. "I've been with them for less than a year. I'd *like* to keep working there but who knows if that'll be possible after this merger." She used air quotes around the word *merger.*

"But…it is a merger, isn't it?" I asked.

"More like a takeover," she wrinkled her nose in distaste. "Not a hostile one. Gun is all about it. I think he's ready to walk away and hand over the reins to someone else, which is weird. You'd think he'd want to see this drug he's been working on for six years come to market before bailing."

It *was* odd, particularly since Gun had told me how Nolan-Volz was his way of proving himself to the world after his career had been tainted by the mess at Orvex. And now that his company was coming close to introducing a miracle drug to the world he was looking for a quick exit? It didn't make sense.

Another thing that was odd was Charity herself. My first impression of her had been completely off. I had her pegged as a Bond Girl type. But here, after downing the two glasses of champagne Marcus had offered her and with her high-fashion clothes hidden beneath shapeless nylon, her sophistication had melted away to reveal something else entirely. Her bored-sexy voice now shaped itself around the vocabulary of a typical California beach girl.

Marcus was smiling, seeming to enjoy her company

more than he had anticipated. "Gun and Charity," he mused as he continued to snip. "The odd couple for our times."

Charity laughed with him and started to shake her head but noted the reflection of Marcus' suddenly sour expression. She immediately took the hint and went all-statuesque. I felt an instant connection to the woman.

"The article I wrote was mostly about the merger...or rather, the take-over," I amended, swiveling back and forth in my chair. "That and Gundrun and his career. I didn't get to delve as far into the details of Sobexsol as I would have liked. It sounds like it could be a game changer."

"Could be," Charity acknowledged with a shrug, which she quickly checked after getting another look from Marcus. "Lots of drugs claim to help you get off other drugs. But Sobexsol could conceivably get you off all of them and then some. Of course, it won't help those who are reaching for a bong because their cat just died. But for those who have addictive personalities, people who get addicted to *anything*, drugs, alcohol, gambling, sugar, Sobexsol could be their salvation. It's designed to stop or at least dull those addictive impulses. If Gun could have held out a few more years he could have sold Nolan-Volz for billions."

Whoa. I hadn't fully understood what this drug did before but if it could actually do *that*, game changer didn't quite cover it. Maybe if I took Sobexsol I wouldn't crave coffee and vodka. I made a mental note to never, *ever* betray my besties, Smirnoff and Starbucks, with that usurping whore, Sobexsol.

"I understand the clinical trials are going great," I said to Charity. "Are there any side effects?"

"So far they're pretty mild," Charity said. "A few cases

of mild insomnia, minor hair loss--"

"Hair loss?" I asked. I could see London sitting before me, his palm up filled with the hairs that had fallen from his head.

Look at me. See me dying. You're witnessing my murder.

"*Minor* hair loss, and it's temporary," she emphasized her eyes following a freshly cut lock floating to the ground "But you know, it's early days. We have years more of trials ahead of us before Nolan-Volz can make any definitive claims."

"Can you overdose on this stuff?" Marcus asked. "It would be a cruel irony to overdose on a drug designed to cure you from your addictions."

"Yeah, that would be," Charity laughed. "But of course you can overdose on *anything*. You take too many Tylenol and there's a good chance you'll end up in the ER. But if you take Sobexsol as directed there shouldn't be a problem. At least that's what the *very early* results seem to suggest."

"But, just theoretically, if someone was stupid enough to take too much Sobexsol at once, what would happen?" I asked and then forced a giggle, keeping the mood light. "What could happen if you take too much of an anti-addiction drug? Do you have an irresistible urge to join the Mormon Church?"

Charity smiled sympathetically at my attempt at a joke. "Well, it's designed to alter your neurotransmitter levels so, I don't know, if you take too much it *could* mess with your brain. Apparently a couple of the rats they tested the drug on went a little psycho when they were given really high doses. That's why it took so long for the FDA to agree to let the company move on to trying it on people. But that was before my time at the company. What I know is, if you take the right dose and don't do anything stupid like mix it up with a bunch of other meds that it shouldn't be interacting with, you should be fine."

Could London have been poisoned with toxic levels of the very drug he helped develop? That's some Marie Curie kind of twisted bullshit.

I glanced down at my phone. It was already eight-thirty. We had gotten off to a late start and the three of us had spent the first part of the night chit-chatting about random, totally inconsequential things as I tried to establish a report. Anatoly had told me he would be home around ten, which could mean nine-thirty. I *really* needed to be home when he arrived so it at least looked like I had kept my word.

"It's funny, I did know one other person who worked there a while back," I said, off-handedly. "Did you know a guy named Aaron London?"

Charity let out a groan. "*That* freak? I mean, no offense but he's out of his mind."

"So you did know him," I said with a little smile, looking back up at her. "But I guess he wasn't always like that. At least that's what I've heard."

"Yeah, I've heard that too but I didn't see any evidence of it," Charity replied. "When I got there they had already restricted his lab access. I don't know why they didn't just let him go. Every week he seemed to get a little more hysterical and a lot more disheveled. His wife was already having issues by the time I got my job so maybe that's what pushed him over the edge. I met her once, in my first week of work. She came into the office with him."

"I've met her as well," I said with an encouraging smile.

"What was your impression of her?"

"Um…I guess it's mean to say this now but, she was *weird*, right? I understand she was an addict so that probably explains a lot. They were the perfect dysfunctional pair."

"She was an addict?" I asked surprised.

"That's what I heard. She got hooked on pain meds or something. Would have been nice if she could have hung around long enough to take part in the Sobexsol studies… actually, no. What am I talking about? Family members of Nolan-Volz employees can't take part in those anyway."

I was still stuck on the whole Anita's-an-addict thing. Of course there were a lot of highly functional people walking around this country who secretly huddled up in bathroom stalls doing lines on their lunch breaks. But I couldn't imagine Anita being one of them. Perhaps she had beaten it. "I don't think she needs help anymore," I suggested, cautiously.

Charity's expression changed to one of complete shock. Like I had uttered some kind of blasphemy. Then she forced a little laugh. "You're funny," she said in a polite tone that let me know I definitely wasn't funny…which was good because I wasn't *trying* to be funny.

"Did Gun think London was nuts too?" I asked. I caught Marcus' eye in the mirror. I could tell he was silently cautioning me, *keep it casual. Don't make it an interrogation.*

"Gun *hated* London," Charity's laugh became genuine if a bit rueful. "I have no idea why he kept him on as long as he did. I asked him once and he told me he and London used to be close friends. London's bipolar and…well, I don't know if he stopped taking his medication or what, but he was seriously weird by the time I met him. But I guess it wasn't always that way? So maybe Gun had some lingering loyalty? I really don't know."

I slowly swiveled my chair back and forth. Gundrun had told me he and London had no personal relationship at all.

"A man named Gun being friends with a man named London is almost as improbable as the Charity, Gun thing," Marcus noted. "I swear there are so many ways you could go with this. If he gets a little out of hand you could advocate for Gun control. His wife could say she likes to play with her Gun. If my name was Gun I'd always talk about myself in the third person. Every time I had sex, right before the moment of climax I'd yell, *Gun's ready to shoot*! It would be my trademark."

Charity gave him an odd look and then burst out laughing again.

"Well, he seems like a nice Gun. He's the Gun who tried to help London get back on track," I said, in a rather clumsy attempt to get the conversation back on track.

Charity waggled a perfectly manicured finger at me. "Actually there were many days when I thought Gun was aiming to kill London," she said with a broad smile, still riffing off the theme. I swallowed hard and Marcus narrowed his focus to Charity's hair his mouth pulling itself into a small frown.

But Charity didn't seem to notice the shift in mood. "There was this one day, I got back from some errand Gun had sent me on and I heard Gun in his office *shooting his mouth off* at London."

It was amazing how quickly Gun jokes could get old. Although Charity didn't seem to think so.

"I'm not being fair," she continued. "Most of the yelling

was actually coming from London but still, I heard Gun too. I couldn't make out what they were saying but the *tone*! Gun was *pissed.* I've never heard him go off like that before." She let that land, smiling proudly.

"What was he going off about?" I asked, forcing a smile. "I assume it wasn't about gun rights?" The things I'll do to get information.

Charity laughed again, delighted with our new game. "No, no. At least I don't think so. I couldn't fully hear them. I *think* it might have had something to do with Sobexsol. I did hear them mention *that* a few times. You know the day London was fired they had to actually have him escorted out by security?" she asked, her voice becoming hushed as if Janice Joplin hanging on the wall over there might overhear us.

"Why?" I asked, leaning forward.

"He went from crazy to psycho. His wife had been gone for several months by then and he was in this downward spiral. Gun asked me to deliver some papers to his office and I got there to find that he had pinned a whole bunch of other papers to the wall. Lots of confidential internal documents and memos that really shouldn't have been on display. And some other stuff that…I don't even know what it was. It was like in a movie. And he was ranting to himself, sweating and coughing…it was kind of scary. I went back and told Gun and he just turned white. I didn't know you could lose so much color in the space of a second. And then he just flew past me, sprinted down the hall into London's office. There was more shouting, I think someone actually *threw* something, obviously that would have to have been London who did that since Gun has too much dignity. I heard Gun yell about how much he had risked to help London and his wife…I think he was referring to his decision to keep London on so long. Gun should have fired him *way* earlier. But London wouldn't hear it. Next thing I knew security was running up and literally dragging London, kicking and screaming out of there. It was wild. The craziest thing that's ever happened at Nolan-Volz during my time, that's for sure."

"Wow," I whispered. "From what you're telling me, it sort of amazing Anita didn't leave London sooner, addiction or no."

Charity locked eyes with me in the mirror, her expression puzzled. "Who's Anita?"

Marcus stopped cutting.

I swiveled my chair back and forth again, trying to keep my expression neutral. "Aaron's wife?" I said, casually. "Isn't that her name?"

"I never heard anyone call her that," Charity said, now looking really confused. "Her name was Anne. And she didn't leave him. She's dead. She killed herself nine months ago."

# CHAPTER
TWENTY-EIGHT

"Every great artist must also be a great liar. Slaves to honesty have no imagination."
--Chaos, Desire & A Kick-Ass Cupcake

She's dead. The words kept pounding against the inside of my skull as I drove away from the salon. The woman I had been talking to was not London's wife.

Oh my God, the woman I've been talking to was not London's wife! She showed up at the hospital right after he arrived there. How did she know to come? But of course there's only one way she could have known that.

I decided to take residential side streets home. I was way too distracted to navigate serious traffic. And what about Anita's daughter? Who the hell was that? Robin to her evil Batman? Seriously, what was going on??

Gun lied to me about not knowing anything about London's social life. Anita and Catherine lied to me about their very identities. *Everybody* was lying to me. And they were lying so well! There was a momentary, distracting glare in my rearview mirror as the car behind me went over the speed bump I had gone over a few seconds before, it's headlights bobbing up just long enough to cause a reflective glare.

Anita, Catherine, Gundrun, these people could teach courses to spooks they were so good at subterfuge and deceit. Well, maybe not Gundrun, I kind of knew he was lying but pulling off the whole wife thing? That was a different level.

I turned onto another residential avenue as new ideas and theories bubbled and boiled in my head. Anita had to be the killer. But then it was hard for me to believe Gundrun didn't fit into this picture somehow.

I glanced in my rearview mirror. Nothing behind me but one set of headlights.

The same set of headlights that had been behind me on the last street?

I shook my head and let out a nervous chuckle. *Don't get paranoid. Just because people are lying to you, stalking you and possibly trying to kill you, that doesn't mean you should be paranoid.*

It wasn't a very reassuring line of reasoning. I slowed and turned onto another quiet street, eyes on the rearview.

The other car turned too.

Oh. Shit.

Okay, so I was being followed. By a woman who was impersonating London's wife. Or maybe by Gundrun, or the teenage girl who called herself Cat, or by the man with the black hat. There was no good option among them. I took another turn.

The headlights followed.

Was it a Zipcar? I couldn't tell from this angle, in the dark of night. And really, did I honestly care if I got murdered by a Zipcar driver versus say, a Prius driver? It was really the murdering part that was the problem.

I glanced at my car's clock. It was nine twenty. I could be home in about ten minutes and then maybe, *maybe* Anatoly would be there. Or maybe he wouldn't.

"Shit, shit, shit!" Here I was eager to get home so it would look like I didn't lie to Anatoly (again) about going out but now if I *did* get home before him I could get myself killed. And if I didn't get home before he did…well that might be better because the person following me might be less inclined to kill me if there was a witness around. But then *Anatoly* might kill me. Or at least break-up with me.

Shit, shit, shit, shit!

I stabbed at my car's touch screen and called Dena.

"Not a good time." Her voice sounded even deeper and grittier than normal.

"I'm being followed," I said taking another turn. Oh my God, the headlights kept coming! Why wouldn't they just go away!

"Okay, so here's a thought. Maybe you're *not* being followed. Maybe you're being paranoid. There's a great mental health…er…*spa* in Washington State I'm trying to get Jason to check into. Maybe you should consider it too."

"I don't need a psychiatric ward," I snapped. "Listen to me. Yesterday someone in a Zipcar tried to run me over."

"Wait, what?" Dena asked, her tone suddenly changing. "Are you sure?"

"Of course I'm sure! And here's the kicker, London's wife? Her name's Anne, not Anita and she's been dead for months! I have no idea who the psycho bitch I've been talking to is! And Gundrun basically threatened me, and some freak in a black hat has been following me around.

And one of these people left me a *note*, Dena! Taped to my front door! An anonymous threat! So no, I'm not being paranoid. I'm not being crazy. I. Am. Being. *Followed!*"

There was a ten-second pause on the other end of the line. Finally I heard Dena exhale deeply. "Shit."

"Exactly!" I turned another corner. Oh God, the headlights took the same turn ten seconds later. "What do I do?"

"Um…okay, give me a second, I have to release Jason from his handcuffs."

For a moment I actually forgot about the driver behind me.

"Fuck, where'd I put the key…" I heard her mutter then she stepped further away from the phone. I heard muffled voices on the other end of the line, including what sounded like a note of alarm from Jason immediately followed by a harsh shush from what I presumed to be Dena. "Forget it, he can stay chained up for a little while," she said, coming back to the phone. "This is important."

"Um…okay…if you're sure...what were we talking about again?" I glanced up at my rearview mirror. "Oh, right! Okay, so I could just drive home but if Anatoly's not there--"

"You can't go home!" Dena said urgently. "You'll be leading this asshole right to your house!"

"Right, right, okay. So what do I do?" I had made a bad call with this street. No streetlights whatsoever. Even most of the houses were dark.

"You're in a car, right? Please tell me you're in a car."

"Yeah, I'm in a car. I'm half way between Marcus' salon and my place."

"Go to the police station."

I hesitated for maybe a moment too long.

"Sophie, I know you and the SFPD haven't always been BFFs but you can't be fucking around with this. The only place you can safely go right now is the police station."

"Okay. I really don't want to--"

"Sophie!"

"Right, I'm going to the police station." I thought about it for a moment before asking, "should I Waze it?"

"Don't Waze it," she said, sternly. "The last thing you should be doing right now is taking short-cuts through dark residential streets."

"Um, right, of course not," I choked out. "That would be stupid."

"Yeah, stay on the busy streets. This is one of those times you should be thankful for traffic."

There was not one other car on this dark residential street.

I fumbled for my phone and went to navigation, desperately punching in *police station*.

"Uh-oh," my navigator voice chirped. "It seems you're currently driving. If you are a passenger say or press *Yes*."

"Yes!" I screamed.

"Sophie, are you okay?" Dena asked. "What happened?"

"Nothing I just--"

"I'm sorry, didn't get that," the navigator voice said. "Are you a passenger?"

I was going to die. I was going to die because of the failings of voice recognition software. Siri was literally killing me.

I pressed *Yes* on my screen this time instead of saying it. But I must have not pressed the screen in quite the right way because it went back to the home-screen without any help at all.

I glanced in my rearview mirror. The headlights appeared to be getting closer.

"Dena, if I die I need you to check in on Anatoly from time to time. Same for Mr. Katz and Ms. Dogz. Do not let Anatoly give away Ms. Dogz in his grief."

"You're not going to die and real men don't give away their dogs. Have you figured out where the nearest police station is yet?"

"I'm trying but my navigator isn't being cooperative."

Dena let loose with a series of expletives. "Your navigator is going haywire *now?*! They say all this technology is improving our lives but is it? Is it really? Are we better off than we were ten years ago or just more entitled and exponentially frustrated?"

"Yeah, I really don't have time to do a deep dive into the societal impact of modern technology right now," I said, tersely.

"Okay, right. Sorry. I need you to keep driving, don't slow down and then carefully try to type in the information again."

The headlights were now reflected even brighter in my rearview. I stepped a little harder on the gas, held my breath and tried one more time to get this navigating, hard-of-hearing, virtual bitch to take my typed commands.

"In three hundred feet take a left."

"Yes!" I screamed. "Thank you technology gods. Thank you!"

"Is it keeping you on a busy street?"

"Um…" I turned left as directed. So did the headlights. I

thought I could hear the sound of traffic a little more clearly now. "I think that's in the cards."

Three quick turns later I was on a major...well not major, but not exactly minor, thoroughfare. "I'm on a busy street!" I exclaimed.

"But you have been this whole time, right?" Dena asked suspiciously.

"Um..." I glanced in my rearview mirror. Now there were lots of cars behind me. Was one of them *the* headlights? I still couldn't tell if any of the cars in my rearview were Zipcars.

"Your destination is coming up," my navigator informed me.

"My destination is coming up," I repeated for Dena's benefit. "I'll just pull into the police station and...oh... wait...Dena, what if the police station doesn't have *parking*?"

"Police stations have parking," she said, a little too dismissively.

"*Do they*?" I challenged. "Do they really, Dena? This is San Francisco! Parking is never, ever, ever a given! I could have to drive around the block *slowly* for a half hour with this freak on my tail and...oh look, they have parking."

"Shocker," Dena replied.

I took a sharp turn into the small parking lot behind the station, making my wheels squeal from the sudden change in direction. Not a good look when pulling into a police station. I took another deep breath and claimed the first parking spot I saw, putting my car in park but not turning off the engine.

"Are you there?" Dena asked.

"Yeah," I was looking behind me, waiting to see if anything followed me in.

"Go into the station, Sophie."

"Maybe just being in the parking lot is enough," I said, hopefully.

"Don't be an asshole. Go into the station."

"And tell them what?" I asked. It was a small lot with only a few visitor spots but at the far end, there was a sectioned off area in which the cop cars were plentiful.

"Oh, hmm, let me think…maybe you could tell them that you were being followed." I pulled gently on my seatbelt. Another black and white pulled into the lot. "And if that doesn't peak their interest," she continued, "toss in the fact that someone is leaving threats on your front door and that someone recently tried to kill you. I think the cops will be interested in attempted murder…it's sort of their thing."

"Okay, so about that…"

"Oh for fuck's sake, what is it, Sophie? What aren't you telling me?"

"Nothing, I'm telling you everything. But the note? It said, *be careful, Sophie.* Someone taped it to my door at, like, three in the morning."

"Yeah, okay, sounds pretty threatening to me."

"Uh-huh," I watched a cop and his partner walk into the station. Neither had noted me. "But would you say it's something I could bring to the police and expect them to do… well, anything?"

"No, but coupled with the attempted homicide…"

"A Zipcar almost ran me over and then it took off. I *think* it was blue, but it was dark and it happened fast." I clicked off my navigation, making all the virtual streets and suggested short-cuts disappear with a tap. "Also…I mean, how many near misses are there in San Francisco? I think there's, like, nine hundred pedestrians hit a year here? And almost five hundred hit and runs? I'm going to go in there and say I was almost hit by a car and the driver didn't stop and I think that's suspicious?"

"Sophie, you can't just hang out in the police station's parking lot."

"Can't I?" I asked in a tone that would suggest I was posing a philosophical question. "Maybe--"

Someone tapped on my passenger window. I literally screamed and jerked back, causing my seatbelt to tighten. But it was a cop.

"Sophie? What's going on?" Dena shouted.

"Nothing," I replied apologetically and rolled down the window.

"Ma'am, are you all right?" He had salt and pepper eyebrows, a small gap between his front teeth and skin the color of coffee with a dash of cream. It was the kind of face you wanted to talk to…until you saw that it's attached to a body wearing a uniform.

"Me?" I asked, self-consciously. "I'm fine." I could hear Dena sigh through the Bluetooth speakers.

"We saw you pull in on the cameras a few minutes ago. Were you planning on coming into the station?"

"Planning?" I repeated. "No I…I mean, I didn't originally *plan* on coming here at all--"

"Tell him, Sophie!" Dena snapped.

The salt and pepper eyebrows lifted in surprise. The way he was angled I couldn't quite see his hair, but there was something going on with that. "Who do we got on the line?"

"Dena," Dena said, irritably. "My friend Sophie here

came to your station because another car was following her."

Salt-and-pepper-gap-tooth-man looked at me with new interest. "Someone was tailing you?"

"Yeah," I said, sheepishly. "I guess I just got a little freaked out and figured I'd try coming here."

The cop pulled out a notepad and seemed to be about to jot something down while crouched by the window, then thought better of it. "You want to come out of the car for me? It'd be easier to talk that way."

"Dena, I got to go."

"Text me when you're on your way home."

I hung up and turned off the engine before getting out of the car.

Cornrows. This cop had cornrows. He was like the new Black Ken, all clean cut and representing. "Do you know who was following you?"

I shook my head, he took a note.

"Any chance you got the license plate?"

"No, I mean, I was driving so…"

"Totally understandable. How about the make or model of the car?"

I shook my head again. "It was dark."

"Oh," Officer Cornrows replied. No, *understandable* this time. "How about the color?" he asked hopefully. "Did you happen to notice the color of the vehicle?"

I gave him another head shake. "All I could really make out were headlights. I think they were kind of square-ish in shape. Does that help?"

He put his notepad away and offered me a sympathetic smile. *Of course that didn't help.* "If you see him again, I encourage you to get some of those details. It might be helpful if next time you call us *while* you're driving, that way the 911 operator can direct you and we can pull him over while he's still on your tail."

"*While* I'm driving. Oh, gosh, that makes sense." I was surprised Dena hadn't thought of that.

"There's not a lot I can do for you right now--"

"Can I ask you something?" I interrupted. "If someone put a GPS tracking device on my car, would you be able to find it?"

Officer cornrows blinked, taken a little off guard. "Um, is it visible?"

"I don't think so," I said, slowly, trying to make him understand. "If I knew that I wouldn't need anyone's help trying to find it."

"Right." A couple of other cops came out of the station, talking and laughing loudly. They both gave us a second look but didn't bother to stop as they went to their own cars. Officer Cornrows followed them with his eyes as he considered my question. "Maybe try a mechanic?"

That's what London had said he had been told. "Tell me this then," I asked, "if someone *did* put a GPS tracker on my car, would that be illegal?"

"Huh, let's see. We know car manufacturers do it all the time with their built in GPS systems or emergency road assistance software, rental car companies do it sometimes too with their vehicles and that's definitely on the up and up…"

"So, no then," I finished for him as another cop car pulled into the lot.

"A private citizen doing it?" Officer Cornrows asked, doubtfully. "Maybe." The cop who had just parked got out of his patrol car and gave my officer a friendly wave. "Hey Errol," Cornrows called to his redheaded work-buddy. "Lemme ask you somethin'."

"What's that?" Errol (who the hell names their kid Errol anymore?) lumbered over to us. His steps were heavy, a symptom of his considerable size. Errol was not a man you would want to mess with.

"Is it illegal for a private citizen to put a GPS tracking device on someone else's car?"

"Huh?" he put his hands on his hips and studied the ground as he thought it over. "Well, if they did it without the other person's permission and then used it to, I don't know, follow them around town or somethin' then…maybe it could be used to strengthen a harassment case? Or if it messed up the car I guess you might get them on defamation of private property. I don't think there are any specific laws about GPS though."

Our legal system hasn't caught up with our technology!

Those had been London's words. I had spent that whole meeting rolling my eyes but he was right.

"Thank you," I said, politely, "for your help. I think I should probably head out now."

"If you see that guy again, just give us a call," Officer Cornrows said, a little patronizingly. I suspected he didn't believe anyone had followed me at all. To him, I was just another San Francisco head-case.

And why wouldn't they see me that way? That's exactly what I had thought of London. I was *becoming* London. I stepped back into my car, my mind going to that weird Shakespearian text on London's old phone. I started up the engine, but before I could pull out I heard my own phone chime. A text.

My hand was actually trembling as I pulled my phone from my bag. If the text read *Out, damned spot* I was going to lose it.

But the text was from Dena. I read it. And then I re-read it, and then re-read it again. Her words, while not Shakespeare, were alarming:

Hey Soph, Jason and I have a bit of a situation here. Do you still have that lock-picking kit?

# CHAPTER
TWENTY-NINE

"I'm convinced that the secret ingredient in every per-
fect marriage is a healthy dose of denial."
--Dying To Laugh

Anatoly stood in the foyer, arms folded across his chest as I walked through the front door. Ms. Dogz was on one side of him, Mr. Katz on the other as if he was some sort of Disney hero who had been able to call on his animal friends to help him fight the villain. I had a horrible feeling I was the villain.

"I know--" I began, closing the door behind me.

"Damn you." The words weren't all that indicting in and of themselves. He had said them enough times before. But his tone now, his inflection…it turned the words to ice.

"Anatoly, I had to do this. If you would just listen to what I found out, you--"

"Enough." Ms. Dogz looked up at him with a certain degree of alarm. Mr. Katz simply licked his paw. "Do you not care at all about your word?" he asked. "You'll be forty soon--"

"Low blow," I snapped. "And I'm still a few years away,

thank you very much!"

"At what point do you start acting like an adult?" he went on, almost as if I hadn't spoken. "You have no respect for me, for your own safety, for rational thought--"

"If you would just let me tell you about my night you'd find that I've been exceedingly rational today."

"Rational? I have never met a woman as smart as you who acts so stupidly. You--"

The doorbell rang, cutting Anatoly off and inciting Ms. Dogz to let loose with a series of barks.

Anatoly moved his gaze behind me to the windows on either side of the door. "It's Dena," he said, coolly.

"Oh. Right." I turned and reached for the door that Ms. Dogz was already scrambling at. But before I opened it I paused and looked back over my shoulder. "I know how angry you are right now. I get it and you have the right to be. But for right now...would you mind getting out your lock-picking kit?"

"I'm not contributing to your breaking into any more apartments," he said, a little menacingly.

"Yeah, that's not it." I cracked open the door so as not to let Ms. Dogz out. Dena met my eyes and gave me a what-are-ya-gonna-do smile. Jason was standing a few feet behind her so he couldn't be easily seen from the window. He was wearing jeans, no shirt and a leather jacket draped over his shoulders. His hands were behind his back.

I grabbed Ms. Dogz by the collar and pulled her back as Dena strutted past me in leather boots. Dena was the only person on earth who could still strut with a limp. "I think I accidentally kicked the key into the heating vent," she said. Jason walked (no strutting for him) right behind her looking more irritated than embarrassed.

"What's going on here," Anatoly asked, warily as I closed the door and released the dog.

Dena yanked the jacket from Jason's shoulders and turned him around so Anatoly and I could see the handcuffs that kept his hands in place. Curious, Ms. Dogz went up to sniff them before sniffing Jason's ass.

"I've never had this issue before," she admitted, studying her handy-work. "A lot of the newer cuffs have a safety latch so you can open them without keys if you have to. But this is an old pair so…"

"Oh good God," Anatoly grumbled and turned to go get the picks.

"I assure you, God has nothing to do with these proceedings," Jason called after him with a grin.

Dena stepped a little closer to me and asked in a hushed voice, "How did things go at the police station?"

"I told Dena that was bad advice," Jason interjected before I could answer. "Never, ever get the cops involved. They're just the warrior class of a hierarchical and oppressive societal structure."

"Um, yeah," I glanced briefly over at Jason, "I have no idea what that means." Turning back to Dena I said, "Whoever was following me took off and I didn't get any details on the car. They couldn't help me."

"Fuck," Dena muttered under her breath.

Anatoly returned with the kit in his hands. He walked around Jason. "Let me take a look at the lock." He got down on his knees so his face was eye level to the handcuffs. It also placed him eye level to Jason's ass. "We're not doing it this way," Anatoly said, authoritatively as he quickly got off his knees. "Follow me."

Anatoly turned and walked into the dining room. I tailed him and Dena, Jason, Ms. Dogz and Mr. Katz all tailed after me. Had we a tuba and a baton we could have been our own marching parade with just the gentlest nod toward S&M-love. Anatoly took a seat in a dining chair. Jason walked over and turned his back to him, offering up his chained wrists. It was probably a minor improvement in that Anatoly was no longer on his knees but Jason was still shirtless and handcuffed and his ass was still essentially in Anatoly's face. It was going to take a while before I would be able to scrub that image from my brain.

Jason beamed at me as Anatoly looked through his kit. "So you finally understand that corporate America is trying to kill you."

"Corporate America is not trying to kill me," I replied, taking a seat at the other end of the table. "Anita London, or whatever her real name is, *she's* the one trying to kill me."

"Why do you say that?" Anatoly asked distractedly as he studied the cuffs. He then shook his head and muttered, "I didn't know they made locks like this anymore."

"Like I said, old cuffs," Dena explained taking a seat next to me.

"Tonight I discovered that this Anita London person is not who she claims to be." I glanced over at Anatoly but he only had eyes for the cuffs. "London had a wife but she's *dead*. She committed suicide nine months ago! The person I've been talking to is a fraud!"

"So wait," Jason said, thoughtfully, "how does corporate America figure into all this."

"Oh my God, Jason, it *doesn't*," I snapped. "I don't

know who this woman is but--"

"I know who she is," Anatoly said, calmly as he continued to fiddle with Jason's lock.

"What?" I asked, confused.

"Anita London, I know who she is," he repeated.

I exchanged looks with Jason, then Dena. "Who is she?" I asked.

"She's Anita London," he answered, simply.

I groaned, in no mood for dumb humor.

"I'm serious," he continued. "I've done my research. Her name is Anita Jaynes London, she goes by Anita Jaynes at work. She and Aaron London had been married for twenty-four years."

"No, you're thinking of Ann London," I corrected. "*That's* who Aaron married and she's dead."

"She did go by Ann for a long time," Anatoly noted. "And as far as all her public records are concerned she's very much alive and currently employed with a start-up tech firm…God damn it, who designed this lock?"

"I'm not going to be stuck in here forever am I?" Jason joked, then added, in a more worried tone, "Am I?"

"I can get you out, but it will take a minute," Anatoly growled.

"I don't understand," I began, but the doorbell interrupted me.

Everyone in the room froze with the exception of Ms. Dogz who went running to the door, barking all the way. Mr. Katz blinked once, kitty language for, *only a dog would be stupid enough to volunteer for the front line.*

What was outside my door…at ten o'clock at night, without an invitation?

Anatoly pushed his chair back from Jason's ass. "Let me handle this," he said coolly, getting up to confront whatever danger waited on the front steps.

"I'll come too," Jason volunteered. "I've studied kick-boxing."

"I'll bet on the dog's teeth over your feet." Anatoly turned and strode out of the room, not waiting for further argument.

Dena and I looked at one another. What if it really was someone who had come here to hurt me?

Dena reached deep into her hobo bag and pulled out a rolled up whip.

"First a leash, now a whip, it's like you carry an entire Red Room in your handbag," I whispered, trying to lighten the mood and distract myself from my own mounting anxieties.

But Dena wasn't listening. Slowly, she got up, unfurling the whip before taking a broad stance in front of both Jason and me, ready to defend us. She looked like an action hero from an 80s popcorn flick. Indiana-Dom.

But the first sound we heard from the foyer, aside from Ms. Dogz's incessant barking, was not the blow of a fist, or the cocking of a gun. It was a voice. A happy voice. Mary Ann's voice.

"Is she okay?" I heard her asking. "Is she here?"

Anatoly said something unintelligible and Mary Ann came bursting into the dining room carrying a large, rectangular, yellow, Tupperware container and wearing a huge smile. Ms. Dogz was at her heels eagerly sniffing her jeans. She stopped short as she took in shirtless-Jason with the handcuffs and leather-boots-Dena with the whip. But then she just shrugged. "Okay," she said with cheery dismissiveness. She put the Tupperware down on the table and gave Dena a quick hug. She briefly contemplated giving Jason a hug too but ended up just indulging him with a smile and an awkward wave from two feet away. Apparently embracing shirtless men in handcuffs was a bridge to far.

Of course when it was my turn she rushed over to me and threw her arms around my neck. "You were *followed*?" she said, disbelievingly. "How scary!"

I pulled back. "How'd you know?"

"I texted her," Dena informed me as she folded back up her whip and Anatoly re-entered the room. "It was too crazy not to share."

"I should have called," Mary Ann admitted, "but I just had to check in on you and see for myself that you were okay! Last time I talked to you...I mean you *said* you were okay but that was only after you screamed and I heard the car peeling away."

"Yeah, I probably should have called you back after that," I said, abashedly. Mary Ann pulled up a chair, as if sensing the one to my right was meant for Dena

We both looked over at Anatoly who reclaimed his seat. Jason immediately turned around and backed up into him so Anatoly could continue his rescue mission.

Mary Ann's forehead creased as she studied the two men. "Okay," she finally said, with her trademark cheerfulness, indicating that she thought it best just not to ask.

"Anatoly was telling us he tracked down some information about Anita London but..." I shook my head and turned back to Anatoly. "Don't you think you may be looking at a different Anita London than the one I've been talking to?

You've never seen her."

"I'll happily show you ID shots of her but it doesn't change the fact that a woman named Anita *was* married to Aaron London, they didn't divorce, they have a daughter together, and she's not dead. However, it appears that Anita and Aaron have maintained separate residences for over half a decade." His tools scraped against the metal of the handcuffs as he spoke. "This investigation is less than a day old. Give it more time and I'll find out more details."

"It's only been a day since *you* signed on to this investigation, but I've been working on it for almost a week." Ms. Dogz came over to me and lay down across my feet, a clear sign of solidarity.

"You've been spinning your wheels for almost a week." Anatoly dropped the tool he was using back in the kit and brought out another.

"What are you two even talking about?" Dena snapped, falling back into the chair beside me. "Just put a fucking sign in your front yard saying *Done With This Shit.* Let these crazy people know you won't be poking around anymore and your problems will go away overnight."

"Blasphemy!" Jason shouted. "Sophie has an obligation to expose these corrupt, drug-pushing-overlords to public scrutiny. She has an opportunity here to lead the crusade against Big Pharma and their sinister plans for the failing State of America!"

"The failing State of…" I began but Mary Ann leaped to her feet.

"Guess what I brought everyone!" she exclaimed and hurried over to her Tupperware, opening it to reveal half a dozen cupcakes. A small, sculpted tower of light brown frosting with chocolate sprinkles decorated each one. The cupcake itself was a rich cocoa-brown. "There's six here and five of us," she handed one to me and then one to Dena. "I think the extra one should go to Sophie since she's the one people are trying to kill." She moved over to Jason and Anatoly, handing Anatoly one first. She seemed a little confused about what to do about Jason. "I guess I could..." she extended the cupcake toward his face. Jason opened his mouth eagerly waiting. It was enough to make Mary Ann rethink. "Oh, I have an idea," she said, pulling the cupcake away before Jason could take a bite. "Dena why don't *you* feed him? It'll be like practice for when you feed each other cake at your wedding?"

"We're not getting married," Dena said at the same time Jason declared, "Marriage is a puritanical conceit of a society desperate to create conformity!"

"Um...okay," Mary Ann said, her cheeriness wavering, but only a tad. "I still think maybe Dena should feed you?"

"You want a bite of my cupcake, Jason?" Dena asked, uncrossing her legs and spreading them wide, holding her cupcake right in front of her crotch.

"Okay, eww, no." Mary Ann shook her head vigorously, showing the first signs of irritation.

I smiled and took a bite of my cupcake. "Oh my God," I exclaimed my mouth still filled with rich chocolate cake and the surprise of a creamy ganache filling. "This is insane!"

Anatoly and Dena exchanged looks and then both took a bite of their own cupcake.

Anatoly's eyes widened. "Wow."

"You *made* these?" Dena asked.

"Yes?" Mary Ann responded, uncertainly.

"You are going to be a great fucking mom," Dena replied taking another bite.

"Hey, I'm being left out here," Jason complained as Anatoly tried yet another pick on the lock...

...and it worked. The handcuffs came loose, dropping to the floor as Anatoly unfastened them.

"Holy shit," Dena leaned forward, pressing her forearms across the top of her knees. "One bite of Mary Ann's magical cupcake and you were able to free Jason."

Jason was rubbing his wrists where they had chaffed against the metal. "Thanks man, I owe you."

"Yes you do," Anatoly said with a breath of relief. He pushed himself away from Jason's butt once and for all and started back in on his cupcake. Jason, now free to feed himself took the cupcake Mary Ann offered.

For a few seconds, we all fell silent as we nibbled away. Eventually I looked up at Anatoly again. "I haven't been spinning my wheels," I said, trying not to sound petulant.

"No," Anatoly agreed with a sigh, before taking another bite. "That was overly harsh. I just wish you would try to proceed with some modest degree of caution."

"Fair enough," I mumbled, my mouth full again.

"If you two insist on pursuing this," Dena interjected, "maybe you could just be a little more discreet about it?"

"Maybe, *maybe* it's not corporate America trying to kill you personally," Jason finally admitted as he munched away. "It could just be one corporation this time. I'm willing to give you that."

Oh my God! This is what Mary Ann had been talking about! It really is impossible to be a bitch when you're eating a great cupcake!

"It would be helpful if I could find out London's stated cause of death," Anatoly mused. "Anita told you it was congestive heart failure but she hasn't published an obituary yet and while I'm sure the hospital filed a death certificate it's unlikely to be available for a while."

I let out a frustrated sigh and looked down at my cupcake. Of course we couldn't take Anita's word on cause of death, I couldn't even take her word for being Anita. Charity had been *certain* London's wife had died. She had been working with him when it happened for God's sake. So many things weren't adding up. Speaking of which… "What about the underlined headline?" I asked.

Dena, Jason and Mary Ann all looked at me. I hadn't told any of them about that headline.

Anatoly's face darkened even as he took his final bite of the cupcake. "I'm following up on that," he said, cryptically.

There was something about Anatoly's tone. It invited no questions but also filled me with a vague sense of dread.

"What are we talking about here?" Dena asked, picking up on a shift in mood.

I hesitated and then shook my head. "Nothing, it was just a headline about Nolan-Volz being absorbed by a bigger company."

"I'm the one who told you about that headline," Jason mumbled through a mouth full of cupcake. "I don't get what you mean when you say it was underlined."

I shifted uncomfortably in my seat. "It's a figure of speech," I finally said. "I just meant, it was important."

Dena gave me a look. She was one of the few people who could almost always tell when I was lying. I gave a subtle shake of my head, indicating that now wasn't the time. For reasons I couldn't explain it suddenly felt like an issue that needed to be dealt with more sensitively than the rest.

"I appreciate all of your concern," I said, carefully. "And Mary Ann, these cupcakes are beyond belief. But...it's been a very long day and I'm more than a little exhausted." I looked up at my friends, silently asking for understanding.

Dena gave me a nod and pulled herself to her feet. "Time to call it a night, guys." She walked over to Jason and linked her arm with his.

Mary Ann got to her feet as well. "I'll emailed you the recipe for the cupcakes," she said, helpfully as I stood up to give her a hug goodbye.

"I'll use it," I said definitively. "I'll walk you guys out."

"Thanks again for helping me escape my chains of servitude," Jason called back to Anatoly as Ms. Dogz and I escorted our guests to the door. Under her breath I heard Dena mutter, "You *love* servitude."

Mary Ann gave everyone another quick hug before trotting down to her car. Ms. Dogz sat on the porch looking after her. Funny, the dog was new to this house and yet she never tried to run away from it.

Dena held back a moment. "Meet me in the car, okay Jason?" she asked as she handed him the keys.

He hesitated a moment but then nodded leaving the two of us alone.

"You can't break up with him yet," I said as I watched him go. "It would be cruel to break-up with a man within twenty-four hours of chaining him up."

"I'm not breaking up with him...at least not tonight," Dena said with a sigh. "Probably not tomorrow either, or anytime soon…then again…oh, who knows?"

"I'm sorry," I said, leaning against the door frame. "I'm so sorry I complicated things between the two of you."

Dena gave me a half smile that seemed to be infused with both forgiveness and weariness. She shifted her gaze to where her car was parked. The headlights were off but you could see the faint glow of Jason's cell as he fiddled with it from his place in the passenger seat. "It's frustrating how someone can be so perfect for you in some ways and so totally wrong for you in others," she noted.

"You still think Jason and I are being paranoid conspiracy theorists?"

"I think what *you're* doing, asking potentially violent people provocative questions is…well, it's a bad idea," she said, thoughtfully. "But you're not seeing things that aren't there or buying into crazy conspiracy theories the way he does." She nodded toward her car. "They need a new dating app, one where dominant chicks like me can find men who are both submissive and grounded in reality."

"Sounds like a winning pitch for the next tech expo," I suggested, smiling.

Dena allowed herself a small smile as she turned her gaze up to the night sky. "So what's next?"

"London's daughter said she'd meet with me tomorrow, probably here although I haven't heard from her since she said she would." A white moth flew toward my face and I impatiently swatted it away. "I don't understand what's going on," I admitted. "Charity was very clear, Aaron London's wife is dead. And when I match that theory up with the things Gun told me it kind of makes sense. Gun never actually said London's wife left him. He said he *lost* her. But then

Anatoly found all these records that say otherwise, so..." I shook my head. There were no obvious answers.

Dena let out a humorless laugh. "It would appear that not making sense is the one consistent characteristic of both Aaron London's life and death."

"Yeah." I agreed with a sigh. Ms. Dogz who was still on the porch turned back to me and cocked her head to the side.

"How are things with you and Anatoly?"

I looked away, suddenly feeling teary. "I've been screwing up," I admitted. "I...I don't know why I keep pushing him. I know I need to talk to him, but it's just been so hard."

"Try talking to him again now," Dena suggested, "while you're both still under the spell of the magical cupcake. As for the rest of it," she reached forward and squeezed my hand, "just be careful, Sophie, okay?"

"I'll be careful," I said although I wasn't sure I even knew what that meant anymore.

Dena's tight-lipped smile let me know that she knew the worth of that promise. She headed down the porch steps and started walking toward the sidewalk but then stopped and looked back at me. "Maybe my problems with Jason can be solved if I just add another guy to the mix. It's been a while since we've done a three-some. If Anatoly has any friends who might be game, let me know."

I watched her go, wondering how many problems had been worked out through ménage a trois'. Even when things between Anatoly and me weren't perfect I never wanted anyone else...except maybe Dwayne Johnson. If I thought The Rock was available for a three-way, I might have to make the pitch to Anatoly.

When I came back, I found Anatoly still at the dining

table, his now empty cupcake wrapper crinkled up in his hand, eying the last remaining cupcake the way…well, the way I usually eye pictures of Dwayne Johnson.

"I know what you're longing for," I teased him.

He dragged his eyes away and smiled up at me. "I've been told that one's yours because you're the one people are trying to kill." His smile faded a little. "I'm not going to let that happen. You know that."

I disappeared into the kitchen and then came back with a butter knife and cut the cupcake in half. "I'm glad you still want to keep me alive." I handed him half.

He gently took my offering and lifted it as if toasting me. I returned the gesture with my own half-a-cupcake and bit into it the same time he did. "You haven't been forthcoming with me lately," Anatoly said after a moment of chewing. He angled himself to face me. "You've misled me…occasionally lied to me."

I flinched but said nothing.

"I've been secretive with you as well…in the past," Anatoly continued. "How many years had we been together before I told you I had an estranged wife? That I had once been part of the Russian mafia? I told myself I was protecting you but instead my secrets put you in danger."

"Yeah, but that's all over now," I said with a shrug, my mind briefly touching memories of our tumultuous trip to Vegas before coming back to the crisis at hand.

"Is it?"

There was a touch of insecurity in his voice. Anatoly was never, *ever* insecure. I looked up into his eyes, trying to read his thoughts. "Is there more?" I asked, warily. "Are you still keeping a secret from me?"

"Only that I knew…I *know* that had you chosen to leave me over those secrets it would have been understandable. I knew when we came back here I had a lot to make up to you."

This was a confusing conversation. Anatoly's secrets had been exposed years ago. And yes, it was because of those secrets that I had faced some danger in Vegas and it's what had brought Alex Kinsky temporarily into my world. But none of that had any relevance to what was going on right now.

"You were right, I was in denial about London," he continued. "Am I also in denial about us?"

I blanched, the words hitting me hard.

"After we got back from Vegas I thought you and I had reached a good place. We weren't arguing anymore. We were being more open with one another. We seemed to be approaching a kind of stability I've never had with anyone." He leaned forward, his eyes searching mine. "And now you seem intent on taking us backward."

I pressed the palm of my hands into my legs. "I haven't been writing," I whispered.

He hesitated, his eyes lowering to the floor as if looking directly at me after such a confession was somehow disrespectful.. "I've wondered about that," he finally said. "I didn't want to ask or interfere with your process. And I'm sure the challenge of moving on from Alicia Bright is harder than it may seem to the outside world."

He *had* known. He did see me and yet in some very important ways, he apparently still didn't get me

"I hate stability," I said, quietly. "I can't abide *safety.* This peace you're trying to bring into our home is destroying us."

Anatoly gave me a wry smile. "Most people like peace."

"We're not most people. It's not coincidence that we've spent most of our years together arguing. It's not a flaw in our relationship, it *is* our relationship. I mean, okay, fine, you should have told me about your past. You seriously screwed up on that one. But you can't change all the rules just because you took the game too far one time. I *like* that we've been arguing again lately…we just need to learn to keep those arguments within certain confines. We need the heat of the conflict without the venom. A relatively high degree of chaos works for us. How could you think otherwise?"

"We've been together almost a decade now," Anatoly said, sounding worrisomely tired. "In that time we've both aged and possibly matured. Is it unreasonable that we might outgrow our taste for madness?"

I didn't want to have this conversation anymore. I didn't even know how to process it. Of course I knew one sure (and highly enjoyable) way out of it. My wince turned into a sly smile as he lifted his eyes back to mine. "If you want to slow down with age that's on you. Me?" I got up and eased myself onto his lap, wrapping my arms around his neck. "I'm clinging to the recklessness of my youth."

Anatoly's hand moved to my waist, the other to my thigh. I expected him to lean in and kiss me but he kept me waiting, his eyes moving over me. When he finally made eye contact again I thought I saw a touch of sadness. But it was then that he leaned in, his lips brushing against mine as he pulled me to him.

When he finally pulled back his expression was serious.

"Tell me," he said, his voice low, "what do you think happens when you build a house on lava?"

I bit down on my lower lip and let my hand move down his shirt, to the button on his jeans, lower still until I cupped him, feeling him harden and the denim fabric strain. "I can't say for sure," I said, softly. "My guess is things get really hot."

Anatoly laughed and brought his mouth to the nape of my neck. He whispered something in Russian against my skin. I didn't understand the words, but if I had to guess I'd say they translated into *you're impossible.*

CHAPTER
THIRTY

"Sunrises are the sunsets of masochists."
--Dying To Laugh

When I opened my eyes the next morning Anatoly was crouched by the bed, his hand on my shoulder as he gently shook me awake. Shades of pink had slipped around the corners of our window shades giving everything a romantic glow. Mr. Katz was still at the foot of the bed, Ms. Dogz sitting in the doorway, a little bit of dog food on her nose making it clear that Anatoly had already fed her. I stared at the light through heavy lids. "We don't get up until all the pretty colors in the sky are all gone," I grumbled.

Anatoly smiled and kissed my cheek. "You can go back to sleep if you like. I need to get an early start on the day. There's a lot I need to figure out. I don't suppose there's any chance you're going to stay home today."

I hesitated and then gave a small shake of my head... small because it's very hard to shake your head without physically removing it from your pillow.

"That's what I thought," he sighed and then right on top of the bed where my right hand clutched the sheets, he lay down our gun.

Immediately I was sitting up, the sight of loaded steel in my bed having the effect of downing ten cups of coffee all at once. Mr. Katz lifted his head long enough to glare at me then immediately went back to sleep. Mr. Katz was very laisssez-faire about guns.

"Keep it on you," Anatoly explained. "It's the responsibility of those who covet danger to also prepare for it."

"I don't plan on coveting *that* much danger." But then I thought about the note left on our door, then the Zipcar that had almost killed me. I took the gun in my hand. "I'll keep it on me."

"Thank you," Anatoly sighed in relief. He got up and turned to leave.

"Anatoly?"

He stopped and turned back, raising his eyebrows expectantly.

"Is there something you're not telling *me*?"

He looked at me, seemingly confused. "Like what?"

"Like about that guy who was killed in Golden Gate Park?"

His expression darkened. "Ah…it looks like that might have been gang related. The victim had tattoos that indicate he might have been part of a gang. It doesn't fit with anything we've learned about London but…it's important," he said, almost more to himself than to me. He turned to leave.

"Anatoly," I said, stopping him. "Any chance it's a gang you're familiar with?"

He paused a moment too long then said over his shoulder "The Russian mafia has had dealing with them in the past, back when I was working with them. But that was a long time ago. In and of itself it doesn't mean anything. Regardless, it's one of the things I'll be looking into today." He started to leave again.

"Anatoly?"

He laughed softly and turned back around again. "Yes?"

"Gundrun Volz's assistant remembers London well. She…she was *so* sure his wife had died. And Gun didn't even think London *had* a daughter. I'm not questioning the results of your research…but I tried to find Catherine online and…" I shook my head. "What kind of teenager doesn't have any social media accounts?"

Anatoly reached into his pocket and pulled out his phone. He tapped the Facebook app, typed something in and then handed it over. There was a profile picture of Catherine on a private account. Her thick blonde hair hung over her shoulders and she wore a Victorian style nightgown as she stood in the middle of a stage, her arm flung out as she seemed to stare out at an audience. The name on her profile was Cat Jaynes.

"She's on Instagram too, although both accounts are set to private," Anatoly said. "Her legal name *is* Catherine London but on her social media..." he gestured to the screen rather than finish his sentence. "That's why you couldn't find her."

"I am such an idiot," I said, quietly. "Every time I talked to her she referred to herself as *Cat*. Although I wouldn't have known to look for her under her mother's maiden name." I stared at the picture for a few more seconds. So she was really London's daughter. But why didn't anyone know about her? "She wants to meet," I said, quietly. "I invited her to come here."

Anatoly smiled. "Nice of you to volunteer that without my prying it out of you. I'll come home for that. What time?"

"I don't know, she never called me back to firm up the details and I haven't been able to reach her since she proposed the meeting."

Anatoly's eyes narrowed with suspicion.

"I swear, I'm not keeping anything from you," I said, stifling a yawn. "She may be blowing me off…she's probably blowing me off. But if she does call me back, I'll tell you, okay? If you promise not to try to control me I promise not to try to keep you in the dark about what's going on. Fair?"

Anatoly's mouth twisted into an amused grin. "Control you? It would be easier to control a hurricane. There's coffee waiting downstairs."

"Have I told you lately that I love you?"

He didn't say anything but I could see the reciprocation in his eyes, right before he turned once again to leave. Ms. Dogz trotted after him, determined to see him out. Anatoly must have almost been at the top of the stairs when he called back to me, "Keep it on you."

I reached out and let my fingers trace the ridges of the handgun. "I will," I said softly although I knew he wouldn't be able to hear me. I wouldn't use it of course, but it did feel good to have it there.

I sighed and lay back down against the pillow, listening to the front door open and then close. It was so early but now I was so awake. How to use the time?

Eventually I convinced myself to get out from underneath the covers. With both Mr. Katz and Ms. Dogz tailing behind me I went to the kitchen and poured myself a cup of coffee.

"Why do you think Cat is using her mother's maiden name?" I asked Mr. Katz.

Mr. Katz walked over to his food bowl and swished his tail letting me know that my questions were not his priority. I ushered Ms. Dogz into the backyard and then got the kitty kibble out of the pantry and poured her a bowl.

Maybe Cat was pissed at her father. If Anatoly was right about everything it would certainly appear that Anita and London had been separated for some time. Whatever it was that drove them apart, maybe Cat had sided with her mom.

I sipped at my coffee as I watched Mr. Katz eat. "I'm missing something," I said aloud. Mr. Katz was still too busy eating to care.

I left him there and went into my office. I had the manila folders Jason had left for me. I flipped through them, paying particular attention to the personal notes. There was one line that I kept going back to:

I've been a husband to her in every way that matters.

That was a weird qualifier. In what ways hadn't he been a husband to her?

I then pulled out the note from his work:

Eight months in: Subject had half a glass of wine and then stopped, without wanting more. Can stand among smokers without wanting a cigarette. Minor hair loss, but that seems to be tapering off.

Eight months in... that didn't make sense. This was clearly notes on the results of a clinical trial. The only drug that Nolan-Volz was developing was Sobexsol and they had started clinical trials less than a year ago. London had stopped working there six months ago. Soo…how did that add up?

And speaking of timing issues…

I went to my desk and pulled out the anniversary card from my top drawer. I studied Anita's note.

> *My love,*
>
> *Ours was a forbidden love, too powerful to deny. Seven years later I still feel the power of our love every day. I know how much you've sacrificed for me and I know I'm not always the easiest person to live with, but never doubt how grateful I am to have you in my life.*
>
> *Yours Always and Forever,*

Anatoly had told me Anita and London had been married twenty-four years.

"Oh," I whispered to myself and and then louder, "Oh!" Mr. Katz strolled into the room and looked up at me with mild curiosity.

"I think I figured this out!"

He blinked his eyes at me while simultaneously swishing his tail. That's kitty language for: *Took you long enough.*

CHAPTER
THIRTY-ONE

"Dear God, don't let today be another learning experi-ence."
--Dying To Laugh

I sat in my car, parked right across the street from Nolan-Volz, a large travel mug of coffee in my hand and a handgun in my purse. I watched as workers trickled in through the front door. Some in jeans, some in suits. It was just a little after seven forty am so these were the early birds looking to impress the powers that be. I was *never* out of bed by this time of day, but this was a worthy cause to sacrifice both sleep and tradition for.

She didn't show up until eight twenty-five and my coffee mug was empty and my bladder uncomfortably full. I spotted her when she was still half a block away and immediately got out of my car, impatiently waiting for a few cars to pass before jaywalking across the street to greet her.

"Charity!" I called out, just in time before she went inside.

She turned, surprised. But when she saw me her face lit up. "What are you doing here?" she asked but before I had time to answer her hand went to her head. "Look at my hair!" she squealed. "All this time I've been trying to blow out my curls or pull them into a braid or a bun and then your brilliant friend gives me the perfect cut and hands me some products and *look*! My curls are gorgeous! Aren't they gorgeous?"

"They're gorgeous," I confirmed. "Hey, do you have a minute? I need to ask you something."

"Um," she looked back at her place of work. "I really need to get in there. Gun likes me to arrive before he does to get everything ready for him and *he* always arrives before the other executives…"

"He's not in there yet," I assured her, bouncing on the balls of my feet as I tried not to think about how much I needed to pee.

"How can you be sure?" She asked, now glancing at the time on her phone.

"I'm sure because I've been watching."

Immediately she looked up, now with a new level of curiosity, and maybe a little wariness. "Why?" she asked as a car drove by, Sergeant Pepper blasting from its speakers.

"Look, I told you I knew Aaron London and that I had met his wife, the thing is, I didn't meet his wife until a few days ago."

"But…" she shook her head, indicating that was impossible.

"Yeah, I know what you told me," I said, still bouncing. "She's supposed to be dead. But the thing is, I *met* their daughter."

Charity shook her head again. "Someone's messing with you. I'm telling you, his wife was Ann and she's dead."

"What did she look like," I pressed.

"Blonde...well, not naturally. She had these great, dark eyebrows. She wore her hair past her shoulder blades and it was always kind of wild...like I just-had-sex hair."

I thought about Anita London. She probably wasn't naturally blonde either although her eyebrows were a light brown, not really dark. But that could be a dye job too.

"She had tan skin," Charity went on. "Well, maybe not tan exactly, she had an olive complexion."

I wouldn't call Anita's complexion olive, but it was sort of a subjective term.

"And of course she was tiny, barely above five feet. And that British accent really set her apart. It sounded almost sexy when she was on the phone."

And now there was no doubt. *We were not talking about the same person.* "This woman, Aaron's...wife, did she go by the last name London?"

"No," Charity said, with a little laugh. "I was told she thought a British woman living in America with the last name London would be a little too on the nose. She kept her maiden name."

"It wasn't Jaynes, was it?" I asked.

"Not even close," Charity said, tilting her head to the side. "Her last name was Keller."

Anne Keller. The woman London lived with. The woman he loved. But not his wife.

"Charity, what would have happened to London if he had given Anne samples of Sobexsol before the clinical trials had begun?"

"Are you serious?" Charity asked. "You could go to jail for that. Hell, if he was caught? He could bring down this entire company."

# CHAPTER
THIRTY-TWO

"My husband and I see the world differently. When he hears the word decadent he thinks scandalous, sexual adventure. I think chocolate cake."
--Dying To Laugh

I knocked three times on Anatoly's office door and waited. When he opened the door and saw who it was both his eyebrows shot up into his hairline.

"You never knock," he noted.

"Well, *somebody* told me he was trying to bring stability or some such crap into our home. I figured I'd meet you half way and refrain from barging into your office without knocking."

"That's nowhere close to halfway."

"Whatever, I need to talk to you." I pushed past him and plopped myself down on the chair in front of his desk.

"I need to talk to you as well." I looked over my shoulder to see he was grinning. Not just smiling, *grinning*. There were teeth on display and everything.

"What's going on?" I asked, suspiciously.

Anatoly walked past me and sat down in his chair.

"Ladies first."

I studied him for a moment. He *knew* something. Something big. But then so did I. I couldn't decide if I was more eager to hear his news or to brag about my recent discovery.

"I was sure Anita was a fraud," I said, opting for the latter. "Particularly when Charity told me his wife was named Anne but I was wrong."

"I'm aware of that," Anatoly said with a little half smile.

"No, no, not the way you think I was wrong. I was right that someone was lying about being London's wife, but it wasn't Anita. It was Anne Keller."

"Who?"

"Anne Keller," I said again. The sun was coming through the window behind Anatoly, forcing me to squint. "That's the woman who he had introduced as his wife to everyone he met over the last seven years. Anne Keller took Anita's place in London's life. Anne Keller was Anita London's imposter. And like London, Anne is now dead."

"Anne was the usurper," Anatoly said, thoughtfully. He stroked the stubble that clung to his chin. "That's motive."

"Damn straight!" I slapped my hand against my knee. My God, how long had it been since Anatoly and I were truly on the same page. This absolutely rocked. "And there's *more!*"

Anatoly lifted his eyebrows, silently inviting me to continue.

"I think London was giving Anne Sobexsol before it was approved for clinical trials!" I reached into my purse and took out copies I had made of London's personal notes and slammed them on Anatoly's desk. "I'm guessing Gundrun knew about it," I continued as Anatoly picked them up and started to scan them. "Or at least that he knows about it now."

"When did they start clinical trials on Sobexsol?" Anatoly asked.

"Less than a year ago."

He looked up from the papers and met my eyes. He was putting the pieces together the same way I was. "If you're right, London was giving Anne access to the drugs before they were even supposed to be giving it to humans. And if Gundrun knew…." Anatoly's eyes glittering with something that looked a lot like satisfaction. We were finally figuring this thing out!

"And read those notes!" I said, walking over to him and shuffling through the papers in his hand until I saw the one I wanted him to read. "Read that one. It sounds like Anne is falling apart here…London is *definitely* falling apart by the time he wrote this. Maybe the long-term side-effects of this drug aren't so hot."

"That seems plausible," Anatoly agreed.

"That would explain why Gundrun is so eager to have Nolan-Volz absorbed by another company," I said excitedly. "And his assistant thinks he's planning on leaving the company soon. He knows the drug is never going to make it to market."

"Again, that's possible," Anatoly agreed. "Maybe even probable."

"Yeah, but…" I faltered, looking up at him. "That would mean that all those people who *are* part of the clinical trials…Anatoly, they're being poisoned."

"Only if we're right," Anatoly cautioned. "And we might not be. All of this is pure speculation. And if we are right it's also possible that London's girlfriend didn't take the pills as instructed or that she mixed them with something else. A lot of things could have gone wrong. But no matter how you play it, if Gundrun knew what was going on he could lose his company *and* go to prison."

"Right, okay," I said doubtfully. Speculation or not I *knew* I was right. And those people taking that drug right now...

I shook my head. I couldn't get caught up in the horror of it yet. I had to be calculating and figure out how to prove my suspicions or at least get the authorities to investigate. "What did you need to talk to *me* about?"

"Anita London," he said, quietly. "The start up she works for develops GPS technology. They're working on developing miniature location device instruments that are so accurate and so discreet they could earn them military and government contracts."

"Government contracts," I repeated, uncertainly. "You mean this technology could be used by..." my voice trailed off as I thought of the possibilities.

"By the CIA and FBI," Anatoly finished for me. "And of course the NSA."

"Holy shit," I whispered, suddenly feeling nervous. "She actually put a tracking device on London's car."

"And possibly yours," Anatoly warned. "Wherever you're parked, leave your car there. You can take an Uber home."

"Anatoly, we're in a commercial area...in *San Francisco*. You know my car's in two hour parking. I'm lucky I didn't have to park it at a meter."

"Leave the keys with me, I'll move it somewhere else,"

he advised.

I rubbed my right thumb against my left palm as I tried to decide if this was truly the most plausible theory. "But… Gundrun has even more motive to kill London than Anita."

"I still think it was Anita," Anatoly said, in a rather definitive tone.

"Why?"

"Because there's one more thing I found out today."

I leaned forward, waiting for him to proceed.

"Anita," he said with a smile, "has a Zipcar account."

CHAPTER
THIRTY-THREE

"Discomfort leads to innovation. Dissatisfaction leads to creativity. Happiness leads to champagne. I choose happiness."
--Dying To Laugh

I couldn't stop writing. The words were spilling from my fingers. I was typing so fast my hands were beginning to cramp. Ms. Dogz was on one side of me, Mr. Katz on the other, watching in wonder as I created new characters, new adventures and a brilliant story.

I had left Anatoly's office via Uber three hours earlier. I now *knew* Anita was the killer. Anatoly had warned me that it was still a flimsy case. We needed hospital records to show the possibility that London had been poisoned. We needed information from the hospital about whether or not Anita was called when London was brought in or if she just conveniently happened to show up. And most of all, we needed records of exactly when Anita had checked out Zipcars.

None of that was information Anatoly would be able to get on his own. So he was going to talk to a contact he had at the Police force, a senior detective, and see if he was willing to take the matter up. That was the benefit of not repeatedly pissing off the police over the years, they were more likely to help you when you needed a favor. It was ironic that of the two of us, it was the one with the mafia past that had managed to maintain a good relationship with the cops, but there it was.

Of course if the police *refused* to help us, we could always reach out to hackers to get the information we needed. We were living in the center of Silicon Valley after all.

And tomorrow we would voice our concerns to the FDA.

Regardless of what route we would end up taking, right now I just had to wait and waiting was making me antsy and anticipatory...and prolific.

I was averaging ten pages an *hour*. Anita had killed her husband and revitalized my career.

That was an awful thing to say...even to yourself. I stopped typing for a minute so I could focus on feeling guilty.

And then I was back at it, baby!

Seven pages later Ms. Dogz started whining. I stared at her uncomprehendingly as she trotted to the door and stood there expectantly. I looked down at Mr. Katz for clarification.

Mr. Katz blinked twice which is kitty language for *These dogs aren't smart enough to use a litter box.*

"Oh," I said aloud, "you have to go out!" I pressed save and pushed myself away from my computer, grabbing my phone just in case Anatoly called with more news. "This way, Ms. Dogz."

Ms. Dogz trotted after me through the house until we got to the laundry room where I disarmed the alarm (I had told Anatoly I would keep it on and for once I was following through with a promise) then back through the kitchen to our little backyard. I was really enjoying being a dog-person. I suspected Mr. Katz would always be first in my heart but it *was* nice to have an animal that wasn't always so judgy.

As I held the door open for Ms. Dogz, I studied the kitchen. I should make dinner tonight…well, not dinner. If you lived with someone who could whip up Duck a l'orange at a moment's notice you stopped cooking.

But you didn't stop baking.

I smiled to myself and pulled up Mary Ann's email on my phone. The recipe was a little more complicated than I was used to, but I could totally pull it off.

Look at me, writing, baking and catching murderers!

I hummed to myself as I pulled out the mixing bowls, hand mixer, sifter and everything else the recipe required. After doing her business, Ms. Dogz joined me in the kitchen, watching the floor carefully so she could pounce on any bit of food I accidentally dropped. I stepped aside and let her lick up the little bit of sugar I had spilled. That was another wonderful thing about dogs! Three seconds after I made the mess it was gone! Ms. Dogz left me with a sparkling, saliva-cleaned floor…which is a little more disgusting than bleach cleaned but whatever.

I mixed, sifted, mashed, melted and all the rest of it. I didn't have cupcake liners so I greased the hell out of a muffin pan and poured in the cupcake mix, leaving the newly made frosting in the refrigerator. Sadly, my frosting didn't have the consistency of Mary Ann's. It was runnier and didn't look nearly at appetizing. But it tasted nearly as good so I didn't beat myself up about it. These cupcakes that I was putting into the oven were a reflection of the positive turn my life was taking. These were my magical cupcakes of empowerment. I made a quick detour by going outside to get the mail and then strode back into my office.

"I am woman, hear me roar," I said proudly to Ms. Dogz who had taken to following me everywhere.

And the writing gods were still on my side. The words were spilling out as I got lost in my little fictional world, steering my protagonist into danger only to pull her out at the very last minute. I was brilliant!

Except I lost track of the time. I was alerted to that particular mistake by the smoke alarm in my kitchen.

Ms. Dogz immediately jumped to her feet and started barking. Mr. Katz leaped onto the chair on the other side of the room, his back arched and his eyes wide. "*Shit!*" I hissed and rushed out of the room to the kitchen, Ms. Dogz close at my heels. I had to stand on the kitchen island to reach the alarm and turn it off. The smoke wasn't *that* bad. But when I got down and took the cupcakes out...well, they weren't looking too hot. I studied their blackened surface. "I can save these," I said aloud and tried to take one out of the muffin tin, burning my fingers in the process.

"Okay, try again." I turned the tin over and with the help of a butter knife got the muffins out. They landed on the counter with a thunk.

I was pretty sure baked goods should never thunk. Using a clean dish towel, I gingerly picked one up. It was *way* heavier than a cupcake should be. This was more like a cupcake paperweight.

In an act of pure desperation I arranged them on a plate. "It's possible they still taste good," I explained to Ms. Dogz. She looked at me doubtfully. "Well, with frosting?" I ventured. They had become just cool enough to touch and I lifted one to my lips. "I bet it's still salvageable," I assured her and tried to take a bite.

Tried because it was actually much too hard to sink my teeth into.

This could not be explained by burning alone. Somehow I had managed to completely fuck up my empowerment cupcakes. I looked down at Ms. Dogz who gave me a look that…while not judgy, was not impressed either.

"I'm going to take these out to the garbage, before Anatoly comes home," I told her. "This will be one more secret between the two of us, okay?"

She tilted her head to an angle that I now understood to mean, *whatever you say.*

I marched out of the kitchen, plate in hand, ready to just dump it in the garbage in the garage…

…except when I entered the dining room I heard the front door open and close.

Anatoly wasn't supposed to be home for hours.

Ms. Dogz went rushing forward, barking her doggie head off. And then the barking stopped.

"Hey, Sophie, I've missed you!"

It was a girl's voice that said the words. A teenager's voice.

Carefully I walked to the foyer to see Cat, clad in jeans, a long sleeved tee and a long red, checkered scarf crouched down in front of Ms. Dogz, scratching her behind the ears. When she saw me she jumped up, as if a little stunned. Her knapsack swung from one shoulder as she stumbled back a step. "Oh! I'm sorry!" she blurted out. "I didn't know you were here…I knocked but you didn't answer."

"Oh," I glanced at the door. Last I checked someone not answering the door was not an invitation to let yourself in.

"Normally I wouldn't have just barged in," she said, clearly anticipating my questions. "But I heard an alarm and I thought I smelled something burning so I thought…I just thought I should try the door and it was open so…" She blushed a little and looked down at Ms. Dogz. "I'm sorry."

"I was baking," I said, still feeling disoriented. I had forgotten to lock the door after checking the mail. How careless could I be?

"Oh…you're making…um…are those muffins?" she asked, looking down at the plate.

"Yeah, um, they're more like novelty cupcakes."

"Novelty like novelty toys? You…bake novelty cupcakes?"

This girl barges into *my* house and then insults my magical, empowerment cupcakes? No. Just no.

Except…were her actions really so unreasonable? She smelled something burning so she tried the door. In a certain light that would seem like the responsible thing to do.

And in *any* light Cat was a tragic figure in the truest sense of the word. Her father had left his family for another woman, then lost his mind and *then* was murdered by her mother…who was about to go to jail for it (or she would if I had anything to say about it). "I'm not much of a baker." I looked down at the lumps of hard, wasted sugar and flour on my plate. "It's been years since I tried my hand at it and I think another long baking hiatus may be in order."

Cat smiled at my comment. She seemed softer than the last time I had seen her. Less angry and more vulnerable. "I love baking. I'm always making things for my friends and my parents. I've been baking even more lately to, you know, distract myself. Look." She reached into her bag and pulling out a Ziploc bag filled with sugar cookies (my least favorite kind of cookies). "I brought these for you," she said shyly as she handed them over.

I placed them on the corner of the plate filled with my novelty empowerment. "I wasn't sure you were coming," I said. "We never set up a time."

"Yeah, I know," Cat gave an apologetic shrug. "I wasn't able to really plan this. My mom has been hovering like crazy since my dad died. I thought she was going to be at work all day but she took the first half of the day off so she could…I don't know…hover some more I guess. She's weird sometimes."

Yes, weird and homicidal. "Care to come sit down?" I led her into the living room and placed the cupcakes on the coffee table but held on to the cookies. Ms. Dogz sniffed at the chocolate and then turned her nose up. Ms. Dogz, who used to live in a place overrun with insects, rotting food and trash, was disgusted by my cupcakes.

I claimed the armchair and gestured for Cat to take the couch. Mr. Katz entered the room and took a seat by my side, eyeing Cat warily.

"Do you like cats?" I asked. "I mean, you kind of have to if your *name* is Cat, right?"

Cat offered me a strained smile. It was likely a familiar joke to her. "When did you meet my father?" she asked.

"The day he died," I answered truthfully. "I wasn't

dating him." I hesitated a moment before asking, "did you know the woman he was living with after your mom? Anne Keller?"

"Of course I knew her," Cat said off-handedly. "She was my mom's best friend before she hooked up with my dad."

"What?" I gasped.

Cat shrugged and fiddled with her scarf. "My mom used to go by Anne too. When I was little, they were the two Anne's. The fun AA," Cat laughed. "That's what they called themselves. The Fun AA. Although I guess Anne was the more fun of the two. She was definitely the one who liked to party the most. Mom always told me that guys loved Anne. She just didn't know that one of those guys was my dad."

Oh, no wonder Anita killed him. I might consider killing Anatoly if he took off with Dena or Mary Ann. Of course if he made a pass at Dena or Mary Ann they'd kill him for me. Now I felt kind of bad for wanting to put Anita in jail.

"When was this?" I asked.

"Oh, like seven years ago…a little over that I guess. She came over to our house all the time when I was a kid. I remember a few times when my mom and I would be baking…we baked those cookies," she said, gesturing to the Ziploc in my hand. "They're kind of our specialty, *really* good. Anyway, we'd start baking and then mom would say, *Let's invite Anne over for this. She really wants to learn how to bake*." Cat rolled her eyes at the memory. "And then Anne would come over and drink wine with dad and the two of them would watch us bake. That was Anne."

Although I wanted to be attentive to Cat's baking stories my mind was sort of stuck on the seven years part. I hadn't really thought about the number before. Seven years was a long time. If Anatoly cheated on me with one of my girl-friend's I wouldn't wait seven years to murder him.

"Were you close with your dad?" I asked, a little distractedly.

"When I was little? Yeah, I guess." She crossed her legs at the ankles and then re-crossed them with the other leg in front. "It was too weird after he left us. My mom didn't want me spending any time over there and Ann didn't know how to act around me anyway. Dad never filed for divorce because he knew my mom was going to make it super difficult but he acted like he was married to Anne. He even gave her a stupid ring." She tugged gently at the ends of her scarf. "Are you going to try my cookies? I promise, they're *so* good."

"Oh, yeah…" I opened up the Ziploc. Ms. Dogz was immediately on her feet and trying to get her nose in the bag.

"No!" Cat said, firmly to the dog. "That's not yours." She looked up at me with an apologetic smile. "Sugar's really bad for dogs. Don't let her eat it."

"Oh, I won't," I said, pulling the cookie close to me. "After Anne Keller…um…when she…"

"When she offed herself?" Cat filled in for me, without a trace of discomfort.

"Yeah," I said with a nod. "Did you see your dad much after that?"

"My mom and I would go over there sometimes in the couple weeks after she died. Actually my mom went over there a lot. Dad was a mess…I mean, not like he was toward the end, but he was definitely hurting. And my mom…I don't know. I guess my mom just decided she was going to forgive him, which is kind of pathetic when you think about it."

"Wait, after everything they went through she was ready to be his friend again?" Anita did not strike me as being that magnanimous.

"She was ready to be his *wife* again," Cat corrected.

"Oh." Now I was beginning to understand the timing of the murder. "So he left her, for her best friend no less, and she was *still* willing to forgive him if he'd take her back and he said…no." God that had to hurt.

"Wrong," Cat said with a shake of her head. "He said yes, and *then* he said no. They were back together for, like a month. And then he pulled away again. Sold his condo, moved into that ugly apartment. He would invite me over sometimes but he didn't want to see Mom. I didn't get why but then, I didn't know about you."

"Cat, it wasn't me. I know you don't believe me but--"

Cat held up her hand. "It's okay. My mom and dad were all kinds of dysfunctional. For a little while, I thought he would come back to us because…I don't know, I thought he was just better with my mom than he was with Anne. Mom says he didn't even need to take his bipolar meds when he was with her."

I pressed my lips together. I could tell her that while he may have been able to function without medication in the years he was with her mom he was eventually going to need medication regardless of who he was living with. It was the nature of the disease. But why ruin her romantic fantasy that her mother was able to keep his demons away by her mere presence? Soon she would have to reassess her opinions about her mom, but not yet and not about that.

"I even thought that when he started to really lose it he would turn to my mom for help. My dad…he used to lean on her and if he had leaned on her again he would have gotten better. But he didn't." Her voice cracked and she angrily swiped at her cheek. "I guess they just weren't meant to be. I get that now. I'm really just here because...well, I miss my dad." She met my eyes. I saw no sign of the tears she had just made a show of wiping away.

But then maybe that was because she had just wiped them away. I needed to stop being so suspicious and just listen.

"I can't tell my mom that," Cat went on. "I can't talk to her about him. I thought maybe I could talk to you."

Oh God, this was hell. I needed her to know I hadn't been sleeping with her dad. But now she was here because she thought I *did* have a relationship with him and therefore could mourn with her.

"Hey, are you going to try that cookie or what?" she asked again with a smile. "I'm beginning to to be insulted! What is it, you don't trust me to know how to bake?" she looked pointedly at my own weak attempt at the art.

"Sorry." Her red scarf didn't suit her coloring. Pink would be better on her. "Of course I trust..." but then my voice trailed off.

I knew that red scarf. I had seen it in London's apartment the first time I went in.

But not the second.

Someone had removed the scarf between my two visits. Anita had told me that neither she nor Cat had ever been in that apartment before. So either Anita had been lying to me or Cat had been lying to her.

I looked down at the cookie in my hand. "You must have been very angry with your father." There had been a cookie tin in London's kitchen. The ants around it had been dead.

"I was," she said flippantly. "I'm not anymore."

"Because now he's dead."

She didn't say anything for a moment and then gave me a cool smile. "I guess that has something to do with it."

"You said you played Catherine of Aragon in a school play." I looked back up at her, trying to keep my voice calm. She had been surprised I was home. Was that because she was tracking my car that was now parked by Anatoly's office? "Are you really into theater?"

"I like to act," she said, cautiously. "I like lots of things. I'm a member of the robotics team too. And the softball team."

"What play is your school putting on now?"

Cat studied me for a moment. Mr. Katz swished his tail.

"Macbeth," she said quietly. "We're putting on Macbeth."

Carefully I put the cookie on the edge off the coffee table. "What's in the cookies, Cat?" I whispered.

"The usual," she said calmly. "Butter, sugar, eggs, vanilla…and a little bit of rat poison, just for you."

I jerked my head up to meet her eyes but she was already flying across the coffee table, her hands out like claws. I instinctively raised my arms to protect my face as she literally straddled me in my chair but then I felt her squeezing my neck, making it hard to breathe.

Oh fuck that.

I grabbed her hair and yanked, hard. She screamed and I pushed her off, coughing. Ms. Dogz was barking, looking confused as to where she should place her loyalty.

My gun was in my purse, which was in the office. I just

had to get to the office. I started to run. Cat lunged for me but she wasn't fast enough. I looked over my shoulder just in time to see Ms. Dogz sniffing the sugar cookies that were now on the floor.

"No!" I screamed running back to stop her. But I didn't get far, Cat was on me again, knocking me to the ground. I felt her fist hit the side of my head, causing an explosion of pain to vibrate through my skull. Again her hands with to my throat. I tried to pry them off but she was surprisingly strong and the blow to my head had made me dizzy. I reached up to the surface of the coffee table, groping for anything I could use as a weapon as she continued to squeeze.

My hand wrapped itself around a cupcake.

With every bit of strength I had I smashed that cupcake against her head. It made an audible sound and Cat cried out in surprise and pain. I hit her with it again and again. My baking skills were so bad I was actually able to weaponize my empowerment cupcakes! The repeated impact was enough to get her to loosen her grip. I pushed her off me and turned over on my stomach. I tried to crawl in the direction of where Ms. Dogz had been but when I lifted my head I saw the poisonous cookies still laying on the floor, but no Ms. Dogz. And then the red scarf was around my throat and I was in an even worse position than before.

"I didn't want to do it this way!" she was screaming. But I didn't really care what she was saying anymore. I was *not* going to be strangled to death by a high school drama geek. That just wasn't the way I was meant to go out.

I flailed at her, but now, with my face pushed against the floor and the scarf getting tighter and tighter around my neck…it wasn't working. *Nothing* was working.

And that's when Ms. Dogz chose a side.

Seemingly out of nowhere she leaped onto Cat, pushing her off me, snarling and growling all the way. I heard Cat scream as she bit into her arm.

"Sophie, stop it, it's me! Sophie!" But it wasn't helping.

I struggled to my feet as Cat got bit again. She screamed but it was my whistle that got Ms. Dogz to stop. She backed up a few feet as she continued to growl.

Cat looked up at me helplessly as I glared down at her. "Sophie bit me," she cried.

"She's not your Sophie, anymore" I snapped. "That's Ms. Dogz, and she's *my* bitch now, bitch."

 # CHAPTER
THIRTY-FOUR

*"I considered watching the solar eclipse but I didn't
have the right glasses and I've been told that there are
more enjoyable ways to go blind."*
--Dying To Laugh

In the early morning, less than forty-eight hours after the
police came to my house to take Cat away, less than forty-
seven hours since Anatoly had taken me in his arms, kissed
me passionately and tended to my rapidly forming black-eye,
less than forty-four hours since I had called Dena to tell her
the whole story, and less than twenty-six hours since I had
called Mary Ann to ask her where I had gone wrong with the
cupcakes, I sat with Charity in my car across from Nolan-
Volz. I had stopped her from going inside and asked her to
sit with me for a few minutes while I caught her up on a few
things. Now, on her lap, was a newspaper. She read the
article detailing Cat's arrest. She looked up at me, and then
read the words again. "I can't...I can't believe this."

"London had been taking Gaba," I explained to Charity.
I watched her through my dark sunglasses (which were
necessary to hide my black eye). "The particular Gaba pills

he was taking came in big, clear capsules. So Cat just ordered up a bunch of clear capsules and filled them up with all the drugs in the medicine cabinet. The Abilify that London used to take *before* the Gaba and then all of Anne's old pills. Her allergy pills and...other stuff. Apparently there were a *lot* of pills. When filling up capsules proved to be too time consuming she just sprinkled the pills into the sugar he sweetened his coffee and oatmeal with, mixed it into baked goods she made for him and so on thereby making sure he was getting drugged all the time. She replaced Anne's pills with over the counter stuff that looked similar enough. It's not like London was checking on it. Of course, after London died Cat cleared out the medicine cabinet, otherwise it might have been discovered that the drugs were all mixed up and not what they were labeled."

"Why?" Charity whispered. "Was she really trying to kill her own father?"

"Maybe?" I ran my fingers over the steering wheel as I watched the doors of Nolan-Volz. "Aaron London had rejected both her and her mom for this other woman and when the other woman was out of the picture, he rejected them again in an even more humiliating way. It's possible she thought that if her dad got sick, he'd turn to her mom. Then she'd stop poisoning him, he'd get better and credit...well, her mom."

"Seriously?" Charity asked.

I shrugged. "Maybe not. Maybe she *was* trying to kill him. What *Cat's* saying is that she was just worried about her dad. She knew he had ditched his prescription for holistic medicine and she was trying to trick him into taking the pills he needed. But I'm pretty sure that's bullshit."

"But...to mix a whole bunch of pills together...some of them weren't even his...you know what that could do to a person?"

"Drive them crazy? Cause hair loss? Congestive heart failure? Yeah, I know. And by stalking him in Zipcars...she was full on gas-lighting him. The thing is, London was already kind of losing it due to the loss of his girlfriend and his decision to go off his meds. So people just saw his descent into madness as the natural progression of things. They didn't suspect."

"Wow. Just...wow." She finally looked up from the paper and patted her perfect curls. "And you figured all this out because I told you he was married to Anne?"

"That and some other things. I had actually thought Anita was the killer but I didn't take into account that Cat had access to all the things that would have enabled Anita to stalk and kill London." I glanced out my window just in time to see Gun walk into Nolan-Volz. *Perfect.* Charity hadn't noticed so I simply looked away and gave my full attention to her. "Anita brought her work home with her, so Cat used the tiny little GPS devices to place on London's car. They're so small if you put them on the underside of a vehicle they're practically invisible. I got the one she planted on my car removed yesterday and the mechanic told me that if I hadn't been able to tell him exactly what to look for he never would have found it."

"Wow. That's so Mission Impossible."

I laughed. "Yeah, kind of. She was also using her mom's Zipcar account although she wasn't an authorized user. But I guess if you're planning homicides, abiding by the user agreement for Zipcar isn't really your number one concern."

"Wow," Charity whispered for about the eleventh time. "Well...thank you for sharing this?" she said uncertainly. "I can't believe someone I knew was murdered. He *was* a dick but...wow." She handed me back the newspaper. "I'll tell Gundrun. I really have to get into work now—"

I put my hand on her arm. "Don't go into work today."

She looked at me askance. "I can't just play hooky. Gun will be in there any minute now--

"He walked in two minutes ago," I said, quietly. "I saw him."

"What?" She exclaimed and then immediately reached for the handle of her door. "Oh God, he's going to be pissed."

But I kept my hand on her arm, holding her firmly. "Charity one of the drugs that Cat poisoned her dad with was Sobexsol."

"What?" she turned back to me. "But...she couldn't have. She doesn't have access."

"She *shouldn't* have had access. But London apparently had lots and lots of it in his medicine cabinet."

"He *stole drugs from the lab!*" She sounded almost awed now. "Do you have any idea how illegal that is? Oh my God, when Gun finds out..."

"Gun knew," I said quietly.

"*What?*"

"Cat told the police that she overheard her dad on the phone with Gun, talking about how after three years on Sobexsol Anne started having suicidal thoughts, intense anxiety and whatnot."

"But the clinical trials started less than *one* year ago."

"Exactly," I said with a sigh. "She was taking the drugs

before it was even supposed to be tested on humans. You're the one who told me Gun and London used to be friends years ago. The police think Gun let London give the drugs to Anne as a favor, and maybe to help get early data that would help them further develop and perfect the drug. The FDA was dragging its feet on its approval."

Charity just stared at me, then shook her head. "You're taking the word of a murderous child."

"Yeah, I am," I admitted. "And under normal circumstances, I'd say that was ill advised. But why would she lie about *this*? Cat didn't think there was anything wrong with Anne being on a clinical trial. She didn't know Anne wasn't allowed to have those drugs. And the thing is…I think the long-term side effects of Sobexsol are…problematic. I think it may cause some level of psychosis…or at the very least severe depression. Those people who are taking the drug now in the approved trials? They could be in trouble. Gun should be stopping the study. But instead he sold the company. He's planning on taking his share of the profits from the sale and getting out before things go down hill."

Charity blinked and then looked down at the paper again. "And the cops…you said the cops believe this too?"

"Well, not exactly the cops. The Feds."

"*The Feds!*"

Charity looked across the street at the Nolan-Volz office. "This is too crazy for me."

"Me too," I admitted. "At first I thought that London's murder might be part of some grand conspiracy but there was no conspiracy. Just an accumulation of lies and misdeeds by a bunch of different actors that unwittingly came together to form a big, giant mess. Maybe that's what most conspiracies are, you know?"

Charity gave me a weird look. "I have no clue what you're talking about. And honestly, I'm not sure I want to know all this. I just want to keep my head down and got to work."

"Charity, I like you," I said, sincerely. "Marcus likes you too. And you really helped me out whether you knew it or not. That's why I'm trying to help you out by telling you not to go into work today."

"Because why?" she asked, exasperated.

"Because that." I pointed out the window just three, no five, no *eight*, black sedans pulled up in front of Nolan-Volz along with four black vans. Men wearing jackets that said, FBI started pouring out of them and going into the building.

"The place where you work is being raided by the FBI. It's a good day to call in sick."

CHAPTER
THIRTY-FIVE

"Stalkers all over the world should be on their knees, thanking Facebook for giving them legitimacy."
--Dying To Laugh

"You've been distracted lately," I said as Anatoly sat on the edge of the bed to put on his shoes.

He looked up, bemused and let his eyes roam over the tussled bed sheets. "I assure you, you had my full attention." He then reached forward and put his hand under my chin, guiding my face toward him. "Are you complaining?"

I smiled as I brushed my lips against his. "No, you weren't distracted for *that*. You're never distracted for that."

"I aim to please." He went back to putting on his shoes.

"Still," I noted, "when we're not making love, you've been distracted. And you've been acting...I don't know, just kind of weird."

"You're imagining things," he said as he got to his feet before adding, "again." I watched as he retrieved his shirt from where I had thrown it on the floor. He had already been at work today and now, at nine-thirty at night, he had to go in again. Such is the life of a private detective. "I think this will be the last stake-out I'll have to do in a while," he noted.

"After tonight I'll be able to provide my client with more than enough evidence to prove that the guy they're paying workman's comp to isn't really injured. Still, it may be a late night. Set the alarm after I leave."

"See, that's what I mean." I sat up and pulled the sheet over my chest as I leaned against the headboard. Mr. Katz was sitting next to Ms. Dogz on the floor, proving all prejudices can be overcome with time and exposure. "It's been two weeks since Cat's been arrested. Why are you still so intent on having the alarm on whenever I'm home alone?"

"It's just a smart idea," he said, vaguely.

"Something's going on," I pressed.

He sighed and then leaned over and gave me a more lingering kiss. "Everything's fine. I'm simply protecting what I love."

"Anatoly—"

"How many pages did you write today?" he asked as he pulled on his jacket.

"Twenty three," I said with a smile. "If this keeps up I'll have it all wrapped up by the end of next month." I cocked my head to the side. "Is there something you're not telling me?"

He put his finger to my lips. "I'm not telling."

"Why not?" I demanded.

"Because," he said, leaning over and giving me one last kiss on the forehead, "you like secrets."

"Anatoly," I said again, but this time I was interrupted by my phone dinging with a text message. I picked it up from my nightstand. It was a multimedia message sent to both Dena and me from Mary Ann. I looked at the picture and gasped.

"What is it?" Anatoly asked, pausing on his way to the door.

I held it up. "It's a pregnancy test," I whispered. "It's

Mary Ann's pregnancy test!" I leaped out of bed and started jumping up and down. "She's pregnant, she's pregnant, she's pregnant."

"Wow," Anatoly said appreciatively. I stopped and looked down at myself, realizing only then that I had been jumping up and down while completely naked.

"Don't get any ideas," I said grabbing my robe and quickly pulling it on. "I have to call Mary Ann! Oh my God, I'm going to be an aunt!"

"You already are an aunt," Anatoly noted. "You're sister has a son."

"Oh, right." I immediately checked myself. "Jack. I do love my nephew Jack. Very much. He's…he's got that Tasmanian Devil vibe going for him and…um…well…"

Anatoly laughed and shook his head. "You don't have to explain Jack to me. Give Mary Ann my congratulations and remember to set the alarm."

I dropped down on the edge of the bed again and stared at the picture as Anatoly made his exit. I couldn't drag my eyes away from those two beautiful blue lines.

As I heard the front door open and close I looked over to Mr. Katz and Ms. Dogz. "This requires champagne."

The fact that there was no one there to share it with me didn't really matter. I got up and sort of skipped out of the room. I would pop a bottle of champagne, pour it in a glass and then call Mary Ann up to toast her over the phone.

She was pregnant!

Ms. Dogz tailed after me, down the stairs, through the living room and into the foyer on our way to the dining room and kitchen…

…except once she reached the foyer she stopped.

I turned to see what was up and saw her staring at the door.

And then she growled.

Seriously? Weren't we done with all that?"

"Huh." I pressed my face against the window. The porch light was already on but I couldn't see anyone. I looked down at Ms. Dogz. "I really don't think there's anything out there."

When she looked unconvinced, I sighed and cracked open the door. I still couldn't see anyone so I opened it all the way and stepped outside. She followed me, taking a few steps out, sniffing the air.

"See? There's no one here," I said, turning around...

...to see the note taped to my door.

I froze. The words were very simple, very clear.

Miss me?

But Anatoly had just been here. Which meant that someone must have put the note on my door not minutes ago, but seconds ago.

Ms. Dogz started barking and I whipped around.

Standing in my walkway was a tall man wearing black jeans, a black T-shirt and...a black baseball cap.

I froze, my eyes wide. The man's head was down. Then slowly, ever so slowly, he looked up.

Alex Kinsky stood before me, his green eyes crinkling at the corners as he smiled.

I didn't say a word. I couldn't even find my voice.

He reached into his pocket and took out a few dog treats, which he tossed to my bodyguard. Ms. Dogz sniffed them and then gobbled them up.

"You're not very good at heading warnings," he said, leaning back on his heels, folding his strong arms casually across his chest. I could see burn wounds on his neck. Reminders of the fire we had both escaped.

"The note?" I whispered.

"And the underlined headline."

"What...the article about the body they found in the

park…" but I didn't finish my sentence. I was just completely unprepared for this encounter.

"I need your help, Sophie," he said, with a lazy smile. "And I think you need mine."

"I don't need anything from you," I said. "You need to leave."

"I'm afraid you're wrong on your first point. However I understand if you don't want to talk here, in the privacy of your home, in the middle of the night." The way he said *privacy of your home* made the words sound suggestive and borderline inappropriate. "We can arrange to meet tomorrow in a more public setting if you'd prefer. But before we make those arrangements, why don't you answer my first question?"

"Your first question?" I repeated.

"Yes." He took his cap off, revealing his strawberry blond hair, which he ran his fingers through before reaching into his pocket and tossing a few more treats to the dog. He then took a few steps forward, a quiet smile on his face. "Did you miss me, Sophie?"

I stared at him, then down at the dog. My life would never be boring. There would always be danger and chaos. Sometimes it would come in the form of a whacked-out teenager and sometimes it would come from a former mafia associate. But it would always come.

And then I found myself smiling back. "Meet me in Union Square, tomorrow by the Macy's Christmas tree at five pm."

"You're not answering my question," he pressed taking another small step.

I sucked in a sharp breath and put my hand gently on Ms. Dogz head. "I don't know if it's fair to say I missed you," I admitted. "But…" I hesitated a moment, causing Alex's smile to get a little bigger, his eyes a little brighter..

"But?" he asked.

"But," I said again, "I'll admit, I can't wait to find out why you're here." I ushered Ms. Dogz inside and quickly closed the door, locking Alex out. I would set the alarm and get out my gun, just in case he got any ideas.

My next adventure was about to begin.

# ABOUT THE AUTHOR

Kyra Davis is the New York Times and USA Today best-selling author of the *Sophie Katz Mystery* series and the *Just One Night* series, The *Pure Sin* series, and the stand-alone novel, *So Much For My Happy Ending.* Her books have been translated and published in seventeen different countries. After spending the majority of her life in the Bay Area, Davis now lives in Los Angeles County with her husband, son, fabulous dogs, and an endearing but occasionally moody leopard gecko.

Find out more about Kyra Davis and her books at www.kyradavis.com

Printed in Great Britain
by Amazon